# UNCLE BRUCKER the RAT KILLER

A Novel of Tall Tails and Other Dimensions

# Leslie Peter Wulff

Night Shade Books
New York

Night Shade books may be purchased in bulk at special discounts for sales promotion, corporate gifts, fund-raising, or educational purposes. Special editions can also be created to specifications. For details, contact the Special Sales Department, Night Shade Books, 307 West 36th Street, 11th Floor, New York, NY 10018 or info@skyhorsepublishing.com.

Night Shade Books™ is a trademark of Skyhorse Publishing, Inc.®, a Delaware corporation.

Visit our website at www.nightshadebooks.com.

10 9 8 7 6 5 4 3 2 1

Library of Congress Cataloging-in-Publication Data

Names: Wulff, Leslie Peter, author.
Title: Uncle Brucker the rat killer / Leslie Peter Wulff.
Description: New York, NY : Night Shade Books, 2017.
Identifiers: LCCN 2016038963 | ISBN 9781597808941 (paperback)
Subjects: LCSH: Teenage boys--Fiction. | Uncles--Fiction. | Rats--Fiction. |
  Fourth dimension--Fiction. | Time travel--Fiction. | Imaginary
  places--Fiction. | Imaginary wars and battles--Fiction. | BISAC: FICTION /
  Fantasy / Urban Life. | FICTION / Fantasy / Contemporary. | GSAFD: Fantasy
  fiction.
Classification: LCC PS3623.U44 U53 2017 | DDC 813/.6--dc23
LC record available at https://lccn.loc.gov/2016038963

Print ISBN: 978-1-59780-894-1

Cover design by Claudia Noble
Cover artwork by AJ Frena

Printed in the United States of America

To Sandy, for everything.

Shot dead most of them with my 22.
Maimed an equal number.
Killed three with a stick bat.
The rest died of fright upon my arrival,
except just one I had to wrestle.

—The Rat Killer

# 1

The rats killed my grandmother on May 24, 1998.

It's a famous case, a well known fact. You can read about it in the Journal on May 25th of that year. Front page headline: RODENTS SUSPECTED IN FATAL MAULING OF GRANDMA THOMPSON. You can look it up in the Tri-County Times too, if you can find the old copies, but I got my information from Uncle Brucker the Rat Killer. He knew a lot about everything but mostly he knew about rats.

Spring 1998 was the wettest spring on record. Two weeks of rain and the ground was spongy. Earthworms squirmed to the surface, gasping for air, and gophers slept above ground. Squirrels made nests in the tallest trees, trying to find the sun. Bluebirds lost their direction in the dark clouds and tumbled to the ground, and so did the chickadees and night-flying falcons.

The rats had a fat day feasting on the suicide birds.

"Only the fish were happy, coupla frogs," said Uncle Brucker.

"But what about the rats?" I asked him. "Weren't the rats happy? I mean with all the dead birds to eat up?"

"You'd think so, wouldn't ya? Breakfast, lunch and dinner droppin' out of the sky. Rats crawlin' around, munchin' here, munchin' there. But remember, we're dealin' with rats, and rats are miserable creatures."

I was twelve and a half years old at the time of this conversation. I had just run away from home for the first time. I ran so fast I felt like I was still running, more than four miles to the old house.

Uncle Brucker stood at the back door when I ran up. He didn't tell me my father had called and he didn't say my father was coming to get me. He didn't say anything at all. He just handed me a can of Coke and I knew all about it.

Then we sat side-by-side out front in the double rocker and waited for my father to show up.

That's where the rats murdered Grandma Thompson, right there in the doorway. They ganged up on her and murdered her at the front porch of the old house. Scratch marks all over the front door, scratched-up porch boards.

Uncle Brucker had a thick beard that hid his face. It moved in and out of his mouth when he talked, sweeping the words out. He stroked that beard a twisty way.

"You see, after a feast, a rat likes nuthin' more than a good sleep. And boy did these rats feast. A sparrow, coupla chickadees, barn bats for dessert. So you see the situation here. On May twenty-fourth the sun came out steamin', swellin' up the rat holes while the rats were out feastin' and bloatin' in the sun. And everybody knows a bloated rat can't fit in a swollen rat hole, and a cranky rat will turn vicious and attack an elderly person. Poor Grandma Thompson, she opened the front door and they were all over her. She didn't have a chance, one old lady against a horde a bloated rats, killin' just for killin', chewin' just for chewin'. Hunger had nuthin' to do with it.

"After the funeral I went on a rampage and kilt about sixty-three rats with my twenty-two. Shot 'em right up their butts stickin' out the rat holes."

Uncle Brucker twisted something out of his beard, held it between two fingers, put it back where he found it. He leaned back in the big rocker and put his feet up on the railing. I stretched my legs out all the way but they didn't reach.

I was listening for my father's Malibu. If the tires squeal when he steps on the brakes at the stop sign it means I'm in trouble.

In a while I heard the Malibu coming around the corner. My father drove right through the stop sign. He didn't step on the brakes and he's coming down the road and I was in big trouble.

I took a last sip of Coke before I had to go.

"Is that why they call you the Rat Killer?" I asked.

"Nah, that ain't why," he said. "Grandpa Thompson named me that when I was little cause I used to kill rats and eat 'em until I found out they wasn't squirrels."

"How do they taste?"

"Pretty good when you think they're squirrels," said Uncle Brucker.

# 2

The rats murdered Grandma Thompson and rats were responsible for Grandpa Thompson's death too, though they didn't kill him outright.

"Grandpa Thompson drowned, but if you ask me the rats did him in," Uncle Brucker told me the next time I ran away.

After Grandpa Thompson died back in 2003, Uncle Brucker moved into the old house. It really was a great runaway home. The screened-in porch stretched across the front, around the side, all the way to the back door. The crawl space under the porch made a great hiding spot or clubhouse area. Big droopy willows shaded the front lawn and tall pine trees leaned over the barn out back. The back yard was way bigger than any baseball field.

For years Uncle Brucker let my father store his junked cars on the property, but my father never worked on them and he never came to tow them away. Uncle Brucker moved the junked Camaro and a junked Scout into the tall grass that grew around the barn.

We were sitting next to the Camaro in the junked Monte Carlo.

He was teaching me how to downshift and telling me more about rats.

"The rats had it in for Grandpa Thompson," he said. "Rats hate anythin' that hates them, and they got a way a knowin' what hates 'em. . . . That ain't second."

"I know."

"Wrong way downshiftin'."

"I'm just passin' through."

"And Grandpa Thompson hated rats more than anybody hated anythin' cause of the way they ate up Grandma Thompson. All this hatred brought an influx of rats and a few wayward squirrels as well. Rats are attracted to what they hate and they will not eat anythin' unless they really hate it. Ever watch rats eat? Rippin', chewin', and gnawin'. Rippin', chewin', gnawin'. It's like they're murderin' all over again. Strange, innit? Rats love to eat but they hate what they're eatin'. And rats love eatin' what they hate so much they will rarely stop eatin' even when they look death in the face. That's when Grandpa Thompson did his killin', when they was eatin'. He crept up behind 'em and shot 'em in the pudnuts. Grandpa Thompson kilt an average of eight hunred rats a year, though he tapered off somewhat near the end."

"Eight hunred a year!" I said. "That's a lot a rats to kill."

"No kiddin'," said Uncle Brucker. "Think about it. That's eighty rats a month based on a ten month year. Lucky for Grandpa Thompson we got twelve month years so that made it easier for him."

"Grandpa Thompson kilt more rats than you?"

"Yes he did. Many more. Grandpa Thompson was the greatest Rat Killer in Bowen County."

"I thought they call you the Rat Killer."

"They do."

"How come they don't call Grandpa Thompson the Rat Killer?"

"Cause I already had that name for years, and that's what counts. It's like Venezuela, down south. Lots of countries wanna be called Venezuela, but Venezuela got called it first."

Uncle Brucker lit a cigarette. I noticed the way he smoked. He inhaled, flicked the ashes, exhaled—a three-step process. It looked like he blew out more smoke than he took in. The shrinking cigarette disappeared into his shaggy beard.

For a moment I thought he would set fire to his beard, but Uncle Brucker knew how to smoke a cigarette without setting fire to his beard.

When he finished he flicked the butt onto the driveway.

"See what I just did?" he said. "Never do that when there's rats around, flick a butt in a driveway. Right now there's no rats around so it's OK."

"But I don't smoke."

"Then don't worry about it."

He lit another cigarette.

"Worry about what?" I asked.

"Smoker rats. Certain species of rats will comb a driveway lookin' for butts. Smoker rats can't light a butt. They find one lit, they'll pick it up and smoke it. Then they never leave you alone. That's how Grandpa Thompson died. He was a chain smoker. Walked down to the pond one mornin', flickin' butts all over the place without understandin' the consequences. Smoker rats followed his trail, screechin' and fightin' for the butts. By the time he got to the rowboat there was hunreds of 'em. He tried to row away but they swam out to the boat and capsized him. Grandpa Thompson went straight to the bottom cause he had a habit of keepin' his spare sinkers in his pockets."

"Too bad he kept his sinkers in his pockets," I said. "Then he wouldna drowned so easy."

"Nah, he still woulda drowned. When Grandpa Thompson didn't have sinkers in his pockets he carried a lot of spare change."

"Enough spare change to weigh him down?"

"Don't take much," Uncle Brucker said. "Coupla dollars in quarters will sink a full-grown man. Who knows how many nickels he had?"

## 3

The night had sneaked up on us and we were sitting on the porch in the dark. The overhead bulb had burnt out or maybe Uncle Brucker didn't turn it on. The crickets were already making a lot of noise. Two cats fought somewhere on McDermott's property. The streetlight clicked on at the corner and a thousand moths came around. No breeze. The rats are out there, you can put your money on that.

I learned a lot about rats from Uncle Brucker every time I ran away from home.

"Rats evolved in many directions over the years," Uncle Brucker explained. "You got your straight line and you got your divergent lines of development, and there's rats we don't know how the hell they get here. Rats got their own ways about 'em, but they don't look like much. You won't know 'em just by lookin', you know 'em by what they do—like the tangerine rat. Looks like your everyday rat, but only a tangerine rat will peel and eat a whole tangerine. Another rat, the dandy rat. Looks like every rat. Sleeps like every rat. But when the music's playin', only the dandy will get up on two legs and dance, and only a dandy will dance a waltz. You see a rat dancin' on all fours—-that ain't no dandy rat. Dancin' to another tune? That's a common rat. . . . Gotta be a waltz."

Uncle Brucker knew more about rats than anyone knew, and he knew a lot that no one knew. He knew the facts and he knew the stories. He wasn't the type who read a book about another person's experience. He went off and learned stuff on his own.

"What's the biggest rat?" I asked him.

"The biggest rat by far is the big East Kalahari Desert rat, which can get much bigger than a Old Guinea King rat, dependin' how old. How big can he get? Oh, I'd say a old Old Guinea King rat can weigh in at seventy pounds. But a female big East Kalahari Desert rat'll put thirty pounds on that. I've never seen one in the States."

"How come?"

"Never looked. Don't have to look cause I know the facts. Some folks come over, want to show me their rats. I tell 'em call first, and don't bring no bogus rat. A genuine odd rat I'll take a look at for ya. The other day this fella calls, says he's got a hunred pound rat cummin' in from Africa. I say, 'You're lyin', fella. I know the fact.'"

"What's the fact?"

"Fact is big rats don't travel well, especially on steamers. A thirty-five, forty pound wharf rat's got a chance, but a sixty pound bilge rat'll never make it, cause the crew eats 'em. A small rat they don't bother with, but a big meaty rat the engine crew will roast in the boiler and feast on for the duration of the voyage."

I leaned back in the big porch rocker, stretched my legs out all the way and put my feet up on the railing.

"What's the smallest rat?" I asked my Uncle.

"The smallest rat I've seen is a nick rat. No biggeran a nick, about so big. . . but I don't know the smallest for sure. There may be rats so small we don't even know about 'em."

Uncle Brucker wrote down notes for his Proposals, and he kept a Journal for Additional Ideas. He thought-up two books on rats he'd been working on. One of his books is the *Specialized Rat Encyclopedia, From A to Z*.

In the preface to the *Specialized Rat Encyclopedia, From A to Z*, he explains that rats are curious and intelligent creatures capable of adapting to situations. For instance, a family of rats living in a public library can learn to read an abridged dictionary. A gas station rat will putter with four-cylinder engines and perform minor electric repairs. At Multiple Tire in Matacham, station rats taught themselves how to drain the oil and use a spark plug wrench.

"What's the other book about?"

"The other book is a collection of true rat stories from around the world," he said. "Everybody loves a rat story, cause there ain't nuthin' like 'em."

A greenfly flew through a hole in the screen. He swiped it and knocked it to the floor where it buzzed and buzz-buzzed.

"I'm tryin' to get one rat story from every country the world over," he said. "But with so many stories mixed in my head, it's hard to keep 'em straight. Someday when I get 'em straight in my mind, I'll write 'em down chronological so they make some sorta sense. At that point I'll think up a title or I'll know one already."

That greenfly buzzed. The mosquitos flew in just to annoy us, but they didn't buzz like that greenfly.

"Damn!" Uncle Brucker said. "Still no reply from the government concernin' my new proposal. What's takin' 'em so long?"

His new Proposal, D-299, was of primary importance. He had worked on it for a long time and finished it early last year. It's a Top-Secret Defense Plan that he couldn't tell me about in case the government decides to accept it. If the government won't accept it, then he'll tell me about it. Or if the government accepts it and says OK, then he tells me. But until that time he can't even give a hint.

Uncle Brucker said, "I hope the government ain't takin' its time, cause I really want to tell you all about it. Right now my proposal is in the consideration stage, and that's stage two."

"How many stages to go?"

"Good question. Stages vary with the proposal. This bein' a prime proposal, top scale, might add up five or six stages. There's committees to go to and meetins to attend, and you know that don't make it easy. So I can't tell you about my proposal yet, Walt. Right now you'll have to wait."

"How long?"

Uncle Brucker thought about this.

In a while he said, "Average one stage per year. Sorry."

Uncle Brucker searched through his pockets. He was looking for something important, and he found it wrapped in a handkerchief in his back pocket. He unwrapped it and handed it to me secretly, palm down.

When he opened his fingers it dropped like magic into my hand.

"Wow!" I said. "It's a real Indian arrowhead!"

It had INDIAN scratched into the side.

"Nah, that ain't real," he said. "What Indian would write Indian on his arrowhead? It's authentic though, except for the inscription. I made this one myself in the Cherokee Indian style, and it's just as good. I wrote Indian on the back so you know it ain't real cause it looks so authentic. It's yours, I'm givin' it to ya. Keep it as a good luck piece."

# 4

By the time I turned 16, my father and I were at war. We fought every day about one thing or another, but the biggest battles were over the missing drill bit and spark plug wrench.

We got along for a day or two, which means we ignored each other and didn't talk. Then if I said one word, he'd get crazy and start in with the orders. Mow the goddamn lawn. Patch the damn roof on the shed like I told you.

And find me my drill bit and bring back the damn plug wrench!

He worked for the highway department during the week. On weekends he repaired cars in the garage attached to the house. He kept the garage door open so you'd know he was in business. Except when his girlfriend Raylene came over, he rolled it down.

While cleaning up one night he noticed the space on the pegboard where the spark plug wrench went. Where was the damn plug wrench? He bought it at Schnells Hardware just last week. He had held it in his hand a minute ago.

He rolled up the garage door and backed out the Subaru, and Raylene came inside and got me and I looked for it, and Raylene looked for it. I know what he's like when he loses track of things, and now Raylene's finding out. You don't want to be within a mile of him until he gets it back.

We searched all over the floor and behind the work bench, and he drove down to Schnells and bought a new spark plug wrench.

Next weekend it was the drill bit. He took it out when he screwed on the door panel of an Altima. My father was supposed to be the Man In Control.

Losing the plug wrench made him short-tempered and hot-headed. And now the #8 drill bit was missing too. Every weekend something disappears. He couldn't take it any more. The plug wrench started a fire in his head. The drill bit fanned the flames. A wildfire blew in my direction and a pumper, a hook and ladder, and a monsoon couldn't put it out.

He didn't need liquor to get ornery. He started out ornery every day. And you couldn't reason with him. He listened only to what played out inside his ornery head.

Across the breakfast table Friday morning, he put the eye on me. He had one silver earring in his left ear and a wrinkled county work shirt on his back. Stick-up wax in his hair. He put a new blade in his razor and a Band-Aid on his chin.

He drank from his coffee mug with his eye on me, and all during breakfast he eyed me. He didn't say one word after I passed him the sugar. How did he get the scrambled eggs on his fork? Beats me, he never looked down at his plate.

He was certain I took his tools. Most likely I hid them somewhere in the garage, but they could be in the basement. He said I did it to get back at him, just to fuck him up. I had the motivation but he lacked the proof. Someday when he figures it out I'll get what I deserve.

He doesn't need my help when it comes to losing things. He lost the plug wrench and misplaced the drill bit on his own. If he ever stops bossing me around, I might show him where he put them.

Finally he said, "I'm workin' on a theory," like it's headline news. "It's called the theory of the missin' tools."

"You work that out all by yourself?"

"It's my theory."

"Sounds like the same old theory's been stuck here for a while. You better jack it up, old man. That theory's got a flat."

"You coulda hocked 'em down at Schnells. Coulda sold 'em cheap on the street."

"That a different theory?" I asked him.

"All part of the same theory," he said.

He glanced at the clock on the wall. 7:30. Time to go to work. He got up from his chair and went to the door. I sat at the table with the bowl of corn flakes.

"I ain't dealin' with you no more," he said with his back to me. "It ain't worth it. I ain't talkin' to you and I ain't listenin' no more either. I don't talk to thieves, crooks, and liars. Startin' now."

"Now ain't soon enough for me," I said as he walked out.

It went on and on between my father and me, war without end. It wasn't just the plug wrench and the drill bit that set him off, it was that plus everything else.

After breakfast I got my pack and walked down to the school bus stop, but I didn't get on the bus. JJ waited at the stop and his twin brother TJ was with him. They watched me cross the street at the corner. JJ turned to TJ and pointed at me.

"School's in that direction," he yelled my way.

Instead of going to the high school, I went the other direction through the woods, crossed the stream behind the strip mall, and went straight to my Uncle's house.

From now on I don't live with my father anymore. I made up my mind on the way over. He can't make me stay and he can't stop me from going. I'm moving into the old house.

From this day on it's me and my Uncle. I never asked him if it was OK. I never even thought about asking. I had run away so many times it was my second home. Now it moved up to first.

My new first home was more than a mile closer to the high school than the old one. Monday I'll walk to school, but today I'm taking off. It's moving day.

But when I got to the old house, my Uncle wasn't home. The Eagle was in the driveway, the Ram parked out back. If the cars are here, he should be here. Where is my Uncle? I sat outside on the porch and watched the school busses come down the hill and head back to the lot on the other side of town.

Reed Weir drove up in his Nissan a while later. Reed was my Uncle's good friend and a good fisherman. They went fishing for bass and brookies on Sundays.

Today he wore a suit jacket and tie and polished brown shoes, and he combed his hair back neat for a change.

"I guess you ain't goin' fishin'," I said.

He couldn't get my father on his cell phone, so he stopped off at the high school first and then he drove out here.

"Your Uncle is at Mercy in Dexter," Reed said. "They took him in last night. He phoned me from the hospital early this mornin'. He didn't sound too good. We better get over there and bring him a beer."

# 5

They put Uncle Brucker in the hospital bed because he had a stroke, his second stroke in three years. The first stroke left him with seventy percent use of his left arm. The second stroke wasn't as bad, but now part of his right side was damaged too.

While he was in the hospital recovering from the first stroke he caught pneumonia and the doctors made him stay two extra weeks. At the end of the first extra week he became weak and delirious. His appetite disappeared. He lost thirteen pounds altogether because he didn't feel like eating a damn thing. His temperature shot up to 102, then 103, then 103 and 1/2. He just wanted to get out of there and go back home and get better.

Last night he pulled the tubes out of his arm and made a break for it. Two orderlies found him in the basement trying to climb through a tiny window behind the soda machine. The orderlies dragged him to his room and strapped him to the bed They were big men, six-two, six-three. He didn't have a chance.

Uncle Brucker hated the hospital. He hated the tall orderlies and the strap-on beds. He hated the big-seat hospital toilets, the bad-tasting water, the smiling doctors, the tubes that go in and out. There isn't one thing he liked about the hospital except Nurse Marnell, who was his dream fuck.

Reed took a beer out of his pocket and stashed it under the bed blanket. He pulled two more cans from under his jacket and rolled them under the bed. In the trunk of his Nissan, Reed saved a six-pack and a Chivas for the next fishing trip, but right now half a six is all my Uncle would get.

Reed got back in his Nissan and drove off to work, and I moved the chair close to my Uncle.

"You got the pen, Walt?" His voice was small.

"I got a pad too."

"Good boy. Now write this down. I, Brucker Thompson, bein' of sound mind though I look like crap and feel like shit, bequeath the house and all my belongin's to you, Walt. That includes my power tools, my coin collection, the Heritage Mugs, and my War Medal and everythin' I took in trade. Keep the mugs upside down so the rats don't get in 'em, and whatever you do, don't dust off my Medal."

Sunken into the hospital bed, buried under the sheets. Tubes going in his arms. Bags of fluid hanging by the side of his bed.

Uncle Brucker's left eyelid sneaked shut, then his right eyelid shut. The color had drained from his face and now he was yellow, but I guess that's a color too. His bent nose got bigger since the stroke. Purple veins popped out on his nose and all over his forehead, having a big party at the temples.

"I don't know nuthin' about dyin'," he said.

Eyes closed, he was quiet for the longest minute and he looked like he was dead, really dead.

"No, you ain't dyin'! Tell me you ain't dyin'," I said.

Then something inside him connected and his chest went up and down in a deep breath, and his eyes popped open and he looked around like he was seeing the world for the first time. And he smiled. Not much of a smile, but it qualified.

"You're right, Walt. I ain't dyin'," he said. "When you're dyin' you know about it. Right now I only know about livin'. I had a feelin' is all, and that shows you feelin' ain't knowin'. What did I say?"

"Feelin' ain't knowin'."

"That's right! Maybe I ain't thinkin' straight, but it's better than no thinkin' at all." Then he saw someone coming down the hall. "There's doctors cummin'! Quick, Walt, hide the beer and gimme that glass a water!"

"What's goin' on?"

"Hide the beer and pass the glass!"

I got the glass of water from the table and he took it with both hands. He drank it quickly, spilling it on his beard. His eyes slid toward the door. The two doctors came down the hall, one door, two doors closer.

"Hello, doctors!" said Uncle Brucker. The doctors looked in. He held the glass with one hand as they walked past the room. With the other hand, he tipped an imaginary top hat.

"Lookin' healthy, feelin' fine, sippin' a glass a water," he said. And he drank some more.

"Why were we waitin'?" I asked when the doctors had gone.

"For health reasons," he whispered. "A person looks his healthiest when he's sippin' a drink and especially healthy when he's sippin' a drink a water. You figure it takes about a minute a drinkin' to be sure you look entirely healthy. Every time a doctor walks by I'm lookin' healthy drinkin' water. I keep lookin' healthy, they gotta let me outta here. They gotta."

He was breathing softly now.

And I was starving. On the bedside table I found half a baloney and cheese left over from lunch. I ate it in four bites even though it was on whole wheat.

Visiting hours end at ten. It was already nine thirty-five. I planned to stick around until the last minute, but Keith Weir came to pick me up early and I had to leave at nine forty-five.

# 6

Two days later. I backed the Ram out of the driveway at three-thirty after I got home from school. Avoiding 94, I took the back roads all way to Dexter and parked in the lot under the hospital.

Now it's nine fifteen. I'm sitting on the floor in a hiding spot behind the door in my Uncle's room. All the other visitors had gone home and the hospital was quiet. There was only me.

Somebody put coins in the soda machine in the basement. The can of soda slid down and hit the tray with a bang I heard all the way upstairs. Soon Nurse Marnell came around to check. She looked in but she couldn't see me in my well-chosen hiding spot. Her perfume smelled up the room.

"You're like a son to me," Uncle Brucker said when the nurse went away.

He felt much better today. His temperature was down, way down. And no tubes.

"I wish you were my dad," I said.

"It ain't somethin' you can choose," he said.

"I don't see him cummin' around here. Do you?"

"That's between me and him."

"It's my mother I hate more."

"Don't hate nobody or you'll end up hatin' yourself."

"Quiet!" Uncle Brucker put a finger to his lips. "Footsteps coming down the hall! Gimme that glass a water, son, and get outta sight. Looks like another one cummin'."

I had it all planned out.

Soon I'll get up and check the hall. If it's empty we'll sneak out of the room, and we won't take the elevator, we'll take the stairs down to the basement and go through the underground lot.

I'll put his clothes in a pillow case and pack the beer and cigarettes in with it, and I'll throw it in the back of the Ram. I'll help him into the passenger seat. I'll clip on his seat belt. I'll get behind the wheel and I'll drive him home faster than any Mustang and I'll nurse him back to health better than any nurse.

He doesn't need anybody but me, and I don't need anybody except him. I had made up my mind. I would never let him die.

"Come on, Unc, we're goin' home."

# 7

Uncle Brucker felt much better after I rescued him from the hospital. The next morning his temperature went down to 100 and he wanted a home-cooked meal. I cooked him a rib eye out back on the charcoal grill. I boiled a whole can of peas. I cut up the steak into little chunks and he fed himself left-handed. He sucked up half a can of Boomers through a straw and said, "I ain't wastin' half a Boomers." Then he sucked up the other half. I gave him a soup spoon for the peas.

Later that week he got sick from leftover pneumonia and his temperature went up to 102 again. Keith Weir offered to take him to the hospital, but my Uncle refused to go back there and lie in another tie-down hospital bed. He fought the idea for a week while his leftover pneumonia went away and his temperature went back to normal.

During the next two weeks his health improved tremendously. For his breakfast I mixed two multi-vitamin cereals, Cheerios and Total. "Gimme three," he said, and next morning I added Wheaties. His appetite came back strong and he put on eight pounds. Bit by bit his body took back what the stoke carried away. Feeling came back first to his left side, then his right side. Then feeling turned into strength.

But I thought he should be careful. Don't move too fast. Rest, sleep in the hammock, go fishing. And lay off the rats!

He took my advice and slept out back in the hammock for one hour every afternoon. He refused to lift anything heavier than a six-pack. He went fishing on Sunday with Keith and Reed Weir and he came back with two big bass and color in his cheeks. He loved to fish, and he bought an expensive reel and fancy tackle. Three more bass and a couple of brookies. The color stayed in his cheeks.

In two weeks he had regained all his energy plus reserve energy for doing extra things such as painting the exterior of the house. That was all he thought about. Painting the house. Finally he had the energy. With my help, he'd get it done. He felt good, very good, and that made me feel good too. He felt good enough to start the job immediately. Get him a roller pan, he had the rollers, we'll finish the job in no time.

He felt so good he swore his vital organs worked better since he had the stroke.

"A jolt like that sends a warnin' to your body and gets the whole system workin' again," he told me. "That'll teach those lazy orgins. Most orgins are capable of doin' a far better job. But after a while they get bored with pumpin' and digestin' and filterin'. It's borin' routine stuff. A stroke tells 'em how it's gotta be. Wise-up you lazy orgins! Do your job! That's what happened to me. That was a revitalizin' stroke, Walt. Coupla revitalizin' strokes and you can really accomplish somethin'."

After dinner he moved to the living room and sat in the recliner and turned on the TV. It was 7:30, time for Cole's Law starring Rad Kielly as detective Boyd Cole.

I don't like that dumb cop show, but Uncle Brucker thought it was TV at its best. It was his favorite but it was on the bottom of my list. Baseball players can't act, to begin with. Washed-up baseball players like Rad Kielly can't play ball and they can't act. Uncle Brucker was always trying to get me to watch a great episode of Cole's Law.

"Have a seat. This is a great show," he said.

"Sure it is," I said.

"You got some problem with great shows?"

"Everybody likes a great show, but this ain't it," I told him.

"There's nobody watches it don't think it's great."

"What about me? I don't count?" I said.

"Maybe you ain't watchin' it close enough."

"I ain't gonna put my head through the screen," I told him.

"You know what I mean."

"Maybe I've done enough watchin' and I don't like what I'm seein'."

"That's a mighty big maybe."

"No biggeran yours," I said.

"How do you know? You ain't measured it," he said.

A few minutes later during a commercial he noticed an ad on the back of a circular that came in the mail.

"Hey, they got off-white!" he said.

Next day we drove down to Schnells Hardware and bought three gallons of exterior off-white for the price of two and a discount roller pan, and I put it in the basement. He had somewhere in the basement a couple of hardly-used rollers that Bill Voght gave him. He was serious about painting the exterior and he thought about painting the dining room, but we had to move all the furniture out first. And where the hell did he put those damn rollers? No hurry, but he wanted to get the job done. Sit down, have a beer. The house ain't going nowhere. Exterior first, interior maybe in the fall.

One night before I fell asleep, Uncle Brucker came into the bedroom and said he owed it all to me.

"It was you who recovered me, Walt, and you did a damn fine job. To you. He sat on the bed and raised his can of Boomers and drank the whole thing. "That's a full toast," he said and wiped his mouth on his sleeve.

He kept his War Medal in the middle of the high shelf in the living room. The War Medal was the one thing he cared about. You could throw out the TV, his rat rifle and everything else. He never cleaned the Medal or dusted it off since he got it because war isn't clean or neat. It was presented to him for one particular battle but in the dust was a history of all that happened over the years.

I'd been staying at the old house since he came home from the hospital, so I guess you can say I moved in.

It was all OK with my father. Raylene moved in with him and he kept the garage door closed, and he was glad to get rid of me.

He drove past the old house once or twice. Once I was out back at home plate with a bat in my hands. Leroy threw a speedo and I whacked it over his head. When I saw the Malibu coming I quit and hid behind the barn until Bones gave me the all-clear. See ya next time, dad.

But there was no next time.

My father never drove by again. Raylene moved in with a guy named Chuck in Neidersville, and her younger sister Crispy stepped in. He wanted to buy a gas station and set up a repair shop. I never found out what happened to my mother. She left when I was eight. My father said he wouldn't know, how would he know? He wouldn't tell me anyway. I took off on my father and my mother took off on me.

Uncle Brucker said what's his is mine. I guess that means the old house is mine too. This includes the barn, an old John Deere tractor and six junked cars my father left that I was fixing up. I had already pulled the front brakes off the Camaro and found an oil pump at Sturdevants in Crawley. New plugs too. I mean almost new. Next, the distributor cap and a not-too-old Diehard I hoped Otto's Auto was still saving for me.

Someday I'll get the Camaro back on the road.

Except for new gray hairs sticking out of his beard, a shaky left arm and a winky left eye, there was no evidence that Uncle Brucker ever had a stroke.

# 8

Uncle Brucker never gave out his phone number and he never advertised. He didn't have to. Got a rat problem? All you have to do was ask somebody, it'll get back to my Uncle.

Saturday morning Mrs. Hobbs from South First Street left a message on the phone. There was a ugly rat caught in the crawlspace under her kitchen. Two days ago her husband crawled in after it, but he got stuck under the floor boards and he can't get out.

We drove out to Mrs. Hobbs' house on South First. I held Uncle Brucker's rifle and he pulled on his leather gloves and got down on his knees and crawled under the house. Moving quietly like a swamp snake, he sneaked up on the rat while it was sleeping and strangled it with its own tail.

Then he crawled over to Mr. Hobbs and offered him a cigarette. Uncle Brucker lit one up too. They smoked and who knows what they talked about down there. Uncle Brucker kept two cigarettes for himself and gave Mr. Hobbs the rest of the pack, and then he crawled out from under the house.

"He ain't cummin' out yet, dumplin'," Uncle Brucker told Mrs. Hobbs. "I'm just tellin' ya what he told me."

"How's he gettin' along down there?" she asked.

Uncle Brucker looked to the house, shrugged his shoulders and smiled a little.

"No complaints," he said.

Mrs. Hobbs had a wardrobe made up of primary colors. Today she wore a bright yellow apron, blue pants, and green shoes.

From South First Street we drove to Parville and checked the traps along Jack's Creek, then from Parville we drove over to Grimley. It was a busy day for the Rat Killer, a bad day for rats.

Uncle Brucker couldn't deal with credit cards, and please don't write a check. He accepted cash for his service, but he'd much rather trade for a toaster oven or a coffee maker.

He'd take almost anything in exchange. He said he made out better this way. He drove a hard bargain and he always got what he wanted. If you want them dead, give a toaster or microwave. Don't give him cash.

Today a retired fireman from Grimley gave him a half-empty bottle of Vodka and a two-finger bowling ball. He took the Vodka and the bowling ball. "If you want 'em dead, give me the blender," he said and he bartered for an alarm clock as well. The woman on Holmes Street baked him a delicious banana cake. She still owed him a toaster from last time. On second thought, he'd rather take the grill.

We parked on a dirt road outside town and I waited while he drank the vodka. Uncle Brucker said it was OK, so I gave the bowling ball to a little kid on a bicycle. By the time we got back to town we had finished off the banana cake and he drank the Vodka.

Wherever the Rat Killer went he attracted a crowd. Neighbors came over to congratulate him for a job well done, old friends stopped by to say hello. Cute little kids and shy old ladies asked for his autograph.

At 48 Crown Street a short man with a bad leg limped over to my Uncle and shook his hand. I couldn't keep my eyes off his daughter.

She was hot! Her jet back hair went all the way down to her waist, cut straight across, and her eyes were dark and slinky. I'd seen her before but I never talked to her. She was a junior in the Catholic high school up on the heights, same grade as me.

I moved a little closer while her father and my Uncle talked, and closer still until I stood next to her. My legs got wobbly, ready to fold, and my heart jumped out of my chest and danced along the sidewalk.

I never felt like this before—so good and so bad, hot and cold at the same time.

Then she turned and I looked into her eyes.

And that's when I fell in love.

"I know you. You're Walt," she said.

"I know who you are. Your name's Renata. Cool name."

"You think so?"

"Sounds like it goes with ya," I said.

"I seen you around."

"I seen you after school at High Mary's. I drive up to the heights all the time. You wear those plaid skirts."

"You got to or else you ain't Catholic."

"You want to go for a ride sometime, get a slice?" I asked her.

"You ain't got a license."

"But I got wheels."

"What kinda wheels?"

"Take your pick. I got the Eagle and a old Camaro I'm fixin' up. I got a Monte Carlo I might fix up too—but that's a maybe. My Camaro ain't here with me or I'd say let's go. That car is fast."

"It ain't fast like Cooter's Cougar," she said.

"What car is?" I said.

Cooter's Cougar had the reputation. It was the car everybody's trying to catch up to, the fastest and coolest car in Bowen county. Chris Christopher couldn't get ahead of it with his GTI, and Firebird Fran ate his dust with a soup spoon.

The Cougar had blacked-out windows. Nobody knew what Cooter looked like because you couldn't see in and he never got out. When the headlights flash on a Friday night you know Cooter's Cougar is on the prowl.

Meanwhile, my Uncle was talking to the man with the bad leg, Renata's father.

"You don't remember me, do you?" he said. "I fought beside you durin' the Second Uprisin'. Just a face in the crowd, I guess. I was there when they give you that fancy Medal for killin' all them rats. You still got that Medal?"

"He sure does," I said. "Sits on a shelf in the livin' room where everybody can see it."

"On the shelf, you say?"

"It's on display. Original dust."

"That so? That Medal might be worth somethin' to the right person—if you're interested in sellin'."

"Not for sale," said Uncle Brucker.

"That's what I thought."

"Then why'd you ask?"

"People change their minds. Nuthin's permanent. Medal ain't worth a nickel up there on that shelf, I'll say that. The right person would pay you top dollar. Change your mind, I could be that person. Dusty Medal like that's hard to find."

Uncle Brucker grabbed my arm and rushed me off to the car before I could say goodbye to Renata.

"Now listen here," said Uncle Brucker, so angry he sounded like my father. "You tell that bastard where the Medal is, you might as well wrap it up and give it to him. Don't tell nobody nuthin' about us. Keep your big mouth shut. You hear me?"

"My mouth ain't so big."

"Just keep it shut."

"Gotta to eat, don't I? Can't shut it all the time or I'll starve."

"And stay away from that girl. She ain't your type."

# 9

I don't care what they say, a shined-up car not only looks good, it runs better too. And the more you shine it up, the faster it goes.

Sunday I woke up early and shined-up the Eagle with the spray wax I keep in the trunk. Uncle Brucker had a tough time getting out of bed so I had extra time and cleaned up the dash while I waited for him. We had a lot of calls to answer and mucho rats to kill.

Finally he came outside. He stood at the screen door with a beer in his hand and watched me for a while. Then he went inside and came out with another one.

When he walked over to the car he had a serious look on his face like he was pitching in the World Series.

He tossed me the car keys but I missed them and I had to dig them out of the seat.

"You're drivin' until I say you ain't," he said, and I slid over behind the wheel and took off. "Easy, make a right at the corner."

I love to drive. Started at fourteen driving the Eagle around the back yard, then last year when I turned fifteen Uncle Brucker let me take it to the streets.

I made a right on Meridian Avenue and then took the back way out of town. I had the Eagle up to seventy going west on 94. Passed a Lincoln Town Car easy and then a Mercedes diesel moping in the left lane. Nobody was in front of me for a long stretch and I took it up to eighty. Uncle Brucker made me slow down to sixty-five when the front end shook. After the rearview mirror fell to the floor, it was fifty-five again.

"Epoxy will fix that," I said, and I kicked the mirror under the seat away from the pedal.

Soon we were in the foothills. We went up and up a twisty road that had a double yellow line all the way. Tall pines grew on both sides of the road and scrub bushes grew out of the rocks. I drove across a rocky stream where icicles hung leftover from Christmas.

I had never been up here before, high up in the foothills where the air is cold all day and the wind comes on strong at night. I kept the Eagle mostly in third gear, took the turns in second.

The Eagle ate up the road.

Somewhere on the road, Uncle Brucker started to talk. Fast at first, like a sideshow pitchman, because he had so many thoughts bunched up inside for so long. Then as he cleared his mind, he slowed down, like a lecturer on a summer tour.

"There's things I gotta tell you, Walt, important things, and they're all true. Some things you'll understand right away. Others might take a while. Don't be alarmed if it comes to you the long way, it's just a slow truth cummin' around is all.

"A long, long time ago, before evolution started, life was different here on Earth," he explained. "These were the Rat Ages when rats had big brains and humans had little tiny brains. For hunreds, maybe thousands of years, big brain rats ran the show. But we have no way a knowin' how long cause rats don't keep track a time. In those days humans lived in holes in the ground and rats lived in fancy garden apartments. Look around you, for every human thing there was a rat thing. Rats drove ratmobiles around town, watched rat-toons on TV. There were rich rat kings and genius rat scientists and fat rat politicians too.

"Cause at that time the meanest ruled. You remember the dinosaurs? Mean tyrants ruled the earth until a big Asteroid crashed and turned day into night. The dinosaurs died off, wonderin' where the sun went. But rats love the night, hate the day. The rats came out of their holes and cheered when the sun disappeared. '*Te-ta*-Asteroid!' they cried. 'Thank you Asteroid! *Te-ta!* Thank you for hittin' the earth!'

"Rats bein' next in line for meanness, they slipped right into the Rulin' Seat and started runnin' things in the meanest way. When things get bleak and can't get any worse, the rats come out, and then things get worse."

Uncle Brucker went on about the Rat Ages, and he took me away. After a while I was no longer riding with him in the Eagle. I was back in the Rat Ages, floating up high with the clouds. Everything shrunk back to how it was ten thousand years ago, and Uncle Brucker's words came together for real down below. Rat kings conquering. Rat hordes crawling out of garden apartments and marching to the ends of the earth. I had a clear view of the Rat Ages as I floated up above, quiet as a blimp.

Everything was piling up, everything my Uncle had taught me about rats since the first time I ran away from home. Floating and listening and thinking and words coming alive. It happened all at once. There was a lot going on, a lot to figure out, and it weighed me down. And then I wasn't floating any more, and I was back in the front seat of the Eagle with my Uncle Brucker.

"How did the Rat Ages end?" he said. "Why did the rats disappear? Well that's the question, innit? Some say their own meanness did 'em in. Others say a whole lotta little asteroids hit 'em right on their heads. Another theory is the Rulin' rats liked eatin' lead, sprinkled it on their meals like it was salt. All we know is they vanished into another dimension and they've been hangin' out there ever since."

"That'll make you sick and crazy, eatin' lead."

"Yes, but they can write with their noses. Some say that's the earliest indication we have of the Rat Ages, and I agree. Crazed nose writins from the sick minds a rats."

"And now they're waitin' in the next dimension, prayin' for the Asteroid to come back," I said. "So's things will get bleak again and they'll get back in the Rulin' Seat."

"Rats are impatient creatures who live for revenge. And what's the worst thing you can do to a human? What's the last thing a man would want to be? I can't prove it right now but I got reasons to suspect they got a way of turnin' people into rats. Nobody knows how they do it. All we know is it's been goin' on for years. Started long ago durin' the crazy days of the Black Plague. You can read about it in the *Medieval Times*.

"Walt, I'm sendin' you a warnin'. That man we talked to yesterday, he wanted to buy my Medal, I don't trust him. And his daughter—-one day they're gonna wake up and they won't be in bed, they'll be in the bottom of a rat hole and they won't know the difference. You're headin' for trouble, Walt, if you keep movin' in her direction. Promise me, you can look but don't touch."

On the way down the twisty road I thought real hard about what Uncle Brucker said.

People turning rat . . . poisoning their genes. It was a small part of a big story. I worked on it as I drove. About 10 miles down the road I put it all together.

"Holy shit, Unc!" I said. "If there's people turnin' into rats . . ."

"Go on."

"And there's no turnin' back . . ."

"Keep goin'."

"And there's more and more of 'em every day."

"You're gettin' there."

"Someday you're gonna have a whole world a rats!"

"Now you see what's goin' on. They're movin' in on us, Walt, takin' over the planet. Once they get evolution back where they want it, it'll be the Rat Ages all over again. And this time they're gonna make damn sure humans never get back into the Rulin' Seat. The government asked me to keep an eye on 'em, and for years I been helpin' out. But I can't do it alone no more. There's too many of 'em out there. I've been lookin' around for a right hand man to help me out. What do ya say, Walt?"

"I'll help you out, Unc. I'll be your right hand man."

"Thanks, Walt. I was hopin' you'd say yes. We can't stop 'em, but we can keep track of 'em."

"How can you tell who they are? Who's gonna turn and who ain't?" I asked him.

"Well that's the next step, innit? Easy, make a right at the corner."

# 10

On the way home we stopped for burgers in Conklin. I was beat from all the driving, but I could drive to Alaska if I had a cheese-burger, a chocolate shake, and a medium twister fry.

"In every town they got their hangouts, but there ain't no town like Conklin," Uncle Brucker said.

We ate at a rundown burger place called Rex's in the old part of town. The broken sign hung low on one side. Any lower, it will hit the top of the door. A couple of nails in the right place will solve the problem, but nobody took out the ladder and climbed up and fixed it.

I pulled into the lot and drove to the drive-up.

"Remember what we're lookin' for?" he asked.

"We're looking for the Three Key Steps to Identification," I told him.

"That's right. What we're doin' is trickin' 'em into revealin' themselves."

On the road down from the lookout at Modak, he explained the Three Key Steps to Identification.

Step 1. Cognistension. You find someone you think might be turning rat, your natural reflex is to turn your head and look at them. What you have to do is observe that natural reflex. Make note of it because it'll point you in the right direction. At this time you might feel a little anxious. Don't worry, that's normal. That's Step 1, and that's called Cognis-TEN-sion.

Step 2. Transposition. So now you think you've Identified a suspect but you won't know for sure until Transposition occurs. The longer you look at them the more they look like rats. That's their inner self showing through, and that's called Transposition. You transpose the vision of a rat over their faces. Step 2, Trans-po-SIT-ion.

Step 3. Genomorphism. The complete manifestation of these rat traits in a physical way. But that don't happen till later. It takes a long time to get going but then it happens overnight. And that's Step 3, Geno-MORPH-ism.

People with rat genes know when they're noticed, especially after Genomorphism occurs. They got an extra rat sense about that. Sometimes when they know they're noticed, they tend to walk away and disappear into a crowd. That's called Stridation. But that's not a step, and it doesn't have a number. It's just a thing they do when they're turning rat.

"Can somebody turn mouse?" I asked him.

"Mice ain't my line," he said.

At last the food came and we took it from the girl at the window. Those twisters are delicious. We smelled them before we got them. Uncle Brucker opened the bag and ate the big ones while I found a place to park.

Right off something made me turn my head and got me looking: the girl at the drive-up window. And it got me suspicious. Her streaky brown hair had bangs over her eyes, and she put on hide-behind make-up that covered her face.

She dropped a quarter in my palm and pressed it down with her thumb. The look in her eye said, "You don't fool me, pal. I know who you are."

"The girl at the drive-up, she's one."

"There's one sure way to be sure," my Uncle said. "Check your fries for Symbols."

Symbols. When they know they've been noticed they like to let you know they noticed you noticing. They'll often give you a Symbol, something out of the ordinary only you know what it means. It's their way of winking at you. A bent fry or twisted fry could be a Symbol.

I picked through the medium bag of fries, looking for Symbols. I found one!

"Look what I got!"

"Twisted?"

"No, folded."

"Let's see that fry."

I handed him an extremely long fry, folded over twice, and he checked it out with a delicate touch. Through the squinty eyes of a police investigator, he considered the too-long, folded-over, untwisted twister fry.

"How do you explain that?" he held up the fry and asked. Not me, he asked everyone else.

The sun went down and the temperature dropped. Store lights flickered in the old part of town. I wouldn't mind the chill but the fries were gone and I was still hungry.

On the roof of the restaurant one lonely light lit up the "R" in Rex's.

The parking lot had emptied out, but we continued Identifying. So far I was at fifty percent, maybe fifty-five. He'll give me the benefit of the doubt. But fifty-five isn't good enough and the benefit ran out.

Maybe I'll never learn to Identify. So many new ideas to understand and big words to go with them. Maybe I'll never catch on.

I thought about the big things I did by myself and what I'd figured out all by myself. The biggest and most important was the rebuilt carburetor I put in the Dart. I did it all myself. It wasn't easy, but I did it.

Then something got into me and I caught on.

"That guy over there in the Corolla," I pointed, and then I Identified another guy in a minivan.

"Don't point," Uncle Brucker said.

The guy in the minivan wore a white cowboy hat pulled over his ears so it would fit under the roof. He winked at the girl at the drive-up window as he passed. She saw him and winked back, and he winked his way out onto the street.

"Let's go," Uncle Brucker said.

The lesson was over. No sense sticking around. This is Conklin, a town meant for passing through. Uncle Brucker's a good teacher and I'm a quick learner and this is the proof.

Uncle Brucker wanted to drive. I moved over and he slid into the driver's seat. He sat up straight because his back hurt and he felt better, and he started up the Eagle.

I know my Uncle. I know him better than anybody. He's proud of me. I know what's going on in his head right now.

"Damn good Identifyin', Walt," I heard him think.

# 11

The gas gauge in the Eagle broke years ago. Put in as much gas as you want, it'll only measure one fourth, at least that's what we figured. But something went wrong as we drove home from Conklin. The Eagle stalled coming out of the lot, but Uncle Brucker got it going again. The engine kicked and the exhaust sputtered on the highway. About three miles from home it finally cut out and we pushed it off the road at the corner by the brokedown Texaco station. Tomorrow morning we'll come back in the Ram with a can of gas and start it up.

Now we walked those three long miles.

It was a bright night with an almost-full moon. A little dent in the side of the moon or it would be full. No clouds, but the stars were hard to find. Well, just one cloud I didn't notice at first, sneaking through the treetops, a fluffy little cloud that looked like sky broccoli. The wind came up, blowing hard in a one-cloud sky. The treetops swayed and the branches squeaked a spooky way, but some squeaks weren't so spooky. The big moon was really big, biggest moon I've ever seen.

Somehow that big puffed-up moon made me want a chocolate shake or vanilla the way TV makes you want things. No place to stop for a shake along the way, unless somebody built a store that afternoon.

I knew my chances for getting a shake were slim, but I kept wanting a chocolate shake or a vanilla shake all the way home.

# 12

Wednesday after school we took the Ram downtown and Uncle Brucker bought me a pair of Identifying sunglasses in Constant Value Stores. The end display on Aisle #8 caught my eye right away. Someone just restocked it. It was waiting patiently for me.

"Choose carefully," Uncle Brucker said. "A good pair of Identifiers will cut through the bullshit and you'll see their inner selves. There's only one pair will work for you, unless you go to China. You gotta find that rightful pair, and you better be sure. I got no money for China."

I chose a real cool pair from the center of the rack. An extra piece of plastic ran across the top for support, and wiggly pads fit the side of my nose. I put the sunglasses on and they slid down my nose.

I tried on the next coolest pair. This pair lacked that extra piece across the top but they stayed up on my nose. A famous French designer signed his name along the right side and a designer from Italy signed her name on the left.

I checked them out in the mirror.

"What do you think, Unc?"

"I ain't wearin' 'em. You tell me," he said.

Me, in the mirror.

"Looks like I got my rightful pair!" I said.

"Wear 'em whenever you're Identifyin'," said Uncle Brucker. "Use the Three Key Steps for reference. Identifyin's easy when you're lookin' through your rightful pair, and they don't notice you noticin' them. And don't let nobody else wear 'em. They dull 'em out for ya."

Uncle Brucker went back to the car and I strolled around Constant Value.

What Uncle Brucker said made a lot of sense. Maybe not right away, but later when you think about it.

A red-haired woman pushed a cart filled with groceries down aisle #7. Her child walked beside her. It all looked regular with my Identifiers off. Put them on, my mouth fell open. Through the glasses, the mother had a gray rat face with an ugly rat nose. And the little rat-face kid had whiskers.

But her hands on the cart were the soft hands of a young woman. I guess that part of her didn't turn yet.

Quickly I looked away to be sure she didn't notice me noticing her.

Next aisle over, a pretty woman shopped with her tall handsome husband. She walked like a runway model who wanted to make it on the screen. The handsome guy was the director. He shaved with the kind of razor that leaves a stubble.

She thought she knew it all, but she didn't notice that her director husband was turning rat. Through my glasses I could see what she'd never expect. Scrawny rat hands and fat rat arms and sharp rat teeth. What she doesn't know about I won't tell her.

I walked through the supermarket like a high noon gunslinger, hunting for bounty and ready for action. You can keep your space ships and hold onto your zap-zap phasers. My hands were made for a six-shooter.

To go with my Identifiers I bought a big brim baseball cap. I put it on when I left the store and wore it to the Ram. You can't tell who I am or what I'm up to in my Identifiers and big brim sport cap. Being a Man of Mystery has its drawbacks, but it beats giving it all away.

Also, I had figured out my own little symbol, a way to let them know I had Identified them. Whenever I Identified someone for sure, I flipped up the brim of my baseball cap and flipped it down again.

Like this. Like that.

Uncle Brucker thought it was a good idea, flipping the brim. "Cool," he said.

I flipped it again.

"Double cool," he said.

# 13

Uncle Brucker told me to keep a RAT GENE LIST for his Government Report. SUSPECTED and INFECTED. I added CUT OFF.

**RAT GENE LIST**

SUSPECTED

Brad

Darcie
Jose Canusy
Bud Faut at Schnell's Hardware
That hot girl with the curly hair outside Half Price Stores
Phil and Darlene Pearson
Hester and Nestor Landers
A lot of kids who hang out at Weidy's
Sam and Debbie
A lot of kids who hang out at the Galleria
The old guy in the ticket booth
Biff Burris (probably)
Milt at the cigar store
Fred Orbis
Mark B. Meaux

INFECTED

Fred Atkins
Patrick
Burt Faut
G. G. Straub
Grant
The two guys from Conklin
Ray Batavia
Rita Burris (too cute to cut off)
The Taylor kids from Colony Park
Garth
Travis
Marty Grover
Walter Wackenreuter

CUT OFF

Theresa
Patrick

Artie Gaetano at Tuskies
Martha Drick, or Dricker, the skinny girl from Colony Park
Grant Barsky
Marty
Loretta
Garth
Travis
Mr. Jastrab, the school janitor
Michael Ostrander
Ms. Nansatter
Jay Waterson
Gini Masterson
Barry Allen Blatters
Randy Garrett
Bowen Taggart

# 14

On weekdays, Uncle Brucker dropped me off across from the high school before he went out on the road answering help calls and tracking rats. He warned me, don't take my Identifiers to school. So I kept them in my pocket and put them on when I got out of the car.

I marched in through the main entrance, past the front office where the Principal sat, and down the hall.

I'm the guy everybody's waiting for. Smiling, my hair combed back the way I like it. New Nikes. Top it off with my Identifiers, I turned a lot of heads.

They're just ordinary-looking sun glasses from Constant Value Stores, but I didn't get them to block out the sun and look cool. Everyone suspected they hid something deep, but they couldn't figure it out and they won't find out from me.

Identifiers on, I see who they are and who I'm not, and I see what they can't see.

"You think you look cool in those shades," Manny said in the hall.

"I got a cool attitude in general," I said.

"Gonna get a pair just like that," said Bones.

"You can get a pair like 'em but believe me they won't be just like 'em," I said. "They're made for me and only me, and that's what makes 'em different."

"Can I try 'em on?" asked Manny.

"No way."

Everybody admired them and wanted to buy a pair, including Charlee. Except Bunky made a face. You wear sunglasses, pretty soon you'll spray on cologne, he says, which means something to him I guess.

I'd wear them all the time, inside and outside, in the bathroom and in bed. I'd wear them all day long. But Uncle Brucker said be careful, don't turn any heads, but I wasn't careful and I did.

The sunglasses got everybody looking my way. The kids pointed to me and whispered to each other. I figured I better cut that out before it goes too far. So then I wore them as I entered the school and took them off in the hall.

I put them in my shirt pocket, sticking out just a little so you'll notice. Through the morning and after lunch, somehow they heated up. By sixth period my pocket was a hotcake. Ordinary sunglasses don't give you trouble. But these are not ordinary glasses. They are my rightful pair. They'd jump out of my pocket and climb onto my face if they could.

In Mr. Dunkle's third period English, I kept my cool, but in the afternoon in history when Mr. Ross wrote on the chalkboard, I couldn't help sneaking a peek.

This is what I saw:

First row, seat one. Franklin Fodor, coming on strong. Nose? Stretched. Ears? Fuzzy. What once were fingers are now claws.

Can't see his left arm but I know what to expect. I wonder what his little brother looks like.

Second row, seat three. The new kid, Jimmy Buscadora. A patch of fur grows up his shoulder and makes a V on his neck. In this case the V stands for rat.

And look at little Fenisha, she ain't half as cute with those whiskers, and there's Sue Coley-Phelps and Peter Feezey and other kids I didn't mention.

I put their names on the list.

# 15

Charlee and I became friends in the sixth grade. Seventh and eighth grade we went different ways, but we've been real good friends from the eighth grade on. She'll always be one day older than me even though she's was born only six and a half hours earlier. Her real name is Charlene but everybody calls her Charlee. She's cute in a funny way and funny in a cute way. She's not hot like Renata. She's smart but she won't eat pizza.

She saw me talking to Bones and Manny.

I said goodbye to the guys and went over to her.

"We gotta talk," she said.

Yesterday in the office she heard Mr. Ross talking to the principal, Mrs. Molasco. Mrs. Molasco was looking in from the hall during Mr. Ross's class and she saw me put my glasses on. She wants to confiscate them. She says they're cheating glasses. I wear them when I take a test and I see all the answers.

"Don't bring 'em to school," Charlee said, "unless you want to get rid of them. She sees 'em, she'll grab 'em."

"She won't get 'em from me."

"Cheatin' glasses," said Charlee. "They sell 'em in the back of magazines. They got a switch."

"They ain't got glasses that can see answers, and there ain't no switch."

# 16

In Mr. Ross's World History class we had to give report on a Great Historical event. I asked can it be World Shaking and he said that's good too. It had to be at least ten minutes long about a Great Historical or World Shaking event of your own choice, and it had to include at least one chart or map or diagram you had to draw yourself.

Last week Charlee gave an excellent report on Mt Vesuvius and Pompeii. For visual aids she had an accurate map and a well-drawn diagram of Vesuvius and Pompeii destruction.

Mr. Ross is a tall man with a long neck. His Adam's apple bounces up and down like a sing-along dot when he talks. His necktie dances around it, except when he sits at his desk it sinks and sits it out. He announced to the class Charlee earned an A for Vesuvius and Pompeii, but I gave her an A+.

Today it's my turn to give my report on The Asteroid That Crashed.

I was determined to make the best report in the class. The ten minute limit didn't apply because I had so much to say. I made my own rules that worked for me.

I worked on the outline with Charlee in the library and at home after school. Uncle Brucker helped me make a Before And After Crash Chart, and I drew a Map Of Destruction with a real-looking asteroid, with rats and dinosaurs running around.

Uncle Brucker coached me in my presentation and he taught me how to be dramatic at all the right moments. But never be overly dramatic. Grab my heart but don't grab it too tight when the Asteroid crashes. Throw up my arms at the end like I'm going to catch the Asteroid and fling it back.

The other students have smart computers to help them out, and their older brothers have smarter computers. But that will only get you so far. If you want to go the rest of the way, ride with my Uncle and me and bring for reference a thick book with thin pages.

I started off by describing the situation when the Asteroid crashed, who knows how long ago. Before ice could form and way before clouds learned to snow. Dinosaurs ran around acting like big shots. They looked down and they never looked up. Or they'd see it coming and move out of town.

I started out slow and quiet. Everyone lean forward and listened closely. When I had their attention, I turned up the volume and added the dramatics.

The Asteroid crashed somewhere in the world south of Texas. It made a hole bigger than a thousand A-bombs. The air turned to charcoal for more than a lifetime. The whole world was in trouble because the sun and the moon disappeared. Things got even worse when the rats came out.

I spoke realistically as if I really lived back then and traveled through time just for this class. My ancestors died when the Asteroid Crashed, so it affected me personally.

I borrowed a metal stand from the music room to display my charts, maps and diagrams. My damage chart showed the Earth with a dent. I forgot one map at home but I'll bring it in. My report lasted twenty-five minutes because I included a lot of statistics and facts. Mr. Ross said it's a record that won't be beat. I ended the report with a question. Hidden inside that question was a warning:

"How would you feel if the Asteroid crashed in your back yard?"

The report was over, and Charlee stood up and applauded. Nobody else stood up, and nobody but Charlee applauded, but she made up for it with enthusiasm.

I bowed to the audience and winked at Charlee the same time, and that's when my Identifiers fell out of my shirt pocket and landed on the floor.

Mrs. Molasco watched me from the hall. She walked in with a mean look on her face, and she bent down and picked up the glasses. Nobody said a word when she walked down the hall to her office.

# 17

Mrs. Molasco's office is on the left when you go in the main entrance to Dodd High. A double-wide window looks out over the sidewalk, the flag pole, and the front lawn. A row of inside windows gives her a clear view of the students in the hall.

Next to her desk, a water cooler with a giant upside down bottle makes bubbles like a guppy. Big green leaf jungle plants grow in pots on the window sill and in big pots on the floor around the room.

Mrs. Molasco sits in the desk chair among the plants and looks out the window. Or she sits on the leather couch on the opposite side of the room with the jungle plants and the water bottle and observes the students out in the hall. Weekdays eight to four. One hour for lunch. Take the summer off.

Now you know what it's like to be the Principal.

She didn't say a word to me when she took my glasses. She could have said "I'll Take These, Please," or "Excuse Me." She walked into the classroom and picked the sunglasses off the floor, and before I could stop her she left the room.

She left them in plain sight on her office desk. I looked in when I walked past. Manny looked in too, and Bones gave me a report between classes. Charlee came with me when the bell rang. I figured I'd sneak in and snatch them with Charlee on the lookout, but the janitor locked up early and Mrs. Molasco went home for the day.

The next day the whole school knew Mrs. Molasco took my sunglasses. She displayed them as an example all day on her desk.

Everybody talked about it in the classrooms and in the cafeteria. Kids I didn't know said hi and good luck and gave me the thumbs-up when they passed me in the hall.

Someone said I phoned Mrs. Molasco at her home yesterday after school, and I disguised my voice and said I was a District Judge. The kid is correct in this matter and I advised her to return the sunglasses immediately, I told her. Don't fool with the law.

Somebody else said I had presented her with an Ultimatum, then I gave her a Deadline. Word spread there was going to be a Showdown: Walt Thompson vs Mrs. Molasco. Principal's office. Two forty-five.

They were Identifiers, not cheating glasses, and she had to return them to the rightful owner. If she doesn't give them back to me by two forty-five I'll walk down the hall past the auditorium, turn at the cafeteria, take a drink from the water fountain outside the teacher's room and march into her office and take them back.

And I'll give her a big chunk of my mind.

At two forty-five Manny and Leroy walked with me to the office. I went in and stood at her desk while she talked on the phone. Manny and Leroy waited outside in the hall. Bones looked in. Charlee stood off to the side behind the door.

She blew a kiss through the air. Good luck, Walt! Good luck!

More kids wandered down the hall. The crowd grew quickly. The bus drivers stuck around for a while, wondering what's going on, and they started up and drove the empty school busses back without finding out.

I wasn't nervous. I was angry and mad. I went from angry to mad and back to angry again. When you're wrong there's reason to be nervous. Make sure you're right, you got nothing to be nervous about.

Mrs. Molasco looked mean from a distance. Close-up she's not mean like you'd expect. She wore her brown hair short and she put on a lot of make-up. She saw the world through dark spooky eyes. Up close she's more spooky than mean.

"Those are my glasses," I said when she hung up. "I apologize for bringin' 'em to school. It won't happen again and I'd appreciate it if you give 'em back."

"You can't have them back. They're my glasses now." She made it sound like a bible quote.

"They ain't cheatin' glasses," I said.

"Ain't?" she said.

"They are not."

"Then what's so special about them?"

"Nuthin'," I said.

"Nuthin? Is that how we teach you to speak?"

"No. I learned that on my own."

The phone rang again. She put my glasses in her desk and answered.

While she talked on the phone I snooped around the office. College degrees, certificates and awards in expensive frames covered the walls above the jungle plants. The degrees proved she was smart. The certificates and awards attested to her greatness.

A calendar hung behind her desk. Under that calendar another calendar stuck out. I took it off the wall and checked it out.

It was the strangest calendar I ever saw. It was all screwed up. Everyday was Thursday. There was no other day except Thursday. Every week had seven Thursdays. I didn't think about it much, it must be a joke or a mistake.

Mrs. Molasco spoke into the phone. The kids in the hall got bored and walked out the front entrance, and their opinion of me went down a few notches. That kid Walt made them wait for nothing. They missed the bus, and now they had to walk all the way home because of me.

Outside in the hall I told Charlee what went on between me and the Principal.

She pressed her mouth tight and serious as she listened. And her eyes got squinty when she's thinking real hard. She didn't like what she heard. Charlee is smart. Her mind has a lot of footnotes. She knows right from wrong, and she's smart enough to know what Mrs. Molasco did was wrong.

She walked right into the Principal's office. Mrs. Molasco looked up from her desk and smiled. Armed with the truth, Charlee let her have it. She talked and Mrs. Molasco listened, and Mrs. Molasco spoke and Charlee listened, and Charlee took her stand and talked clearly and made her point, much like her excellent report on Vesuvius and Pompeii.

Charlee won her over, and she came out of the office with my Identifiers in her hand.

Charlee made an important point that Mrs. Molasco could not counter. The class was not taking a test the day she looked in. We were reviewing last week's test. How can you cheat on a test that's not a test?

# 18

When Uncle Brucker came home that night, I told him what happened at school. There's things I don't like him knowing, but I never keep any secrets.

I told him everything: I went against his advice and took the sunglasses to school and Mrs. Molasco took them from me and Charlee convinced her to give them back.

After an I-told-you-so about wearing the glasses to school, and a you-don't-listen about sneaking a peek in the classroom, and another I-told-you-so about being an asshole who doesn't listen in general, I came to the part about the hidden calendar I found on the wall in the Principal's office, and he put the I-told-you-so's and you-don't-listens to rest.

"What did you say?" he asked.

"I said it must be some mistake," I said. "That damn calendar. Every day is Thursday."

"No, sir. That ain't no mistake," he informed me. "What you saw is a Rat Calendar. Every day's the same to rats, and that day is Thursday. Your Principal knew you didn't cheat with those glasses and that's not why she took 'em. She took 'em cause she don't want you lookin' in her direction. And then what would you see? Keep it to yourself, Walt. It's between you and me and her. Listen to me from time to time. Don't take your Identifiers to school no more and put her name on the list."

# 19

For dinner I fired up two big bass Uncle Brucker caught on Sunday. He said it was damn fine cooking, but don't ask me how it tasted. I can't tell you because I couldn't get my mind off Renata, her long black hair and those slinky eyes.

Later we took out the poker deck and I lost three in a row to the Rat Killer. My mind just wasn't on poker. Uncle Brucker didn't say anything but I'm sure he knew what I was thinking about all along.

One last game. He had shuffled the cards and was ready to deal when we heard a strange knock at the back door.

*Scratch-Scratch Knock! Scratch Knock-Knock!*

"You hear that, Unc?"

"I got ears."

*Scratch-Scratch Knock! Scratch Knock-Knock!*

Now it was at the front door.

"That ain't no ordinary knock," I said.

Whenever Uncle Brucker had to do anything he hated, he got mad and threw something, usually whatever was in his hand at the time. This time he stood up and threw the deck of cards down on the table and the cards shot all over the kitchen floor.

"Don't tell me I got to wrestle that goddam rat now!" he said.

One evening years ago Uncle Brucker came home from a long day out hunting and setting traps. A huge South American grizzly rat was standing in the driveway. He looked mean and he looked hungry, and he blocked my Uncle's path.

"*Ha-cun-da!*" he said. Rat talk for let's wrestle.

You see, what's fair is fair, even to a rat. And the rats didn't think it fair that the Rat Killer can go around shooting them up with a .22 when they have no way of shooting a rifle or even loading it up.

The rat had come to challenge Uncle Brucker to a wrestling match.

Uncle Brucker didn't care much for wrestling but he wasn't about to let a rat get ahead of him on fairness. So he took off his hunting jacket and hung it on a stubby bush.

"*Ha-cun-da!*" cried Uncle Brucker.

Don't think it's easy, wrestling rats. Rats love to wrestle and will never pass up a challenge any time of day or night. Rats have sharp teeth. Rats have claws that'll rip you apart. They have no pity and they don't play by the rules. Rats know moves men don't know, lots of sneaky ones. Besides, it's all in the balance, and rats got lots of balance. I'll tell you right now my Uncle lost the first round. A seventy, eighty pound grizzly on top of you, snapping at the jugular, an inch from your throat. Uncle Brucker was fighting for his life. His life! The next round could have gone either way, but he got his balance back with a punch move and he pinned the rat down.

Then they were even.

Uncle Brucker didn't see the Wrestling Rat again for many months.

Then he woke up one Sunday morning and looked out the window.

And who was standing in the driveway?

The Wrestling Rat. He had come to challenge Uncle Brucker to another wrestling match.

Uncle Brucker figured he'd better get in the mood for wrestling real quick. Now he knows he always has to be in the mood.

Every so often that damn rat comes to town, scratch-knocking for a fight. It's been going on that way for years. My Uncle wins a round, the Wrestling Rat wins the next.

If Uncle Brucker can't wrestle because he's sick or injured, or if he just doesn't show up, the Wrestling Rat would win by default, which means automatically.

*Scratch-Scratch Knock! Scratch Knock-Knock!*

Uncle Brucker sat for a while and drank a can of Boomers. He found a lighter in his shirt pocket and he lit a cigarette, smoked it so quick the ash didn't fall off. Then he finished the beer and wiped his mouth on his left sleeve the way he always wipes his mouth. He really didn't want to go out there and wrestle that damn rat. It was never an easy match for him. Uncle Brucker was only five foot six. How big was that big South American grizzly?

*Scratch-Scratch Knock! Scratch Knock-Knock!*

"You don't gotta wrestle him at all," I told him. "I'll fight him for you any time. I ain't scared a no rat, I ain't."

"Thanks, Walt, but you know I gotta go."

"I know."

"And I gotta go it alone."

"Yeah, I know."

"Me and nobody else," he said.

"I know, I know."

"And I know you know why."

"Cause it ain't just a human and a rat, is it?" I said. "It's bigger than that. If you lose it's like all humans lose. It would mean rats are better than humans, so you got to wrestle and you can't lose."

Uncle Brucker told me I might be called upon to continue the tradition some day. If he died or the Wrestling Rat died, a relative can be brought in to continue the match. Or if he got injured and couldn't wrestle any more, then the tradition will pass down and it will be my turn to wrestle the Wrestling Rat. Me and nobody else. Uncle Brucker pushed open the back door. He knew I wanted to go with him, and he looked sad when he turned and said, "Sorry, Walt. This is between me and the Wrestlin' Rat. No spectators allowed."

Out on the back porch he rolled up his sleeves. He looked up at the night sky. The clouds were breaking up and it had cooled off. A thunder storm was heading our way but it never got here. It was a good night for wrestling, all in all.

"*Ha-cun-da!*" he said, and he leaped off the porch into the night.

When he came home hours later I was asleep on the couch. I woke up when the screen door slammed. He stumbled around the kitchen for a while, bumped into the table, knocked over a chair. He managed to get a beer out of the refrigerator and sit down at the kitchen table.

It was a tough match. He was exhausted. An half-empty can of beer rolled off the table and spilled on the floor. I got off the couch and straightened the chair and picked up the can. He was red-eyed from drinking and he smelled from wrestling, or maybe the other way around.

"Well? Did you win, Unc?"

"Course I did. I always win, and he always wins the next round. Even match."

It was almost one o'clock.

"What took you so long?" I asked him.

"Sometimes we go for a drink is all." And he popped open another one and drank it slowly. Last beer of the night.

# 20

Every day was a busy day for me and my Uncle. He lost a lot of time when he was stuck in the hospital and he thought he'd never catch up. Six days a week, Monday through Saturday, from eight in the morning until six at night, he went out on the road answering calls. I helped him any way I could.

In the evenings after school we took out the government forms and went over the infected list. The list must be neat and straight. Everything must be up to date. The government could call any time so it better be ready.

Uncle Brucker's revitalizing stroke still gave him some trouble with the little things, like tying his shoe laces and using a pen or a pencil. Nobody could make sense out of what he wrote, so that job went to me.

I also made out the weekly schedule, which wasn't easy.

Sometimes he picked me up after school and I went out tracking with him. On the weekends I was his right hand man all day. Everything piled up at the end of the week and this Saturday we were in trouble. We had nine house calls to make, a dozen traps to check. The Ram is due for an oil change, and somebody has to go food shopping if we want dinner.

Uncle Brucker and I got up at seven a.m. and I made eggs and cheese toast for breakfast. To save time we split up the morning. After breakfast I drove the Ram down to Schnells Hardware and I picked up an oil filter and four quarts of 10/40 for the Ram. When I got home I removed the filter and let the oil run out, then screwed on the new filter. I tighten it by hand. Uncle Brucker said it don't matter much so I never use a wrench.

Meanwhile my Uncle drove the Eagle to South First Street for a follow up on Mr. Hobbs. Nothing had changed. Mrs. Hobbs had learned to adjust and he was still under the house. The Rat Killer crawled in and checked up on the situation and they talked about whatever they talked about.

Then he set off to check the traps out on Jack's Creek.

After I changed the oil in the Ram, I drove down to Food Saver with sixty dollars and change I took from the cup in the kitchen cabinet. On the way home from Food Saver I made a right and cruised up the Heights, then down into town past Tuskies, on the lookout. Where was Renata? I hadn't seen her in a week. Then I thought I saw her in the back of a Camry, and I followed it around for a while, staying two cars back to be sure she didn't see me. The Camry pulled over. A girl got out. She had long dark hair and she was cool, but she didn't add up to Renata.

Did I mention my Uncle was scheduled to give a lecture on Rat Talk at the VFW in Wrentham?

# 21

Rat Talk came easy to Uncle Brucker. He had the ability since he was a child. In fact, he may have been born with it. No one realized it was Rat Talk way back then, but it turned out to be Rat Talk all along.

When he was an infant, he kept saying "*Ca-'ta-ka*" to Grandma Thompson and she didn't know what he meant. Later she found out he was speaking Rat for "I want milk." *Ca* means "I like" or "I want." *Ta-ka* is "milk." *Ca-'ta-ka*, "I want milk."

What he was trying to figure out as an adult, he had been speaking all along since he was a kid.

Rats don't have a language like we do where there's a different word for everything, but they do have a way of getting themselves understood. Uncle Brucker got a head start on the subject when he was younger because of his natural abilities. Add that together with his aptitude and you'll call him an expert, which means he had a hell of a lot to say.

So he booked a couple VFWs and a town hall, one roadhouse, the Elk's Club and the rec center in Parville, and this Saturday it was the VFW in Wrentham, which was more than an hour away.

Uncle Brucker understood that lecturing was educational for the audience and lecturer as well. The audience learned about Rat Talk from the lecturer and the lecturer learned about human nature from the audience. He learned that some people were always so impatient, no matter how good the lecture. Others could fall asleep anywhere, anytime. And nobody wanted to be the last person out the door. He had a good reputation as a lecturer and once he was interviewed on a local TV station, but that was because he reported a brush fire and remained on the scene.

I helped him out when I could. He taught me how to speak rat and I caught on quickly. I gave him what he wanted but I couldn't give him what he needed.

What he really needed was an assistant, a lovely lady assistant, about so tall, with red hair. First choice: Dotty the waitress at Mink's Downtown Diner, of course. She wouldn't have to wear fancy clothes, but fancy clothes sure would look nice with her red hair. She could arrange his lecture notes and stand by his side demonstrating good posture. She'd hand out the autograph sheets. He'd be sure to let her know how much he appreciated her, how much he needed her.

After the lecture, dinner and dessert, they'd open a fresh deck at the roadhouse. Any game she wanted to play.

He'd prefer somebody fluent in rat talk, but Dotty would do. He'd already taught her a few words at the diner. She caught on without even trying. And with his help she could learn all four hundred eighty-seven words in the rat vocabulary.

*Di-ch'-ch-ka* means "I love you." Literally, "You are my sex meal." He never had anybody like that, ever. It could have been Dotty.

North through Bowen County, west to Awkwood and Bay Leak by the Bridge. Up the east side of the bridge, down the west side right into the sunset. Mist steamed off the bay and climbed up the bridge all the way to the top. Supersize waterdrops collected on the ironwork, but not one drop fell on me and my Uncle. The sun sparkled the water at no extra charge.

He packed them in in Shankton. He packed them in in West Lindell. It's true a lot of people came to see Gibney the Magician. Maybe East Lindell was a little slow for a town of eight thousand, but nobody was moping around the hall either.

Word spread about the man who knew everything about something that nobody knew anything about: Rat Talk.

# 22

" *is-ka'-tca-te.*" Good evening, folks.
"*Ki'-ch-ja.*" Welcome to my lecture.

There must have been one hundred people at the VFW Saturday night, seats for forty-seven. It was hot outside and hotter inside. Vandals stole the screens from the downstairs windows, and the sweaty janitor refused to open the windows because of the moths. No air-conditioning, and the fans were locked in the basement and the janitor couldn't find the key.

A sign on the wall next to the window said No Smoking, but the smokers ignored it and smoked away. The sweaty janitor didn't care. He stood on a tiny platform they called a stage, and smoked a fat cigar.

Gibney the Magician was scheduled to go on after my Uncle. He was the featured performer and they all came to see him. Little kids and their big brothers watched the magic man practice simple card tricks in the back of the room.

Uncle Brucker told me to check out the place, so I left my Identifiers in the Ram and tried to blend in and not look suspicious.

The key to blending in is looking like you belong. And belong is another word for familiar. One sure way to look like you belong and the place looks familiar is swing your legs in a lazy way when you walk.

So I swung my legs across the lecture hall and through the kitchen in a lazy way, acting like I'd been there many times before.

Remember, you're looking for something suspicious, but you can't look suspicious yourself. It takes practice, you'll make mistakes. You learn how to do that, nobody will bug you and you can snoop around anywhere you want.

The audience was becoming impatient but Uncle Brucker had a lot to say. He knew it was just human nature, but learning Rat Talk was important and he hung in there just to increase their awareness.

". . . Ca-ta-shoes. I like shoes. Here's another example. No word for basketball in Rat Talk. No word for court either. That's right, you use the English fill-ins once again. Therefore basketball court in rat talk is . . . basketball court."

Then a man in the back of the room stood up and said, "I'll give you ten bucks if you shut up."

The man was dressed in black motorcycle leather and he wore a black helmet with red lightning bolts on the sides. All eyes turned to the man of leather and those fiery bolts.

"Take the cash," someone said.

"Don't go home empty-handed," said the sweaty janitor.

"Hey, mister!" Uncle Brucker pointed to the man in the motorcycle helmet. "Take off that helmet, mister. I don't trust nobody hidin' his face. Take that helmet off and show me what I'm lookin' at."

"I ain't takin' it off. I ain't answerin' no questions," the motorcycle man said. "I ain't doin' anythin' you say unless I'm already plannin' on doin' it. Make that twenty and that's my top offer."

The man in the helmet waved a newly printed twenty above his head.

Uncle Brucker watched the bill go around and around, and he considered the offer. He had been offered ten dollars to shut up on several occasions and once he collected fifteen and change for gas and tolls, but no one had offered him twenty bucks to shut up until now.

The door opened and an old man entered the lodge. The audience spread apart as he made his way to the stage. Over his shoulder he carried a burlap sack with a rodent inside.

# 23

The old man held the burlap sack in one hand. He wiped his nose with the other as he walked to the stage. He was old, older than Uncle Brucker, older than anybody, and he was dirty, wrinkled, and bald. He had more teeth in his mouth than hair on his head, if you count the rotten ones.

The old man held the sack at arms length as he looked up at the man on the stage.

"If it ain't my old friend Pete," Uncle Brucker said.

"No, it's Pete," he said.

"Watcha got in that sack there, Pete?"

"Well, Killer," Pete said, "that's what I come here to ask ya. It's some sorta rat, but I never seen such like it before. Got it right here in this sack. It's a good sack. On the way over I says, I says, 'Pete, that Rat Killer fella's gonna be pleased and surprised when he opens this sack.' Been carryin' it all day lookin' for ya. I ain't askin' nuthin' in return, just a buck for my travels and a ride back to town. It ain't the best sack, but it's a good sack, and I couldn't find no other."

He handed the sack to my Uncle who held it in his fist. Old Pete folded his arms at his chest and stepped back and watched. Uncle Brucker put the sack down on the floor.

The rat clawed at the bottom of the sack and chewed at the top but he couldn't get out. And then, quiet.

The rat had calmed down. No one said a word as Uncle Brucker took out his leather gloves and pulled them on, first his left glove then his right. They say you can hear a pin drop. Maybe if you're close enough you can see it drop too, but I didn't have one to find out.

"I'm about to untie this sack, if I got no objections," he said. He spoke up so all could hear. "I don't hear no objections," he said, "so I'll begin after I do my flexin'. Please step back while I'm flexin'."

Uncle Brucker took a moment to flex his arm and leg muscles and get his circulation going.

Then, his blood revved up and speeding throughout his body, he bent down and untied the rat sack.

What Old Pete said was true. This strange dark gray rat looked like no other rat I'd ever seen, either. King-size claws with long curled nails and a twisted nicked-up nose. In many ways it didn't look like a rat at all.

The rat stood frozen for a second or two and then it sprung to life. The people of Wrentham jumped back and knocked into each other. A pretty young lady in the front row turned pale and tilted backwards. Gibney caught her in his arms before she hit the ground.

That rat was quick, but my Uncle was lightning-quick. In an instant his left rat-grabbing hand held the varmint by the neck. With the index finger of his right poking hand he tapped the rat's most sensitive area, between the eyes, and the rat was out cold. It all went so quickly. The audience applauded for a long time after they figured out what my Uncle did.

Uncle Brucker opened the rat sack. He poked the rat between the eyes once again, put it in the open sack and tied it tight. Now it was Gibney the Magician's turn on stage. Uncle Brucker smoked a cigarette in the back of the room and we watched the show.

Later, when the show was over, we hung around and talked, and Uncle Brucker gave out autographs. And the people of Wrentham smiled and shook my Uncle's hand and thanked him for a great evening and for taming that nasty rat.

The lady who had fallen into Gibney's arms rested in her chair. Gibney the handsome magician pulled a cigarette from her ear, and she giggled like a pretty school girl on the way out.

The motorcycle man left a twenty on top of the sack for the Rat Killer. He held the helmet in his left hand. The sweaty janitor watched the Man put the bill down. Later on I looked for it but I didn't find it. The janitor took the twenty when we weren't looking and it's in his wallet by now.

The VFW in Wrentham invited my Uncle to come back in two months for another great show.

We threw the rat sack in the back of the Ram. Uncle Brucker gave Old Pete a buck for hauling the rat around and another buck because my Uncle was a good guy and he felt sorry for his old friend Pete.

He promised to drop Pete off in town, so we all got in the Ram. I got the window seat. Old Pete sat in the middle.

"You smell like piss," I told him on the way home.

"Bite me," he said.

# 24

Uncle Brucker's mind never quit. Ideas formed and thoughts connected 24 hours a day. He never gave his mind a moment's rest. There was always something going on inside his head. As far as I know he never took one day off from thinking.

Uncle Brucker got a wooden cage from out back and put it on the workbench in the barn. Above the workbench, the fluorescent light hummed and blinked. That bulb was older than McDermott's cat and Uncle Brucker never replaced it.

He sat on a high stool at the workbench and examined the rat.

"What we have here," he said, "is exactly what I figured. Rodentas Polaris, known also as the homin' rat or tunnel rat. He's a nasty rat, ugly too, but also very special. His sensitive nose is ideal for sniffin' out the contact point where dimensions come together. A native of the rat dimension, and a frequent visitor to ours, he's adaptable to any environment and will make himself at home anywhere. It don't matter which way his nose is pointin' when he falls asleep at night, because he wakes up every mornin' pointin' north."

After the Second Uprising we pushed the rats back and they've been laying low since then. For six long years the rats have been gearing up, preparing, building the bridges and digging the tunnels that match up one dimension to the next.

Now they were gathering at the other side of the Portal.

A million rat army, waiting for the go code. . . .

But where was the Portal? Where were the rats coming through?

Uncle Brucker was determined to locate that damn Portal and find out for himself. But it wouldn't be easy. All he had to do was what the entire US Army and all its Generals could not accomplish.

Uncle Brucker sat on the high stool out in the barn, and he smiled. It was a big smile on the outside but it was nothing compared to how he was smiling on the inside.

Uncle Brucker had found the answer.

# 25

Nine o'clock in the morning we were back in the Ram. I was driver man, Uncle Brucker rode shotgun. We threw the cage with the rat in the back. Uncle Brucker wouldn't tell me the destination, he just gave directions. And he didn't say street names. Top secret missions like this, you have to lay low and keep the lid on.

"All we gotta do is let the rat loose and follow him to the Portal. Right, Unc?"

"You're right," he said. "And you're wrong. You're right we're gonna let him loose. Yes, you're right on that. But we ain't gonna follow him to no Portal cause that damn rat ain't goin' near the Portal. Old Pete ain't workin' for himself. Old Pete was sent by the rats to confuse us and find out how much we know. Pete says one thing, we gotta figure on another. Sharpen up your pencil, Walt, and grab a sheet a paper. If we want to find that Portal we gotta make a reverse map going in the opposite direction. And then we'll know which way we don't go."

We parked at the edge of town where the sidewalk ends and the woods begin. We waited while a Miata passed followed by a Sunday driver, and then we let the homin' rat out of the cage.

Again, the strange rat stood for a frozen moment. His nose moved left and right and did a nose dance.

The rat took off and we ran into the woods after him.

Uncle Brucker's plan worked only if the rat thought we were following him. That way he'll be sure to lead us in the opposite direction from the Portal.

So we stepped on all the branches we could find and called out and told bad jokes, and we made a lot of noise trampling through the woods so the rat would hear us coming.

Uncle Brucker followed the rat's trail and I followed him and worked on the reverse map as I ran.

We turned east but on the map I drew an arrow to the west. North meant south, left, turn right. I am a reverse cartographer, a map maker just starting out. You can look around but you won't find many like me.

I thought it was a good plan. It sure sounded good when Uncle Brucker explained it to me. But a plan only works when you follow through. I checked my map. It was a mess of squiggles and lines going nowhere. How can you follow through with something that makes no sense at all?

"Hey Unc, where are ya?"

No answer.

Somewhere along the trail I lost track of my Uncle. I made a wrong turn and went off course and now I was paying for it. I didn't know where I was. I didn't know how I got here, and I only had my map to get me out.

I put a big X on the map to mark where I stood, and then things happened that are hard to describe and impossible to explain.

I took a few steps and suddenly the world got wobbly like in a funhouse mirror, only there was no mirror. One moment it was ten o'clock. Then the sun dropped through a slot in the sky and came out at two o'clock. And it was a different sort of sun, a dim washed-out sun that didn't know if it was rising or setting. A wind came out of nowhere, then turned around and went back because it couldn't make up its mind. Everything was sort of in-between and not quite this and almost that, as if the rats had broken the dials on nature's tuner and screwed up the settings. And the wind came out of nowhere again, so strong it pulled the coins from my pockets and ripped the leaves off the trees.

I didn't like being stuck between dimensions. I didn't want to go to some dimension I didn't know about. I was used to living in my old dimension where all my friends live, and I like it here.

Then somebody grabbed my arm and pulled me back.

It was Uncle Brucker.

"Follow me, Walt," he said. "And please, don't dally."

# 26

I was lucky Uncle Brucker caught up to me when he did or I'd be stuck between dimensions, and not just for a day or two, but for the rest on my life.

He pulled me along with my left hand and with the right I held onto the reverse map. It had a big X to mark the crack. It was here, right here on this spot, where the army will build a Portal to the next dimension and sneak up on the rats.

This is important information, and we must get it to General Hardesty immediately so he could start construction right away.

Back on C-Street we got in the Ram and Uncle Brucker drove off before I could close the door.

There's only one person set up with a direct phone line to the General, and that was the Local Liaison. Uncle Brucker could phone him, but he wasn't authorized to use the number, and that meant we had to bring the LL the info in person. For that job we needed somebody who is reliable and ready to go, and I nominated me.

"Tell me where and I'm there, Unc."

"I want to be sure you understand what it all means, Walt. The army gets this information it won't sit on it. Maybe you ain't aimin' the gun, Walt, but your finger's on the trigger, if you get what I mean. The moment the General gets this info, the war begins."

"We're losin' time, Unc. I'll never get it to the LL if you don't tell me where to go!"

"You already know where to go, Walt. You've been there before with me."

Mrs. Hobbs met me in the driveway of her house on South First Street. Today she wore a green skirt with a yellow apron and a red wig. I guess the colors were some kind of signal for those in the know, but she looked like a traffic light to me.

"Walt Thompson?" she asked with a pleasant smile.

"How do you know my name?" I said, and her eyes fired up, and I couldn't speak.

"I asked if you're Walt Thompson," she said, but not right away. "I ask a question, you get the answer or we end it right here," she said.

"Yes, ma'am."

"Yes ma'am what?"

"Yes ma'am, I am Walt Thompson."

"This way, Walt," she said, and her eyes lost their fire, and she was smiling like a sweet old lady once again.

I don't know how she knew my name, but it didn't stop there. She probably knew a lot of other stuff about me too.

I followed her around back to the little window under the kitchen. Mrs. Hobbs unlocked the window with a key. She opened it up and I got down on my knees and crawled in. On the other side of that window, a crawlspace led to the Mobile Control Pod and her husband. Down there in the Communications Room of the Control Pod, a dedicated phone line connected Mr. Hobbs directly to General Hardesty and no one else.

Mr. Hobbs was't stuck under there. That was a cover story, and Uncle Brucker didn't come all the way out here every day just to have a smoke and talk about the weather. Mr. Hobbs was the LL to General Hardesty. For security reasons and for the General's peace of mind, all communication with the General must be cleared with him.

Mr. Hobbs was a pale man with pale eyes that hadn't seen the sun for a while. His thick glasses gave him frog's eyes.

I didn't waste time with words. He was no word waster either. Nothing said, I gave him the reverse map and a note from my Uncle and crawled under the house and out again. I'm not permitted to describe the room under the house or its contents for security reasons, but I can make a list (table, telephone, computer, folding bed, hot plate, TV, dehumidifier, refrigerator, recliner) and you can put it in the room any way you like.

On the way out I thought of what Uncle Brucker said about the rat war. I had handed in the info. It starts right now with me.

I listened but I couldn't hear any gun shots or sirens go off in the distance. No ambulances screaming down the street. That night before I went to bed I checked all the TV news channels but I couldn't find one special report and I didn't see one headline in the papers the next day.

Like Uncle Brucker said, sometimes the less you hear the more is going on.

If that's true I must have started something really big.

**27**

Uncle Brucker expected an official call Friday night or Saturday morning, Sunday at the latest. It was OK'd ahead of time by the LL and the General.

Thursday evening after we watched Cole's Law, Uncle Brucker took me aside in the hall where the neighbors couldn't see us and the postman couldn't hear us and nobody would plant a microphone.

"Keep your hands off the phone and stay out of the kitchen," he said. "And tell your friends don't call. Third ring I gotta answer or the the General will hang up."

Friday. He moped around the house all morning, moving from room to room and chair to chair. He refused to eat his vitamin cereal and he didn't want lunch. He drank only one beer and sat in front of the TV for a long time with the empty can in his hand. All day long he looked like he just got out of bed. His eyes were puffy. His hair was a squall.

Friday night. He sat in the kitchen, telephone on the table, waiting for the goddamn phone call. He had no appetite for the franks and beans I cooked for him. He read the paper twice, filled out eight words in the crossword puzzle, which I thought was pretty good. I got two more. Later I ate the beans. Saturday morning, still no phone call. I got up around ten and found him hunched over the phone at the kitchen table. He had stayed up most of the night but he looked like he hadn't slept in a week.

"You ain't gonna last, Unc," I told him.

"You wanna bet?" he said.

"What's the point in bettin'? You won't be around to pay up."

At eleven o'clock the phone rang.

"That ain't the call," he said after only one ring.

I don't know how he knew it, but he was right.

He handed me the phone. It was Leroy. I told him no calls until tomorrow, only official calls today, and I hung up.

At one o'clock the call finally came through. The phone rang like a bank alarm, so loud I jumped back. Uncle Brucker fell back too. He missed the first ring, then he grabbed the phone like it was trying to escape and put it to his ear.

"Good morning, General!" said Uncle Brucker, standing stiff at attention. "Yes, sir. Certainly, General, sir. You can count on me, sir. I always volunteer. That way you know you got an army without even askin'."

He took the phone into the hall and I couldn't hear him any more.

He hung up and came back.

"That was General Hardesty on the phone," he said. "He promoted me to Top Man In The Field, and he personally volunteered for a special assignment, and you know I can't talk about it until it's over. All I can say is what everybody already knows. Uprisin' Number Three is in progress and me and the army are goin' on the offensive pretty damn soon. Got my squad cummin' over tonight for orientation. Tomorrow mornin', they're leavin' with or without me. It's up to you to give me the go-ahead. No go-ahead, I stay home with you. Think about it while I'm packin' up."

Upstairs in the bedroom, he went through his sock drawer and chose only the best. He found three new-looking tee-shirts and some clean underwear too, and he stuffed them in his pack.

Then he emptied his wallet on the dresser and put back what was important to him. That included an old matchbook with the phone number for Dotty D in Buckston, scraps of paper with notes for True Rat Stories, and around forty dollars in cash.

"I'll be gone two weeks, maybe more," he said. "You'll be on your own. Think you can handle it? Or do I have to unpack?"

"But I wanna go with you. I'm your right hand man, ain't I?" I said.

"That's a position the army don't make a provision for," he said. He found the keys to the Eagle and he dropped them in a bowl on top of the dresser just in case I needed them.

"OK. You got the go-ahead," I said.

"How's the rat list goin'?"

"I started a new page."

"Keep it neat. The Government asks for it, we gotta turn it in."

"I ain't gonna keep it from them," I said.

Next he went to his closet and took out a .22 rifle wrapped in a fuzzy gray cloth. He found two extra clips in the bottom of the closet, and a scope too. He unfolded the stock, screwed in the scope, locked in the clip, and it was a U.S. Army-Issue Rat Rifle Type B.

He thumbed a bullet out of the spare clip and held it in his hand.

"For me?" I said.

"It's a good luck bullet," he said. "Just don't keep it in the pocket with the holes."

"Don't worry, I learned my lesson with the arrowhead."

"And don't shoot it, or you'll be out a luck."

# 28

Uncle Brucker found a beat-up old backpack that got chewed up during the Uprising. It was hidden behind some boxes on the stairway to the attic. He took it down and put it on the kitchen table and unzipped it. He took out an old shopping bag.

I knew something important was in the grocery bag by his wait-until-you-see-this smile.

"What's in the bag?" I asked.

"Oh, nuthin'."

"Gotta be somethin'."

"It's just an old rat TV set."

"A rat TV? Like the commanders use?"

"The very same. I been savin' it for someone just like you."

He carefully took the TV out of the bag. He cleared off the beer cans and he placed it on the kitchen table. One dial on each end, two speakers, scratched up plastic, fourteen-inch screen. The dial on the right didn't work and the rats ate all the O's off the brand name. Made by M T R LA.

"Looks just like an ordinary old TV set to me," I said.

"It's rat made."

"The controls are busted."

"Rats know how to use it."

"The wire ain't got no plug on it."

"It's got rat markins," he said.

"Where are the markins?"

"Right there."

"Where?"

"And on the back."

# 29

At 6:30 we heard it.

*Scratch-Scratch Knock! Scratch Knock-Knock!*

Across the table from me he let out a breath of air and put his head in his hands. But it was different from how it sounds, more like his hands reached up and grabbed his head without permission and now his head was stuck there and didn't know why.

*Scratch-Scratch Knock! Scratch Knock-Knock!*

"Don't tell me I gotta go out and wrestle that damn rat now," he said.

# 30

Uncle Brucker told me stay out of their way and don't ask any questions.

"These people have an agenda," he said. "When they want to say somethin', they'll say it. When they don't, good luck. Now go take out the garbage and wait in the barn until you get the all-clear."

It was already five-fifteen. His squad was scheduled to arrive at six, but five-thirty wouldn't be unusual because his squad was prompt. Each squad member had to enter the house a different way to avoid suspicion. That meant some of them had to climb in through the windows. And don't park in the driveway, park down the road, then walk back to the house.

I carried out the garbage and went to the far side of the barn where Grandpa Thompson used to feed his pigs. It wasn't originally part of the barn, it was a nailed-on shed Grandpa Thompson built for pigs only. Inside, a long wooden trough, an old wicker-seat chair, and three busted windows with a view of the yard. On the wall above the trough, boards with chalk names of pigs: Butch, Lilly, Natty, Fran.

Three boards at the far end had no names on them.

I sat on the wicker seat in the pig shed and wondered about the missing pig names. Maybe one pig was Thor. I'd name my best pig Dynamite. There was some other stuff in the shed but I don't feel like describing it. I'd rather be thinking up pig names. Thor and Dynamite and Mick.

Here I am in my night fort, protecting the old house from marauding rats. Put rifles in the windows, put a cannon through the door. You can't maraud around here.

Sometime later I heard the back door swing open. Uncle Brucker walked across the driveway and stopped to pee on the azalea. He had trouble getting started, then he peed like he'd never stop.

Finally he came over to the pig shed.

"Anybody here yet?" he asked.

"No, not yet."

"Wonder what's keepin' 'em."

Just then we heard a car coming up the hill. Could it be? And we looked to the road but we were fooled. There was no car to be seen. It was nothing but the tricky sounds of traffic drifting across town from 94.

Uncle Brucker made a face like it's a crazy world and we're stuck in it. What can you do? And he walked back to the old house.

He came out with a beer and a can of Coke. He handed me the Coke and leaned back against the shed wall. White paint flakes fell from the ceiling. He brushed a bunch of flakes off his shoulders. There were more flakes in his hair. I guess I had some flakes on me too.

"It's been a long time since I've seen my squad," he said. "Six years since the last Uprisin'. I was hopin' they'd get here early and have time to reminisce. Guess that idea's shot now. Now I gotta reminisce by myself, which takes the fun out of reminiscin'. Looks like that's the way it'll be tonight. You see another way?"

"It ain't so late."

"It ain't."

# 31

Tired, nodding off. The street lights went on up the hill and down on the corner, and the night settled down. Night bugs flew in the windows and beat against the walls. The squirrels chased each other around the loft like it was a race track. A barn bat made circles high above the yard, then flew straight to the streetlight and then I don't know where. The moon went off and hung out somewhere else. I couldn't find it anywhere around here.

Uncle Brucker finished his beer and threw the can in the corner of the shed. I had some Coke left I was saving. He went outside to take a pee and check around.

He came back and stuck his head in the window.

"You still in there?"

"I ain't gone nowhere," I told him.

"Gettin' chilly," he said.

"I got a over shirt I can wear."

"Well, where is it?"

"On the back of the chair."

"You keepin' the chair warm?"

"I ain't' cold. Don't know about the chair. . . . What was that?"

Out there in the woods, a howl. It started out strong then cut off like a howling question. I had heard it before, earlier. Now it was back again, and closer. And another howl too, a long-stretching answer howl. We listened to the answer howl fade into the night. It was spooky.

"What was that, coy dogs callin'?" I asked.

"Nah, it ain't no coy dog. Them's ratfuckers howlin' on a moonless night."

"You mean they're doin' it out there?"

"No, it's cause they ain't gettin' any," Uncle Brucker said.

# 32

Every passing car could have Downtown or Midnight Mary or the Doc behind the wheel, especially since none of the cars stopped near the house. So I checked out every car that passed to see if it stopped up ahead.

What kind of car would Midnight show up in? Probably a turbo Mustang or some other hot muscle car, screeching around the corner, slamming on the brakes. And the Doc? Cough-cough, clank-clank! A creaky old Dodge Dart, still in the family, begging for a tune-up and barely making it up the hill.

I put on my over shirt.

With a Boomers to keep him company, Uncle Brucker reminisced.

He was battling the rats during the Second Uprising. Deep in rat territory, the entire company was surrounded. Midnight Mary gave him the danger signal. Something went wrong, a break in the line, and the rats came through.

After a quick count they came up one man short.

Duffy! They had left Duffy back at the Squad Bar!

Uncle Brucker said, "Our motto is All For One And One For All, and we stick by it. So we all left the battle and we all went back to the bar to find Duffy. Dirty rat trick, spikin' his drink. He was wobbly. The Doc gave him three fast-actin' sober-up pills. Duffy had his finger in the bottle, so maybe four. In two minutes time he was smilin' an I'd-rather-be-killin'-rats smile, and he went off to do just that. A real professional.

"Now we were a Full Fightin' Force. By the time we got back to the front we were off-duty, but we were so full of fight we slaughtered two hunred rats durin' our break. Set a new record for off duty slaughterin'. The Army won't give out medals for battles they can't talk about—it goes against policy. They use a made-up name instead. The War Medal I got says Battle of The By-Pass so no one knows. I ran into General Hardesty after the ceremony and I said, you didn't have to do that, sir, give me that By-Pass Medal. A citation would do just as well. He said, I know what to do and what not to do, and I don't need no pesty sergeant reminding me.

"He's right about that. When you're right, you're right. Sometimes I'm wrong, I admit it. The General don't need remindin'. I was wrong for doubtin' him and I was wrong to say what I said, but I was right about sayin' I said it. So you see, two wrongs can make a right! And it was me made it right, not the General. The Medal? Take it home, he said. It's got your name on it. Put it on your mantle but keep it in your heart. He's that type a guy."

## 33

Uncle Brucker's squad members didn't get to the old house until after eleven. First came Downtown in her old VW. The Doc followed in a Camry not far behind. My assignment was make sure each squad member enters the house a different way to avoid suspicion.

Downtown and the Doc got the front and back doors, Midnight Mary and ex-Lieutenant Willett went in through the two side windows, but Duffy had to get down on his knees and crawl through the little basement window under the dining room. He whined and complained it ain't fair, but what did he expect? That's what you get when you're last to arrive.

I hung out in my room and left the squad alone just like Uncle Brucker told me. Everybody slept on the floor in the living room except Downtown and Midnight Mary. They slept on the front porch outside my bedroom window. The window was open. I lay in bed and they talked for a while.

Midnight Mary sounded nervous. But not Downtown. Every night, on duty or off, she slept in her camo army bag with her rat rifle beside her. She was as cool as an Eskimo pie, as sharp as a carpet tack.

"Just like old times, ain't it Midnight?" said Downtown.

"I wish," said Midnight.

"Old times ain't so bad."

"My nerves ain't what they used to be. I better attend to that."

"You know what they say? If you ain't worried then you ain't prepared."

"That's what they say?"

"Somebody says it."

"Scoot over a bit, will ya, hon?"

"Better?"

"Better."

"Night, Mid."

"Downie."

**34**

Friday, 10:45 a.m. Wearing what was left of his old army uniform, Uncle Brucker stood in the kitchen by the back door.

"I'm off for a two-week assignment," he said. "But I don't know how long before I'll get back. You see guys walkin' around with backpacks like mine, they're probably goin' off to the Uprisin'. Waitin' at bus stops, train stations, there could be an assignment backup. It ain't unusual for an assignment backup to add an extra week or two. So, addin' it up, a two-week assignment can turn into four weeks even when it starts out as two. You got backups to deal with and government red tape, and you know that don't make it easy. Truth is, you never know when you'll get back from a two-week assignment. How do I look?"

"Like Sergeant Brucker," I said.

Camo jacket, holes in the elbows. Green work pants tucked into high white socks. He threw out his army boots years ago so he wore his heavy winter boots. Pack strapped to his back, rifle barrel sticking out the top.

The pack! He slipped it off his shoulder and unzipped it. He had to check it one more time. He pulled out the call-up orders General Hardesty sent by mail and read them once more. Socks, underwear, cigarettes, lighter, map, compass. Everything in order once again.

Then he walked over to his dusty War Medal on the high shelf in the living room and ran his finger through the dust one last time. Beautiful!

That was everything. Nothing more to check.

And now I understood. He was stalling. He was stalling because he didn't want to go to war. Moving slowly, checking his pack, reviewing his orders again and again. Wishing he never answered that damn phone call from General Hardesty. Wishing he didn't have to volunteer.

We stood at the back door for a while, looking through the screen and thinking, looking and thinking about things we didn't say. Now it was past eleven and the Ram should start up easy—if you don't pump it.

He pushed the door open and we walked out into the yard. Midnight Mary waited in the Ram. Everyone else rode with the Doc in the Camry.

It was a bright sunny day but don't ask me for a weather report. I only saw the driveway and the shadows under the trees.

In the short distance from the porch to the Ram, he filled me with last minute advice. He spoke quickly and walked slowly. He had much to say.

"Don't tell nobody I'm goin'," he said. "Don't say nuthin' to the neighbors if they come snoopin' around. It's a Special Assignment and none a their damn business. Remember the three Key Steps." He put his arm around my shoulder. Side-by-side, shoulder-to-shoulder, and he was no taller than me. "If the Wrestlin' Rat shows up and picks a fight, give him this. Watch me. Knee jab to the stomach, left to the jaw. Got it? Like this. Knee to the stomach. Uh! Left to the jaw. Uh! Believe me he won't expect that! Been savin' that move for years. Use it if you want, then get him in a German Headlock. Rats hate that headlock. They don't know German and they got no way a gettin' out of it." He opened the door to the Ram and he slid in. "If that don't do it, try a Cherokee Chokehold. Now, how do you handle the Wrestlin' Rat?"

"Knee to the stomach. Left to the jaw. Uh! Uh! German Head-lock, then a Cherokee Chokehold. What's a Cherokee Chokehold?"

"Oh, man! You had sixteen years to ask me that question. Sixteen! No time to explain it all now." He turned the key and started up the Ram. "A half-hold goes like this. Right arm around the neck, third degree pressure on the thyroid cartilage. Take it from there."

The Ram stalled in neutral and he started her up again. He found a cigarette on the seat and put it between his lips. Midnight gave him a light. I noticed the rust spot on the hood had grown from the size of a potato chip to a pancake. I'll paint it over when you come back, Unc. Promise.

He said a few words to me in rat talk.

"*Gi-'ta-ta-te*, Walt." So long, Walt.

I said a few words to him.

"*Gi-tac-'ta*, Uncle Brucker." Adios, Uncle Brucker.

I stood by the barn and watched him back the Ram down the driveway. He waited while a dump truck and a van passed, puffed his cigarette, then he backed onto the road.

At the corner the Ram stalled out again, flooded. Too much gas too soon. The Ram takes time, Unc. Just don't pump it! He didn't pump it, and she caught on smooth and powerful. That's the beauty of a 5.2 with 230 for you.

Out front by the little willow I saw the red Ram flash through the tree line, Uncle Brucker sitting up straight behind the wheel. Then I couldn't see him anymore, but I heard the engine rev around the bend and up the hill. Then I couldn't hear him anymore, even when I ran to the far side of the yard.

# 35

Uncle Brucker fought the rats in two bloody uprisings. He knew their tactics and he knew their strategies, and he had a War Medal to prove it. He understood that rats were fierce fighters who learned from their mistakes and did not give up easily. Win or lose, man or rat, the war took its bloody toll.

When Uncle Brucker arrived at Base Camp, he got the feeling it wouldn't be easy.

Dark clouds came in low and settled over the Camp. The sun disappeared behind a great curtain of rain. Uncle Brucker and his squad arrived during a downpour. They sloshed across the parking lot to the tents and then the mud started in.

Mud-stuck vehicles at every corner. Blown down tents, tent-poles broken, plastic bags and garbage floating in the street.

They passed young soldiers who looked like they'd been fighting the rats forever and never took a break.

By the time Uncle Brucker located the Command Tent, the mud had taken his left boot and he knew by the faces of the soldiers how tough this war would be.

The Lieutenant in charge observed the squad sign in. He was as skinny as a cadaver, as pale as a corpse, and he had the eyes of a dead man.

"On hold. Next!" was all the Lieutenant would say.

# 36

Uncle Brucker and his squad joined the army to fight rats, not to sit around on hold in the rec tent. But orders are orders and Downtown found a table and opened a fresh deck.

Downie cut, shuffled and dealt the cards faster than you could see. She spent her weekends at the casinos in Atlantic City where she ranked as #2 Eastern Division Marathon Poker Champ. One look into her sharp green eyes could make a tall man swoon. She knew she was a looker, and she dealt that card to her advantage.

Duffy brought a box of outdated snacks to share, mostly pretzels and chips. When he wasn't battling the rats, he was Northeast Snack Rep for EatWell, sales leader three years in a row. He was pumped-up, all the way up. He got his muscles years ago by working out and he kept them by working overtime.

The Doc had no patience for poker or any other card game. With long smooth strokes he cleaned and oiled his rat rifle. The Doc was particular as well as polite.

Ex-Lieutenant Willett cleaned his eyeglasses and held them up to the light once again. He promised his wife he'd change his underwear and socks, every day, dear. She sent him off to war with four 3-packs of boxer shorts and fourteen pairs of gym socks.

Between card games, Uncle Brucker and Midnight practiced important hand signals such as *Go That Way, Follow Me*, and *Rats Ahead*.

*Rats Ahead* you stick two fingers out straight, thumb up.

Wiggle your thumb and it's *Rats All Around*.

Uncle Brucker heard the rats had overrun our first line of defense at the reservoir and were marching toward the Galleria. He also heard the opposite: the rats had been routed. They fought with unexpected resilience. But he also heard the rats were cowards who would rather eat than fight. General Hardesty had the entire resources of the Army at his disposal, and the Air Force was ready to help, but he could not turn back the rats.

People were saying our leaders failed us. Soldiers were losing the will to win. Grandmothers wept when their grandchildren enlisted. People were saying rats are better than humans.

Uncle Brucker wasn't the type of guy who sat on his ass all day. And he paid no attention to rumors. He got up on his feet and found out for himself.

"It don't look right. It don't sound right. It don't smell right to me," he told his squad. "I might be stickin' my neck too far out but I'd say chances are pretty damn good there's a major fuck-up, and I aim to find it and patch it up."

# 37

Orders were stay put, but General Hardesty personally told my Uncle to help out whenever he can, so he said goodbye to the men and women of his squad, and he made his way by foot to the other side of Base Camp.

The huge camp spread across two and a half miles. It took him more than an hour to reach the West Gate. On the way, he filled two plastic bags with garbage and dropped them in the dumpster, grabbed a ham and cheese on rye from the mess hall, and stopped twice to pee.

Artillery shells crackled overhead and mortar shells smacked into the hillside. The offensive had stalled along the main road to the reservoir. The rats were organized, swift and bold. Their sneak attacks came from everywhere and out of nowhere. General Hardesty sent his Pointmen out on patrol, but they could not locate where the rats were hiding. The muddy road left no room to maneuver. The tie-up extended all the way back to Base Camp.

With one eye out for the unusual and the other for the over-looked, Uncle Brucker gripped his rifle and made his way down the road.

He killed two tunnel rats in a hidey hole. He shot another hiding behind a walnut tree. When three swamp rats jumped up from behind a rotten log, he was ready. He sighted through his powerful laser scope and shot all three before the first rat hit the ground. At the frontline Observation Post, just south of the reservoir, the incompetent ruled the confused. A fair-haired Colonel argued with another young Colonel over who goes next for coffee. The sergeants argued about everything else, and the war went on.

Uncle Brucker found a pair of binoculars and stepped up to the window.

Where were those damn rats hiding?

A few minutes for scanning plus a few more for consideration. Add two, maybe three more minutes to put it all together, and in less than ten minutes Uncle Brucker had figured it all out.

"Them leaves don't fit those maple trees," he told the fair-haired Colonel. The Colonel turned and glared at him. "It's walnut branches the rats cut for cover and walnuts don't grow on maple trees."

Uncle Brucker passed the binoculars to the Colonel. He took them. He didn't realize who he took them from, and the Rat Killer didn't tell him.

"So that's where they're hidin'—in the trees," said the Colonel.

"What you need is a soldier who can flush 'em out and pick 'em off," said my Uncle. "He's gotta be familiar with every kinda tree, and an expert rat tracker who talks rat to boot. Then you'll get this army rollin' again," he said with a smile.

It was a word of advice. To the young Colonel it sounded like orders, and he didn't like it. He didn't like the smile much either.

The outraged colonel puffed up.

"I got news for you, sergeant. That type a soldier ain't easy to find in this man's army," said the puffed-up red-faced young Colonel. "Damn near impossible. You find someone fits the bill, send him my way, and my wife will bake you a cherry pie for thanks. You can share it if you want, or you can eat it all your-self."

By two o'clock that afternoon, with Uncle Brucker's help, the army had cleared the rats from the trees.

The armored column pressed forward once again. His work done, Uncle Brucker could stay no longer. Everyone thanked him for his good advice and helpful assistance. The Colonel shook my Uncle's hand and smiled like a kid with a carnival prize. Another soldier passed Uncle Brucker a beer on the way out. Stop by the OP any time, the soldier said, and Uncle Brucker left the OP with a cool brew and a warm goodbye.

"Don't forget about the apple pie," the Colonel reminded him.

"Didn't you say cherry?" Uncle Brucker said.

"Most people prefer apple," the Colonel said.

Another Colonel offered him a lift back to the Command Tent and he accepted. The soldiers came over. Uncle Brucker looked around.

"Where's the vehicle?"

"I didn't say vehicle," said the Colonel. Not the young Colonel, a well-fed Colonel. "I said I'd give you a lift."

And the grateful soldiers took hold of my Uncle and gently raised him and carried him high above their heads, and that was his lift back to the Command Tent.

After he checked in, he found a dry spot, sat on a wooden crate, and took the envelope from his shirt pocket and read his Special Assignment once again.

It's a tough and risky assignment, from General Hardesty directly to the Rat Killer, and it went against his convictions, but it was his duty, and he would obey without question.

Sometimes a soldier is asked to do strange things when he's fighting a war. Things can get even stranger when he's battling the rats.

Uncle Brucker put his Special Assignment back in the envelope marked Special Assignment and resealed it, and he went outside the tent and tore the envelope into a hundred pieces, as the General instructed. And he tore each piece into a hundred pieces, as the General suggested. Between what the General instructed and what the General suggested, he now had, he guessed, maybe a million pieces.

Special Assignment means High Priority. A High Priority Message must be disposed of immediately, and without further thought he held his hand up and opened his fingers. It was a clumpball of pieces, and a breeze came up and the ball unclumped and the pieces blew over the tents of Base Camp into the sky, and flew off wherever they flew off to.

Later, he lay on his bunk and tried to fall asleep, but he couldn't sleep and he didn't say one word to the Doc or Duffy or Midnight for the rest of the day and all evening, not one word.

He was thinking about his Special Assignment.

38

The weather cleared up and General Hardesty attacked the rats from the west. Expecting a sneak attack, the rats fortified the south. But there was no sneak attack down south or anywhere else. Instead of dividing his forces, General Hardesty put all his forces in the west.

The rats were unprepared for this massive attack. Rat defenses collapsed. The Uprising stalled in the swamp fields south of the reservoir. The rats abandoned their outposts and retreated. Rat supplies fell to the roadside, and the Portal was left unguarded. Rat-claimed land overrun, retaken.

After dinner, General Hardesty mingled with the troops. Morale was high and he kept it high with a warm handshake and a happy-ending combat story. From tent to tent, bunk to bunk, he shook the hand of every soldier under his command.

He told combat stories that started out sad, but he had everybody smiling at the end.

One time when he was a lieutenant chased by renegade rats, he tripped on a jackroot and pulled a tendon. Unable to run, Lieutenant Hardesty quickly made a campfire and cooked a roadside stew from a favorite rat recipe. Then he hid in the dark. When the rats stopped at the campfire and ate the tasty stew, he jumped out of the dark and kicked the rats one by one into the fire. Then he ate the stew.

Another time his recon patrol was surrounded in rat territory. "Lie down, lie down," he radioed his men. "Sleep, go to sleep."

Rat vision is based on movement. The rats didn't notice the sleeping soldiers. When the soldiers woke up the next morning, the miserable rats were gone.

It was a long night of firm handshakes and unforgettable stories, but General Hardesty showed no signs of fatigue. Just after three in the morning he came to the bunk of an old friend. That old friend was my Uncle Brucker.

General Hardesty grabbed my Uncle's hand and shook it with respect and admiration.

"It's been a long time, Brucker."

"It's been just as long for me, sir."

"I met this man the day I signed up. I wasn't even a private then," General Hardesty let the troops know.

The tired soldiers had stayed up all night, playing cards and waiting for the General.

"How's every one of you boys?" he asked. "And I mean everyone. How are you? And you? And you?" The General made his way around the tent. "And you? And you? And how are you?" Not one hand was left unshaken.

He was a handsome clean-shaven General with sharp features, always cologned. He had a friendly manner, more like a dad than a General. Many soldiers sneaked around and shook his hand for a second time that night. Finally he was back at Uncle Brucker's bunk.

"Hey, fella. You're missing a boot!" General Hardesty noticed.

"The mud got it, sir," said Uncle Brucker.

The General leaned closer and whispered, "Walk backwards and your boots don't come off so easy. Follow me, old friend. You learn to backwalk like me, you'll never lose the other one."

# 39

Outside, the two old friends backwalked past the tents, down the hill to the main gate, up the hill again. General Hardesty backwalked with great confident strides, but Uncle Brucker just stumbled along on one shoe. He was quiet for a long stretch as he thought about his Special Assignment.

In the hazy distance the Portal looked like a bridge to nowhere. The entrance ramp rose from the muddy staging area and arched high over the tents, then it cut off in mid air and just hung there. Only it didn't end, it matched up with a tunnel in the next dimension. Already the troops were assembling for the final offensive.

Uncle Brucker watched these brave men climb to the top of the iron ramp and step off into nowhere.

Soon it will be his turn to travel the Nowhere Road.

"There's no need to worry, my friend, but I do appreciate your support," said the General as he considered the magnificent camp. He took a deep and satisfying breath. "The sun is back. The rats are on the run. I did some negotiating myself, caught them off guard with an offer and a counter offer. They had no time to read the fine print."

The morning sun crept up behind the camp, pushing the night out of the sky. Uncle Brucker and General Hardesty had talked until dawn. When the sun hit my Uncle's back, a weariness overcame him and he felt like he weighed an extra fifty pounds.

But he had a way of shaking off the weariness and the extra weight and anything else that got in his way when he had a Special Assignment.

The two old friends stood outside the General's quarters.

It was time for General Hardesty to say goodbye.

"You're a good man for a bad situation, Brucker."

"I'm even better in a good situation, sir."

Once again General Hardesty shook my Uncle's hand. The stars on the General's collar sparkled with the rising sun, and with a we'll-meet-again smile he backwalked through the mud.

"Just one last thing, sir." Uncle Brucker drew his pistol and pointed it at the General. "Stop backwalkin'. You're under arrest!"

"Me? Under arrest?" The General's voice was rough and serious in a way Uncle Brucker had never heard before. And his face was hard and mean like something ornery was pressing through. A different General altogether. "Only a General can arrest another General. Sorry, you don't have the authority."

"Got a Special Assignment gives me the authority. And you're still backwalkin'," said Uncle Brucker.

From the bunk tents and from the mess hall, the soldiers gathered around. General Hardesty under arrest! Had Sergeant Brucker lost his mind?

"Let's see your orders," said the General.

"Now you know I can't do that, sir. For the assignee's eye's only. In this case I'm the assignee."

"But I just can't remember authorizing that assignment."

"Well, I don't know what to say about that, sir. Except you once told me you need a ten foot brain to remember everythin'."

"That's true, considering details."

"You coulda' forgot that assignment, cause I don't see no ten foot brain."

"Ain't nobody got a ten foot brain! Now show me those orders or I'm backwalkin' outta here!"

"No you ain't! Take one step backward and I'll shoot!"

General Hardesty's right hand inched toward the 9mm automatic in his belt holster.

"We got a back story, you and me," said the General with hesitation. "Let's take an at ease and fill it in. Second Uprising, Outlet Plaza, back to back at Cookout King. Out of ammo, we beat the rats back with a bag of briquettes and a rotisserie skewer. Then we had dinner at Rita's Place. Don't say you weren't there."

Steady now, Uncle Brucker aimed his pistol at the General, and in the General's eyes he saw his own tiny reflection eye and eye.

Uncle Brucker said, "I wasn't there."

General Hardesty went for his gun.

In the blink of an eye, Uncle Brucker pulled the trigger.

# 40

The General lay in bed in the med tent in front of a row of monitors. The monitors flashed and beeped and purple liquids pulsed through tubes that fed into his arms. And a second row of serious monitors lined the wall under the first row. A team of technicians wearing green smocks and blue gloves checked the colorful tubes. Another team in yellow smocks and blue gloves studied those serious monitors.

Tears in his eyes, Uncle Brucker stood quietly beside the General's bed.

General Hardesty did not look like General Hardesty. The bullet from Uncle Brucker's pistol had turned him into something else. Now he had the sad eyes of a wounded animal. Bandages wrapped his head from ear to swollen ear—boxer's ears.

Uncle Brucker thought about what he had done to the General. The nasty head wound, the animal eyes, the boxer's ears.

"Excuse me," the medic said, and he elbowed my Uncle out of the way. The medic was a huge man with piston-like elbows and the jab hurt. He gave my Uncle a look that said You Shot The General, and that hurt more.

Uncle Brucker stood with the medics for a silent prayer.

"Allow me," he said, and he pulled the sheet up over the General's head.

The soldiers took down the med tent and folded it and loaded it into a truck. Another vehicle took the monitors and the medics and the multi-colored technicians away.

Uncle Brucker looked around.

"All clear!" he said.

He pulled the sheet from the General's body and handed him a towel. The General sat up and wiped the ugly makeup from his face and tore off the bloody bandage and removed the fake swollen tongue and boxer's ears, and he threw it all to the ground. He combed back his hair. A dab of cologne, and the General was the General again.

He grabbed my Uncle's hand and smiled. The smile was for pulling through, the shake for helping him out.

"You did the right thing, Brucker, under the circumstances."

"If I was shootin' bullets, you'd be dead."

"It's tough bein' caught between your convictions and your orders," said the General.

"There's no gettin' around it," Uncle Brucker said. "You gotta go with your orders and let your convictions slide."

"You need a special man for a Special Assignment. Thanks for answering the phone."

Last week a rat impostor fooled the guards and sneaked past Camp Security. He looked exactly like the General. He would have fooled anybody, not just us, the guards said. He made his way to the budget committee meeting up on the third floor of Central Command where he introduced a proposal to cut funding for the Army, but the guards caught up with him before the deal went through, and the Army remained funded.

It was a serious breach of security and it made General Hardesty look bad to the High Command. After a restless night of on and off sleep, he formulated a plan: fake his own assassination and knock himself off. That will put an end to their impostoring.

Uncle Brucker's special assignment: shoot General Hardesty with a prop gun and make it look good.

Most rat impostors are so bad you can't help laughing at them. Bad impostors won't even fool another rat. It takes a heap of determination, concentration and practice, which is a heavy load for a rat to carry. Don't underestimate talent. A talented impostor can make you think he's a man through refined gestures and movements.

It's like this: your eyes can only tell your brain what they're seeing, but your brain can tell your eyes what to see. A talented impostor can put it all together and get you seeing what he makes you think. Of course he has to refine his gestures first, and he must master his movements. That's how impostors do it.

A siren went off in sector #3. Seconds later, the General's battle Jeep pulled up and the passenger door flew open. The General got up from his sick bed. Sirens sounded in section #6 and #21. Mortars sailed overhead and landed in the parking lot. Searchlights glared, gates locked, sentries doubled up and rifles were loaded.

The rats are in the compound! General Hardesty put Base Camp on Lockdown.

General Hardesty stepped into the wide vehicle.

"Outlet City, Uprising #2," said the General. "I stabbed 'em with the skewer. Rita invited us to dinner. Do you recall?"

Uncle Brucker set the General straight.

"It's Outlet Plaza, not Outlet City. And it's Charcoal Dealer. Never heard of Cookout King. I had the skewer, you mixed the drinks. You can call her Rita but she's Sophie to me."

The General passed his helmet to Uncle Brucker.

"Wear it when you need it," he said.

Uncle Brucker took the General's lightweight bulletproof all-weather form-fitting helmet and put it on his head.

He closed the door and turned to his driver.

"To the Safe House!" he said.

# 41

By the time Uncle Brucker made it back to the bunk tent, his squad was torn up pretty bad.

Downie finally got everybody to sit down for a game of poker, including the Doc, when the first wave of rats caught them off guard. She fractured her wrist in two places with a wild swing, three jacks and a six of diamonds balled-up in her fist.

"Gimme that fuckin' bandage!" the Doc demanded of Ex-Lieutenant Willett. Battling the rats had sucked all the courtesy out of the Doc.

The first wave knocked Downie to the ground. The second wave trampled her. She sat on the dirt floor and the Doc patched her up but he ran out of bandages before he could finish the job.

"Duffy's worse, Sarge," said Midnight. "He's bleedin' hard. And we're outta bandages."

"How bad is he?" Uncle Brucker asked.

Midnight looked at Uncle Brucker. When their eyes met she shifted to the ground. What she said next did not come easy.

"He's talkin' about the White Palace," she said.

"Let's put our heads together, soldiers. There's gotta be somethin' we can do," said Uncle Brucker, but already he came up with another great idea.

"Yo, Willett!'

"Sarge?"

"You got any socks left?"

Using the white gym socks the Ex-lieutenant's wife gave him, they bandaged Duffy's leg and taped it. Other soldiers in need of help wandered over, two privates with leg wounds and one gaptooth sergeant with a black eye and bloody forehead.

Uncle Brucker found a spare sock and helped the sergeant tape up his head wound and stop the bleeding.

"Good thinkin' for a General," the sergeant said.

"Me, a General? You're talkin' to the wrong guy," said Uncle Brucker.

The sergeant held a white gym sock in his left hand and he had a 9mm automatic in his right. One step forward and the gaptooth sergeant stood face to face with my Uncle.

"If you ain't the General, then why are you wearin' a General's helmet, sir? Or should I say impostor, sir?"

The sergeant had heard about impostor rats and he felt sure he caught one. Orders are: shoot impostors on sight. That gap between his front teeth spread wide when he smiled at the impostor in his sights.

Uncle Brucker did not say a word as he tucked his shirt in his pants. And his face went blank——you just couldn't read it. Now he had the sergeant halfway puzzled and half confused.

Uncle Brucker tightened his belt and he adjusted the General's helmet. A General's helmet is always tight, his shirt neatly tucked in. He pulled his socks up to his knees, as high as a General's socks, and he stood up straight and tall and he looked down at the soldiers under his command.

And he looked just like a General and he felt like a General and any soldier would swear this man is a General, a great and famous General. Even the President of the United States would call him General, which is pretty much the same as being a General.

"Soldier," said General Brucker. He was speaking to the gap-tooth sergeant with the sock and pistol.

"Yes, sir?"

"Put your pistol in your holster. And soldier?"

"Yes, sir?"

"That sock goes on your head."

# 42

General Brucker woke up with his head in his arms on the long table in the command tent. The strategy meeting was over and the Generals had retired to their quarters for the night. Last thing he remembered they were discussing the new offensive. While they planned the troop deployment he must have fallen asleep.

Uncle Brucker did not ask to be a General. He did not want to be a General. It was not a position that he sought but it came with the helmet.

Being a General means you better not fuck up. It means on the cuff decisions, orders that stick, spot checks and follow-ups, questions you can't answer, questions nobody will answer. He held the lives of his men in one hand, the fate of his country in the other.

General Brucker did his best, as always, but it did not go well.

Alone in the General's Battle Jeep, Uncle Brucker drove east on the mud rut roads past the rat-torn tents and he stopped at the swamp fields on the far side of the reservoir. In these fields the fighting had been fierce. Acres and acres of hard-fought land, everything trampled. Rats and men battled each other and the earth suffered. Like a muddy desert.

Uncle Brucker ached. He had never ached so much when he was a sergeant, but now that he was a General his entire body ached. Every bone, every joint. And he had a General's headache too, which was worse than a migraine.

If he could find the Safe House he would find General Hardesty. Then he would return the helmet and he would be Sergeant Brucker again. Maybe then the headache would go away.

"Pssst!" From the bushes.

"Who goes there?"

"It's me, General Hardesty."

At first Uncle Brucker saw only the bushes. Then, as he walked forward, he noticed the General's handsome face in the bushes. A little closer, he smelled the General's expensive cologne.

"Follow me," said the General.

The General spread apart the bushes and revealed a heavy iron door. He opened the door and Uncle Brucker followed him down the stairway. At the bottom of the stairs they entered a modern living room with a thick wall-to-wall carpet and an eight-foot-wide window with a view of the boat landing and the reservoir. The Safe House was built into the side of a hill.

General Hardesty said with pride, "Some setup, eh? You got your living room over here, small rec room adjoining. Hot tub out back and freezer down below. My design, the mini-bar. Got the idea from a Rad Kielly movie. Care for a drink? OK, you got it."

At the mini bar, the General poured another round. Double Martini for the General, Scotch and soda for Uncle Brucker. The General sat on one side of the bar, Uncle Brucker sat on the other side.

Uncle Brucker usually didn't drink Scotch and soda, but what the hell, he never drank with the General at his Safe House either.

General Hardesty looked so pale, almost sickly. Uncle Brucker thought maybe he was coming down with something. The old Rat

Killer walked like his whole body ached. General Hardesty would be surprised if the old Killer could still outrun a rat.

"We gave 'em hell, General," Uncle Brucker said.

"So I heard. Don't forget the peanuts."

The General pushed across the bar a bowl of peanuts Uncle Brucker hadn't noticed.

"I don't know 'em to forget 'em," Uncle Brucker said, and he grabbed a handful. The peanuts were tasty. His headache disappeared as he chewed. He was more than a little drunk.

It was a magnificent Safe House, fit for a General. Uncle Brucker never saw anything so highly rated before. Top-rated kitchen, top-rated bar, everything top-rated.

General Hardesty inhaled the crisp, filtered air—extra fresh air.

And the mural, a beautiful oil painting of happy forest creatures covered one entire wall. Here fox and deer danced happily together, and early-rising birds flew off, chirping. The painting was called *Wake Up, The Rats Are Gone*.

Another wall was made up entirely of TV monitors. 24 sets, Uncle Brucker counted, 4 high and 6 across.

"You got all the channels you could want, excellent programming too. Multi-screen display. That talk of rats being better than humans is pure nonsense," said the General.

"I was a General too," Uncle Brucker said, "but only for a little while. You gotta be the right type a guy."

Uncle Brucker hoped General Hardesty understood what he was getting at. To help the General along he put the helmet down on the bar directly in front of the right type of guy, a guy with medals on his chest and stars on his collar, a guy with fortitude to spare——General Hardesty.

The General looked real hard at the helmet. He went on staring for a while, and General Hardesty realized it was time to pack his things and leave the Safe House.

"What show is that?" Uncle Brucker asked, pointing to the wall of monitors.

"Where?"

"That rat show."

"That's no rat show! That's the outside monitor. Those rats are attacking my battle Jeep!"

Enraged, General Hardesty slid off the bar stool. He found a key in his pocket and unlocked a little door on the far end of the mini bar. Inside, a shelf just big enough to hold two 9mm Browning automatics and two extra clips.

"Follow me!" he said, and with his helmet on his head and an automatic in each hand, he charged up the stairs.

Outside, the rats waited. Through the tiniest crack under the door came the scent of the General's cologne. General Hardesty opened the iron door and the rats were all over him. They dropped down from the roof and ran across his shoulders and came through holes in the ground.

The General aimed and fired.

Uncle Brucker stood behind him.

"*Ki-ca!*" Uncle Brucker hissed. Scram!

General Hardesty saw his chance and climbed into the military vehicle.

He snapped his fingers. "Keys!"

Uncle Brucker tossed the keys. "I can't stick around here forever," said the General. "In case you haven't noticed, there's an Uprising going on!"

The General didn't drive off right away. He had something to say but he was having trouble with it. When he finally spit it out it didn't sound so good. What he had in his thoughts sounded better.

"Thanks for helping me clear my head, old friend," he said. "See you at Rita's."

General Hardesty stepped on the gas pedal and the Jeep lurched forward. The wheels tore through the dirt and kicked up a cloud of dust. The General sped down the boat road past the landing and then he headed to the highway.

The cloud of dust followed him for a few blocks and then it finally settled down.

Uncle Brucker was alone with the rats.

# 43

Slowly Uncle Brucker backwalked to the Safe House. The trick was to move so slowly the rats didn't notice him at all. It took more than twenty minutes to backwalk twelve feet. During that time night fell and a three-quarter moon came out of the clouds and floated through the trees up above.

In the light of the moon he reviewed the 175 kinds of rats he knew about. By the time he backwalked to the iron door, he had discovered six more.

Slowly, very slowly, he opened the door and slipped inside.

In the kitchen he found cold cuts and beer in the refrigerator. There was a loaf of rye on the counter, and he made a pastrami and cheese sandwich. He took the sandwich and the beer into the living room and he sat in the leather chair and drank the beer and ate the sandwich in front of the wall of monitors.

One button on the remote controlled all 24 monitors.

He pressed that button and watched a Special Report with retired General Rolf Reyes on the military channel.

General Reyes stood in front of a detailed map of Base Camp. He held a long military pointer in his right hand. With the red laser tip of the pointer, he highlighted the intersection where General Hardesty had stopped at a red traffic light. The sky cam zoomed in for a close-up. General Hardesty checked the rearview mirror. The rats were catching up to him. General Hardesty read the sign under the traffic light. No right turn until four on weekdays. A General had to play by the rules. The rats closed in.

Damn those stinkin' rats!

He realized he couldn't make it all the way back to headquarters. When the traffic light turned green he made a left and headed for the TV station.

# 44

Uncle Brucker could wait no longer. He took one more bite of his sandwich, finished the beer and went back to the kitchen.

Four huge pots of stew simmered on the stove. He lifted the lid off stewpot #1, dipped a spoon and tasted it. Then he made a face and spit it out. The stew had too much pepper and a load of onions. The salt bit his tongue. But he had cooked it from a favorite rat recipe, and it tasted delicious to the rats.

He knew it would come to this, and he had started preparing the stew when he first came in. The stew had been simmering all this time! He took the lid off stewpot #2 and stewpot #3 and #4, and he ran up the stairs.

A dark cloud grew out of those four pots, a thick dark stew cloud, and like a tiny tornado it swirled and filled the stairway.

Uncle Brucker climbed the stairs. The thick, swirling cloud pushed him to the top. Pressure built up; the iron door rattled. The unstoppable cloud blew the door from his grip, and the stew cloud broke free into the cool night air.

There is no word for delicious in rat talk. There is no word for tasty either. But there is one word that means more than those words combined. *Ch-'ca-thc*, the greatest of all meals, or a meal to die for. This could be that meal, it smelled so incredibly good.

The promise of *Ch-'ca-thc* overcame every rat that smelled the stew.

Noses pointed upward, furry heads turned, and the rats backed off.

The hell with the Uprising! One whiff of that tasty stew and the rats knew nothing else.

The air above the Safe House had been calm that day. That evening a cool mountain breeze rolled down into the valley. Over the reservoir it picked up speed. By the time it passed over the Safe House it was a breeze no longer. Now it was a wind.

The reservoir wind crashed into the stew cloud and spread the aroma of *Ch-'ca-thc* throughout Base Camp.

# 45

Uncle Brucker watched it all on the Uprising News. The sky cam followed General Hardesty's Jeep down the road to the TV station. General Hardesty pulled over and jumped out at the studio entrance.

Retired General Rolf Reyes met him at the door.

"Come in, amigo, join the party," said Reyes. "Shoulda brought poppers. I ran outta hats!"

General Hardesty pulled his automatic from his holster. "Damn it, I'm low on ammo!"

"Try this!" Reyes tossed a laser pointer to General Hardesty.

General Hardesty caught the pointer in his right hand. The rats rushed through the door and ran along the floor, down into the heating vents and straight up the walls. General Hardesty fired his pointer at the first rat, and the rat froze. For an instant its eyes glowed red from the killer laser beam, then the rat exploded and splatted all over the door.

"Turn it up! Up!" cried Reyes.

General Hardesty set his pointer on full auto and aimed with precision. Rat eyes glowed red, rats exploded as they rushed in through the door.

With their backs to the studio wall, the two soldiers battled the rats. General Rolf Reyes had retired nine years ago after the First Uprising, and he was here on volunteer duty. He did his share of killing and more during Uprising #1 at the Galleria in Dengrove. But he was a much younger man back then and it was nothing like this.

It was too much for the old timer. His pointer weighed a hundred pounds. He could hardly raise his arm. General Hardesty held him firmly around his shoulder. But General Hardesty's pointer was low on juice. One, two more shots and it fizzled out. He took his automatic from his belt holster and checked the clip. Only two bullets left.

General Hardesty looked to Reyes and Reyes looked to him.

"*Ya sabes lo que tienes que hacer,*" said General Reyes. You know what you have to do.

General Hardesty put the automatic to the center of General Reyes' forehead.

The retired General closed his eyes tight and his lips moved in prayer.

But before General Hardesty could pull the trigger something overcame the rats. Their noses tilted up and they turned around, hooked on a scent so powerful it pulled them from the battlefield.

General Hardesty smelled it too. The rat stew!

"My God, they're leaving!" he cried as the rats scrambled out the front door.

General Hardesty stuffed the automatic in his belt holster and fell back against the studio wall. He took a deep breath and slowly he smiled.

"Smell that stew, you old billy goat?" said General Hardesty to General Reyes with the widest of smiles. "I got a hunch who's behind that aroma. Good work, Sergeant Brucker! I'd give that soldier ten, fifteen medals, but I only got six in the box."

# 46

The rats abandoned their outposts and followed their noses to the Safe House and a meal to die for. Down in the kitchen they fought over the stew pots, ripping, chewing and gnawing. The rats broke through the windows and they came up through the floor. Uncle Brucker realized he'd better get the hell out of there, so he stuffed a few cold ones in his pants and went to the kitchen to take one last bite out of his sandwich.

And sitting in the General's chair with his head buried in a stew pot was the Rat Commander.

The Commander looked up at Uncle Brucker.

"*Ah-th'-ta*," the Commander demanded. More stew.

# 47

"Every man's got somethin' he hates more than anythin'," Uncle Brucker told the Rat Commander. "I hate cookin'. I hate pre-parin'. I hate heatin' things up. I only cooked that stew in order to save the General, but that don't make me hate cookin' any less. So, I'm tellin' ya, I ain't cookin' no more stew, you fat miserable rat!"

My Uncle stood firm with his arms folded at his chest.

The Commander sat in General Hardesty's chair, watching cartoons on the TVs. One stewpot in his lap, two more on the floor beside him. His young assistant Grabs stood behind him.

The Commander had arrived at the Safe House as a slim Lieu-tenant, and he ate his way up the ranks in record time. He made Captain about halfway through the first stewpot. After the second pot he promoted himself to Commander. Now he was shooting for Big Fat General.

"How many licks you figure I got left in this pot?" he asked Grabs.

"No more than ten, Commander," Grabs said.

"Commander? You're tellin' me I ain't up to General yet?"

"It's gonna take more than twenty licks to weigh in as a General, and I figure there ain't but ten left in this pot." Grabs shivered with fear. He didn't want to disappoint the Commander. He'd rather chew off his own tail. The Commander's long tongue came out and scooped a glob of stew off his snout. He was watching a Roadrunner cartoon playing on 24 TV's. The Commander laughed and laughed. Laughing, he stuck his head back in the stewpot. Nothing left. Licked clean. No more laughing. The cartoons were not funny. They were sad, very sad.

Grabs turned to Uncle Brucker. "I'm countin' to ten and you better start cookin'!"

"But rats can't count!" said Uncle Brucker.

"One . . . two . . ."

"You get stuck on two."

"Four . . . nine . . . seven . . ."

"And they got no idea what comes after three!"

The Commander hissed. He was fed up with the human's backtalk. He grabbed a can of beer from the floor, slurped it down and threw it across the room.

Drunk he was and fatter than ever, but he wasn't fat enough to be General. Now he had some gnawing to do—on that lazy cook. He tried to get up from the chair but he couldn't move. Too fat to move, not fat enough to be General. He licked the rim of the pot, and with a smile on his face and the taste of stew in his mouth, his heart stopped, and the life went out of him.

He had tasted the meal to die for, and now there was nothing left.

More rats ran down the stairs and piled into the kitchen. They climbed up the stove and dove into the stewpots. The fought each other to death for the chance of a lick. Grabs showed a viciousness

Uncle Brucker had never seen before. He climbed out of a pot and turned to Uncle Brucker with his eyes afire and his fangs dripping.

Uncle Brucker wasn't the type to take any chances. He expected the unexpected. He was prepared for any emergency, and wherever he went he always had his back covered.

As the rats scrambled across the kitchen floor, he opened the refrigerator and reached in. Hidden from view in the back of the top shelf was one last bowl of stew he had saved for an emergency.

He placed it on the floor and slowly backed off.

The rats fought over the bowl of stew. Uncle Brucker ran out of the kitchen and up the stairs. He left the Safe House through the iron door and headed back to his squad at Base Camp.

# 48

The rats gathered their forces and attacked at dinner time. It was all part of a master plan. The tricky rats tunneled under the parking lot and came up through the mess hall while Uncle Brucker and his squad were having dessert. The rats were many and fierce. The soldiers dropped their napkins and fought back with forks and knives. In minutes the rats overran the kitchen, then they ravaged the supply tent. They drank the General's wine and ate what they could find and they fought and ate and drank more wine.

It was a battle feast.

The rats bound Uncle Brucker's arms and legs with hemp rope and stuffed him in a burlap sack. They dragged him by his feet down the street and in the gutters. They threw rocks at him and kicked him and busted bottles in his path, and they laughed when he cried out in pain. They laughed so hard they lost their grip and dropped him, and his head cracked on the curb, and the rats rolled over on their backs and kicked their feet in the air and howled with laughter.

The rats, the miserable rats! What other creature finds such pleasure in pain?

He fought off the pain by thinking of ways humans are better than rats.

Humans use tools. . . . Humans build things. . . . Humans calculate. . . . Humans drive. . . .

The rats dragged him past the rec tent and the mess hall. Drunken rats, cowards and deserters tagged along. There must be something pretty damn important in that sack and they wanted to find out what it was.

"Who ya holen' up, ratso?"

"Can't tell ya."

"We'll give you a drink if you do."

After a drink: "It's the Rat Killer!"

"That's no Rat Killer. You been fooled."

"I ain't fooled by this."

"But everybody knows the Rat Killer's twelve feet tall. He don't fit in that sack."

"Now listen here. That's the way he is before you catch him. You build him up so high, then when you catch him and beat him down he fits in a sack."

"He ain't in there now. . . . That sack is empty!"

Ahead, past the overturned dumpster, a leg disappeared behind a tent. Uncle Brucker untied his hands and feet but he couldn't get the sack off his head. He ran blindly between the tents and tripped and fell to his knees and scrambled to his feet. Finally, he pulled the sack off and looked around.

And he was standing at the foot of the Portal. The rats had chased him onto the Nowhere Road!

Up there at the Portal, the air was turbulent. The ironwork creaked and the bridge swayed in the wind. Uncle Brucker hugged the hand rail as he climbed up the ramp to the top platform. Powerful crosswinds whistled back and forth. Hold on to that rail! The rift between dimensions created a vacuum. The whistling wind was short on oxygen.

The rats had decorated the entire ramp and Portal with blinking lights and streamers. It's their way of celebrating victory. A rat timer turned on the lights at dusk or when they got it to work.

"Come on, you rats!" A cry from below. "They got the timer workin'!"

One by one the lights went on, from the entrance ramp all the way up the bridge. Red, blue, green, yellow, and strange rat colors unseen by humans. A magnificent hundred-bulb collar outlined the portal, and every bulb blinked.

For a moment the rats were still, transfixed by the blinking lights. For a moment Uncle Brucker felt he could knock the rats over with a whisper, and they would tumble down like cutouts and clear a path all the way to Base Camp.

But how long is a moment? The spectacle wore off when the moment had passed, and the rats came on.

He turned to the rats, the miserable stinking rats. They came up the ramp, more rats than he'd ever seen, more than he could imagine, and like a World Champion he raised his arms high above his head.

"Humans teach! Humans cook! Humans prevail!"

The wind blew and the wind whistled. The ironwork creaked and grumbled. The bridge swayed and the railing shook and the bolts shivered. Uncle Brucker took one deep breath and stepped into nowhere, and he was gone.

# 49

My first week alone at the old house went fast. Every night before I went to sleep, I crossed off the days on the calendar. The second week slowed down. Now week #3 was dragging its ass and Uncle Brucker still hasn't returned from his two week assignment.

I walked to school every day. When I woke late I ran every other block. Charlee said her mom will give me a ride when it rains but it never got past a drizzle.

I prepared another World Shaking Event report. I got an A on the last one and Charlee got an A+. This was not an assignment. I did it because I was into it. Charlee helped me out at first and then she joined me. Now it was a dual report and we got Mr. Ross's permission for next week. First I wanted to give a report on the Black Plague, then we decided World War Two was better.

People with rat emergencies called up and left messages on the phone. When I got home from school I called them back and told them I ain't the Rat Killer. He can't make it today but he won't forget about you. Don't give up, he'll get to you pretty soon.

Manny and Leroy came over and hung out. Manny was a good looking guy who rolled his sleeves up like a lumberjack. Leroy wasn't so good looking but he got the girls. They drank my milk and said they didn't, ate the peanut butter and put the empty jar on the shelf. They never threw out their beer cans. It was a perfect house for hanging out, and everybody knew it.

I made up some new rules, and that goes for you, Manny. You can visit when you want, but I tell you when to get out. Fall asleep on the couch, you better clean up before you go home. And don't touch my Uncle's War Medal.

I told nobody, not even Manny or Leroy, about my Uncle's two-week assignment or why he was gone. They just knew he wasn't home.

I worked on the Eagle and the Camaro. With Leroy's help I put new plugs and wires in the Camaro. I get it back on the road, it's a great accomplishment for all mankind, but especially me. Uncle Brucker will be pleased when he sees it.

Leroy came over and we did some body work on the Scout that I forgot to mention. Leroy brought a 48 piece wrench set with him and we didn't need it, but we used his glue gun. We glued the windshield trim and adjusted the hand brake, and then we decided to call it a day or two.

Everything looked good with the Eagle, the Camaro, the Ram and the Monte Carlo. And the Scout too, considering.

# 50

Every evening before dark I put my Identifiers on and drove the Eagle around town, but I couldn't find Renata.

I drove down to Tuskie's Pizza, then I went down Center past Half Price Stores and the strip mall, and up through the heights and Crown Street where I first met her. I couldn't find her anywhere.

I identified a lot of people. Most I didn't know so I wrote down descriptions such as "the man with the black cap in the doorway" or "two kids with cool jackets walking out of Half Price Stores".

But it takes up time when you're on the lookout. You have to keep your eye on the road when you're behind the wheel. So after a while I just made notes and added the descriptions later. Uptown past Holmes and through the Heights past High Mary's down to Tuskies again and made a right at the strip mall and headed back home.

"Nice house. You got the house," Manny said after I got home and sat on the couch with a beer. "If your Uncle was my Uncle, I'd be here with ya. Charlee's cool. Nuthin' wrong with Charlee. But Renata makes up for what she's missin'. A hot babe like Renata, don't waste no time. You gotta move on into action!"

Some girls are hot. Some girls are hotter than hot. Renata, you are a fireball.

## 51

Every Sunday at sunrise Keith and Reed and my Uncle drove out to Jack's Creek with their rods and reels and returned before noon with a sack of bass and brookies. The Sunday tradition began years ago after my Uncle's first stroke.

For the last three weeks he did not join them.

Keith was disappointed, Reed suspicious. They came to the old house and I told them everything I could without blowing my Uncle's cover. When I ran out of facts I turned to excuses.

"He's out Early Trackin'."

"He should be back sometime too late for fishin'."

"He went to visit a relative. I forget the name. A sick one."

After the last excuse Keith and Reed stood on the back porch and refused to leave. Where was the old Rat Killer? Something's up, they knew it, but I couldn't say a word because my Uncle said don't tell anybody about his two-week Assignment.

Keith did the talking. He was in his sixties, Reed somewhere around forty. They have the same amount of hair on their heads. Keith was Reed's father but they looked like balding brothers. Keith nudged Reed.

Keith said, "In all the years I know your Uncle he never mentioned nobody but you and your dad."

"That's because he doesn't talk about the sick ones," I told him. "I don't even know who they are until they die."

## 52

Charlee says she'd rather have a Mustang any day. Camaro's aren't worth fixing up. It's just talk but she gets it from her brother,

I mean her older brother Arnie with the black Mustang. Uncle Brucker's sky blue 327 Camaro had a 4-speed and a vinyl top, and I put on the fog lights and silver mudflaps. Arnie's got a sixteen valve. It flies, Charlee says. But not without a six and you can't get a six.

Charlee came over after school and we were sitting in the Camaro parked under the shady willows by the barn. It's nice out here under the trees with a view of the house and the yard, and we came here a lot. I got the passenger seat. I let Charlee get behind the wheel most of the time.

There's not much wrong with that girl except she likes Mustangs and she won't eat pizza.

"Peugeots," I said. "Peugeots are the safest cars you can buy. There are only a few of them on the road so they hardly get into any accidents."

"Mustang's faster than any Camaro," she said.

"You think so?"

I consider it bad luck to badmouth a car while you're sitting in it, and Charlee knows it. And don't bug me with Mustangs. They have a reputation, but the Camaro's got the speed. Ask anybody, just don't ask Arnie.

"If you don't like the car you're sittin' in, you don't have to sit in it. But don't stick around if you're gonna badmouth the Camaro. . . . Where you goin', Charlee?"

"I guess I'm goin' back home where I can badmouth in peace," she said.

"Wanna sit in the Monte Carlo?"

"Only if I get the driver's seat."

# 53

It was a new Ford Police GT, and it came down the road with the Sheriff behind the wheel. He turned into the driveway and pulled up next to the old house.

"Hideout!" Charlee cried.

By the time the cop got out, Charlee and I had moved from the Monte Carlo to the Hideout in the barn.

We made the Hideout up in the loft years ago. It stretched across the front of the barn. There was a ladder to climb up on the right. First it was a clubhouse, then a rec room and then it was the Hideout.

We cleaned out the loft and put a bridge table up there, and we had candles and an oil lamp in case of a blackout. A picnic bench fit under the roof where nobody could see us. Through the knot holes and the slats in the siding we looked down at the world and thought of ways to fool adults.

I met Charlee before my mother ran off, and that's a long time ago. Our birthdays come up in three weeks. We'll both be seventeen but she'll get there ahead of me. Her hair is short now and not so yellow. Her mother made her wear bangs for years and then said OK no more bangs. She was a skinny little kid. She's always been skinny. In an old photograph, her yellow hair came halfway down her back and her elbows stuck out like bendy straws. She turned out very nice but she was a real skinny kid.

The fat cop sat in the GT and talked to the dispatcher on the radio.

He got out and took his sheriff's hat from the seat and he put it on. His big stomach hung over his belt like a bumper.

The cop went up the steps to the back porch and looked in the kitchen window and knocked.

"Home? Anybody home?" he said. "Walt Thompson! Are you home?"

He glanced at his wrist watch and waited.

"He's lookin' for you," Charlee whispered.

"Good guess."

"He's walkin' over here. He comes in, he'll see us. Walt, what are you gonna do?"

"I'm gonna be cool like you," I said.

The sun came in through the barn slats and made light stripes across the floor and the walls of the loft. It's one reason we made the hideout up here. We liked the stripes.

The cop walked from the house to the barn.

Charlee put her arms around me and kissed me and wouldn't let go.

"Home? Anybody home?" the cop asked.

The cop stood by the barn.

He put his hand out and touched the barn door but he didn't open it. Something over by the pig shed caught his eye. It was the hubcap I had nailed to the wall with the others. I found it last week on the by-pass and took it home, #12 in my hub cap collection.

No doubt in his mind, it had to be the hubcap missing from his left rear wheel.

The radio in the GT squawked a call-up. Three-car accident, call for back-up near City Hall. Another cop car came down the hill with lights flashing, and the Sheriff grabbed the hub cap and followed his stomach back to the GT.

He threw the hub cap in the back seat, took his hat off and tossed it in the front seat, and without leaving a thank you note, he backed out of the driveway and drove down the road.

"Saved by a hub cap," Charlee said. "Want to fool around?"

"OK."

She took off her clothes except her panties, and she untied my Nike's and pulled off my pants. Her panties were light blue with dark blue flowers and yellow frills. She has cute little tits, and she always smells nice. And she had a press-on rose flower tattoo on her thigh, the kind that washes off in the shower.

And we fooled around up in the barn loft with straw for a pillow on an asian rug Uncle Brucker got in trade. Nice rug, but it's better for walking on than screwing around. The barn siding had slats between the boards, and the sun came in and striped the rug and us on the rug and got in our eyes until the clouds blocked it.

But it wasn't the same as last time. She kissed hard. Her teeth scraped against mine and she kissed me harder. She'd learned a thing or two and it wasn't like before, and she's not Renata. Renata has long dark hair and slinky eyes with dark, dark make-up, and she's not like Renata. It was weird thinking of Renata, and Charlee slowed down, and that sent my duck for a dive, and I got up from the rug and brushed off the straw.

"What's wrong?" she asked.

"It stinks up here," I said. "I ain't doin' it where it stinks."

# 54

**M**anny came up with the idea—throw a party.

That's how I'll hook up with Renata. I was going about it the wrong way.

"Listen up, little brother," he said. "Times a-wastin'. You gotta get a strategy and move into action. Instead of cruisin' around lookin' for her, sit back and she'll come your way. Everybody loves to party. Word gets out, she'll show up. You got it made, little brother, and put in a good word for me."

Manny and Bones and Leroy were hanging out in the living room and watching TV and drinking and eating popcorn. I just came in from an evening of Identifying and walked into this.

"It's gonna be a blast," said Manny.

"Guaranteed!" said Bones.

"Saturday night at eight," Manny said. "You'll be there, won't ya, little bro?"

# 55

**S**aturday night. Nine-thirty.

I bought pretzel rods and lots of chips and dip at Food Saver, and I spent another twenty bucks on bags of ice because Leroy said you're gonna need ice. So far only Leroy and Manny showed up. No Bones. We had a shitload of ice. Charlee's big brother Arnie drove up in his Mustang with a couple of six packs. Everybody had a drink but not me.

By ten o'clock the old house was packed. Manny played a dance tune on a portable set-up he brought with him. Leroy and Ida Lena laughed and joked with JJ, and Bones danced and talked with Bethany, smiling and having a great time. Bunky sat with a beer on the couch.

I told everybody, put the beer cans in the garbage. Nobody listened and I went through the house and collected bottles and cans and I threw them in the garbage in the kitchen.

Back in the living room, I sat on the couch and passed a beer to the Bunkster. Bethany came over holding a cigarette and a joint in her left hand. She kicked off her shoes and stretched out on the couch where she smoked and toked left-handed.

Charlee showed up at ten-thirty holding hands with Vernon Verna.

Vernie graduated last year and he lived in the city and went to dance school. Charlee took ballet classes since she was little and she can dance any step. You can tell by the way she moves she loves to dance.

She danced through the living room and danced around me with her arms out like she's dancing on the moon.

"Renata can't dance like me," she said.

Charlee knows I don't like to dance much. She danced with Vernie Verna.

I made up my mind no drinking until Renata gets here. Where the hell is she? OK, so I had a beer. One beer, that's all. Manny turned up the volume on an oldies song I hated and I drank the beer. Charlee took a sip and passed it back. Bunky sat like a leftover on the couch.

A kid named Kip stood by the shelf with the War Medal. He was a senior with a eighth grade mustache and he was hoping for a beard. He drove a little Mazda 3 around. I didn't know him to trust him and I don't trust nobody with that Medal.

"Don't touch that Medal, Kip. You'll mess it up!" I told him.

"Could use a dustin'," he said, and he held it in one hand.

"That's my Uncle's Medal and it's how he wants it. I said put it down."

"And who the hell are you?"

"I'm the guy who makes the rules around here," I said.

I stared at him and he stared back at me. He was taller than me but not by much, but that don't mean nothing for staring.

Then Ida Lena walked over and Kip put the Medal back on the shelf. She walked up to him smiling real sweet at him. He put his arm around her and she touched his wimpy mustache with a little finger.

Charlee came up to me and leaned close and said, "I know you like Renata. I know you do. You lookin' for her tonight?"

"Lookin' but not findin'," I said.

"I know where she is, if you want to know," said Charlee. "She's down town at Tuskies Pizza is where."

# 56

There she is, talking to her girlfriends in front of Tuskies, all dressed in black. Black shoes, black pants, tight black sweater, black finger-nails, everything black. That's Renata.

I hit the horn—nothing. Damn horn won't work!

So I spun the Eagle around and drove right up to her.

"Beep! Beep!" I said. "BEEEEP!"

I wore my Identifiers just to check her out, but they fogged up, so I took them off.

Renata walked to the car real slow. She always knows where she's going and she's never in a hurry for nobody.

And she got in. She didn't think about it, she just got in and slid over next to me like she was heading here all along.

"You don't need no seat belt. I drive smooth," I said.

She had a bunch of bracelets on her arm.

"Seven?" I figured.

"Count the ones on my right arm I got eleven." She shook her wrist. The bracelets jingled. I could fit one finger all the way around her tiny wrist. How did those bracelets stay on? "All different colors," she said.

"Eleven bracelets. . . . That's one more than enough."

"Count the ones at home I got twenty-two in all. They say the rats make 'em but I don't know about that."

"I'll hang that red one off the rearview. You only need twenty-one accordin' to the book."

"What book?"

"I sure would like that red one."

She examined her bracelets under the street lights. She took a while deciding. First she slipped a red one off her left wrist and examined it under the street light in front of Big And Small Stores. Then I made a right on Holmes Street and she slipped a green off her right wrist under the light by Billy's Bargains.

Finally, under the light at RiteWay, she took off a dark blue bracelet and gave it to me, not the red one I had asked for. Blue is OK too. I put it on the column. The red one I wanted would have gone on the rearview.

"You go to John Dodd?" she asked. "You know Jimmy Kosko?"

"Jimmy Kosko? Is he your boyfriend?"

"Was, don't have one tonight."

At the next light I put my arm all the way around her shoulder.

"Who's your boyfriend?" I said, and she moved against me, very quiet and sweet. "Who's your boyfriend tonight?"

"I don't mind if you are," she said, and I looked into those dark eyes for a second time.

"Let's go back to my house," I said.

"OK," she said.

"Right now?"

"I said OK, didn't I?"

I put on the blinker and I made a right heading home, and for a moment everything was great. I felt great. Renata looked great. The trees, the street lights, the air. All great.

Then somebody in a Maxima swerved into my lane and I almost hit him. I stepped on the brake and missed him by about a foot. If my horn was working, I'd blast him.

"Whew!" I said. "Asshole! Who is that asshole?"

"I don't know. I don't know him."

"He waved at you."

"Oh, him. That's Ditch. He's my boyfriend."

"You said you don't have a boyfriend!"

"That ain't what he thinks. Watch out, Walt! He's cummin' after you. You better let me out over there!"

I pulled into the Quality Shoes lot and parked in the front row. Renata tried to open the passenger door but it was stuck again. I went around and yanked it open but she slid out the driver's side instead.

The black Maxima pulled up. Eighteen inch wheels, fender flares and a hood scoop. Two kids got out the front. It was Ditch and this kid Fang was with him. Fang had no front teeth on top. He's a couple of years older than me. I don't know what happened with his teeth. I don't know why but they call him Fang.

Fang came over to the Eagle.

"The Eagle's a shit car," he said. "Gotta wipe your ass every time you drive it."

"Four wheel drive, cruise, heated seats ain't shit," I told him.

"There ain't no heated seats," Ditch said like he knew what he was talking about.

"Takes off like a rocket ship leavin' the earth," I said.

"They don't make 'em with heated seats," said Ditch.

"Park it in the sun, it's got heated seats." Fang laughed.

That's how the fight started. They badmouthed the Eagle and I couldn't just stand there, I had to do something about it.

Fights I lose I don't talk about.

Fights I win I don't know yet.

I drove back to the old house. The lights were on and some-body left the front door open. The party was over. Everybody had gone except for Leroy and Manny. They'd cleaned up the house a little, about as much as you'd expect. Manny carried a turntable that went with his set-up. They were on their way out when I came in and went to my room and got in bed.

I woke up a while later when the back door swung open. A breeze blew through my room and the blinds knocked against the window. Footsteps went from the kitchen to the living room and the far wall with the high shelf and back through the kitchen and out the back door again.

I got out of bed and I went to the living room and checked the shelf first thing. I expected the Medal would be gone, but there it was, up on the shelf, one day dustier than yesterday. It looked like it had been through a lot laying on that shelf.

I opened the back door and looked outside. Nobody hid in the bushes, nobody ran through the woods. I had dreamed up the whole incident and woke up thinking it was real.

In the morning I got up early and cleaned up the place. I didn't notice it until I checked the clock on the wall by the shelf.

It was 8:37 and my Uncle's War Medal was missing.

# 57

Humans invent. . . . Humans build. . . . Humans repair. . . . Humans drive. . . .

Uncle Brucker woke up in the dark.

The pain told him he was alive and the aches told him he was awake, but he could not see. He wiped the dirt from his eyes and he cleaned his glasses with his shirt sleeve but that didn't do much good. The damp earth had soaked through his clothes and deep into his bones, and he ached.

But where was he? And how did he get here?

So he lay there for a while, gathering his aches and pains. He slept again and in a backwards dream that started in a rat hole and ended with a fat rat commander, it all came together.

After he passed through the portal, the rats caught up with him in the tunnel. He fought like a madman, but the miserable rats brought him down. Awake now, he realized he was in the one place he didn't want to be: holed-up in the soggy ground deep in rat territory.

The hole had caved in behind him. He kicked his legs free. The drunken rat guards were buried by the landslide. Uncle Brucker figured he better get out of there before they dig themselves out.

Yes, he was tired. Sure, he was hungry. Add on weak.

But Uncle Brucker had never been in a fix he couldn't get out of, and he wouldn't let this be the first.

Humans don't give up. . . . Humans think. . . . Humans plan. . . . Humans escape. . . .

A voice from the darkness: "This way!" A woman's voice.

"What did you say?" Uncle Brucker asked.

"This way."

"Which way?"

"This way."

"Where?"

"Over there!"

On elbows and knees he crawled toward the voice. He crawled as fast as he could. Up ahead, a circle of light came through. He crawled toward the light and the light grew brighter. Finally, he came to a ledge and he looked down into a great rat hole.

He'd been inside only one rat hole but he'd looked into a few, and he'd never seen a rat hole like this. This was surely the greatest of all rat holes. A central hub of holes. Bottom holes, top holes, side holes came in all around. Poke holes in the ceiling brought in fingers of light. Jagged roots broke through the walls and hung from above. Water dripped from the roots and collected at the bottom, where a drain ditch carried it away.

The busy work rats pushed boxes along the ground. A woman stood alone in the center of that hole. Her arms hung loose, her shoulders sagged. Her body was bent over like a half-chopped tree.

"This way!" the woman cried.

The woman was Midnight Mary!

"I'm cummin', Midnight!" Uncle Brucker yelled.

He grabbed onto a root and swung down to the bottom. But as he came closer he realized Midnight was not talking to him. Midnight didn't even know he was there.

"That way." Midnight spoke to the rats. "Bottom hole, left. Side hole, right."

Under her supervision, the rats moved the boxes from hole to hole.

"Midnight? What did they do to you?"

Midnight Mary slowly turned to Uncle Brucker. In the half light of a poke hole her face was a lifeless mask. The miserable rats had sucked the life out of her, which caused her hollowed-out body to shrivel-up and bend over.

Her eyes! They were eyes of horror. But it wasn't the horror of what she saw, it was the deeper horror of how she saw—horror from the inside looking out.

The hollowed-out woman raised her right arm, and it was heavy. It was a struggle between What She Was and What She Is. She didn't have much of What She Was left, and she used it all to raise that arm. She pointed her finger straight ahead and wiggled her thumb.

Uncle Brucker knew the signal: Rats all around!

# 58

Uncle Brucker heard rat talk coming from below. He dug the dirt out of his ears and backed into a dark hole, where he watched, unseen.

In the back of the hole on a shelf he found a cardboard box. Inside the box, fresh cupcakes filled with raisins and nuts. The hungry man ate one cupcake right away, then he ate another. Boxes of these sweet, delicious cakes filled the hole. He ate another and another.

Down below, the Professor crawled into the great hole.

"Follow me," said the Professor. "I'll show you what we're workin' on in the Rat Factory."

Three ancient gray rats followed close behind the Professor. The white-whiskered Elders were so old and drunk they could hardly move. They stumbled and they sniffled and every few feet they opened their pouches and drank. They drank to the Professor and they drank to his children and they drank to sleep holes with soft pillows of dirt.

The Professor wore a dirty, torn-off apron and wired-together glasses. He twisted the wires around his ears and he brushed back his whiskers with a front claw.

The Elders had come there to check up on the Professor and drink to the occasion.

"Transposition is a thing of the past," the Professor explained and the Elders drank. "It can take years, and still there's no guarantee of Genomorphism. It's a dull, worn-out idea. It ain't even a notion. Here at the Rat Factory we're workin' on a shiny new idea, the rat cake! Every human has a bit of rat inside him. The rat cake helps the inner rat break out. It's packed with super-nutrients that build the rat up, combined with a sharp astringent that shrinks the human down. Eat one, they're gonna want another—and another, and another. Just two cakes will start the inner rat growing. Eat six cakes, you'll get sixty percent rat in three days. Humans can't resist because they're lazy and they got no fortitude. Give the rat inside him a chance, it'll take over. Load the rat cakes in vending machines or ship 'em off to supermarkets and put them on the shelves. In a few months we'll be back in the Rulin' Seat. Humans are done for! The future is ours. That's the notion. You get the idea. It's all packed together in the rat cake."

When the Professor had finished, he jumped with excitement. When the Elders looked his way, he calmed himself down. He sniffed the air and straightened his tail, and with his nose pointed straight ahead he went to the storage hole where Uncle Brucker was hiding.

Uncle Brucker slid back deeper into the hole. He pushed a box of cakes toward the entrance. The Professor reached inside and grabbed a cup cake and held it up for the Elders to see.

And Uncle Brucker saw it too.

So that's what he was eating! Rat cakes. And how many had he stuffed down his throat? Two? Four? Six? It doesn't matter. He discovered what the rats were working on, and that's what matters.

He held a cake in his hand, a perfect little cake, so round and sweet, with raisin cheeks and peanut eyes. But he didn't eat it, he squeezed the sneaky rat cake to a pulp. The raisins came loose and the peanut eyes popped out. He figured the raisins and nuts were safe to eat, so he picked up a few, held them in his hand and popped them in his mouth.

"The nutrients are in the raisins. The astringent is in the nuts," the Professor explained.

Uncle Brucker spit out a mouthful.

Now he was in a tough position, about as tough as it can get. Anybody else would watch his life crumble with that cake. He'd give up and surrender to the rats then and there. But not my Uncle. He doesn't panic when things get tough. He has strength as well as fortitude.

Fortitude!

What the Professor said about fortitude riled him. What does a rat know about fortitude? What rats got, humans got more of, and that includes fortitude. He closed his eyes and breathed deeply. With each breath fortitude filled his chest and flowed through his body, filling him up with I Can Do's. Now he had a whole chestful of fortitude—just like the man he admired most, General Hardesty.

The Elders toasted the Professor. They toasted the Professor again. The Professor had examples to show the Elders and he was an impatient rat. He wanted to jump on the Elder's backs and nip some sense into them but he knew better. Instead, he jumped a little gray work rat who crawled near him. The rat squealed and tried to get away. The Professor came down hard with his big claws and the Elders watched. In seconds he ripped and chewed and gnawed that rat to the bone.

The Elders plugged up their rat pouches and turned to the Professor.

"Bring the humans out!" cried the Professor.

"This way, humans," said Midnight.

The four squad members came out of the shadows. They walked slowly with their hands tied behind their backs. A woman stepped into the light of a poke hole. Her face was black with dirt and part of her ear had been nibbled off. Her left eye was swollen and closed. She had developed a severe facial tick.

Example number one: Downtown.

"Only two cakes, and you can see the brightness on her face," the Professor explained. "Gone is the dumb human look, replaced by that sharp rat look. Humans have fragile brains, unlike rats, because they don't eat enough stew. Next!"

Example number two: Duffy. Face wet with tears. Ankles nipped and bleeding. His right arm twitched uncontrollably. His left arm hung like a dead thing waiting for the funeral. Example number three: Ex-Lieutenant Willett. Number four: the Doc. Twitching, shaking, crumbling remnants of themselves.

"And now, finally," said the Professor with a grin of satisfaction, "the man you've been waiting for, the man we all hate. Bring out the Rat Killer!"

# 59

The Elders drank the rat juice and waited. They waited and drank some more. The Professor crawled into the hole and came back with a sad look on his face. The Rat Killer could not be found.

It had been a fine visit with the Professor. The Elders had much to be pleased about. Only one thing displeased them, and they forgot what it was. No matter, their pouches were low on juice and they were anxious to go home to their sleep holes.

One Elder burped, a second peed in the drain ditch while the third burped and farted. Ha! Ha! He laughed. More farts. Keep laughing, Uncle Brucker said to himself. Keep laughing, you miserable rat! You'll get yours. And Uncle Brucker chuckled to himself, for he realized what was happening down below. . . .

Duffy's left eyebrow twitched. Ex-Lieutenant Willett blinked. The Doc tapped his foot, and then he winked at Ex-Lieutenant Willett. A tremor ran down Downie's left arm and ended in a thumbs up. A twitch from Duffy, another from Downie, and now the Doc was tap tap tapping his foot!

It was all a code, a secret code!

Tap, Doc, tap!

Twitch, Duffy, twitch!

As the Elders drank, the squad made its move.

It wasn't easy, there was so little left of what they were. An arm here, a leg there. But put them all together, they made one hell of a soldier.

With one hand Duffy untied Ex-Lieutenant Willett. Then Ex-Lieutenant Willett set the Doc free. Duffy put his arm around the Doc and steadied him. The Doc put his arm around Ex-Lieutenant Willett.

"This way!" Midnight cried, and forward they charged.

The work rats dropped their boxes and scattered into their holes.

The Professor turned and ran, but he tripped on a root and fell on his face and cracked his glasses. Midnight caught up to him and stepped on his tail. The Professor scratched at the dirt but could not get away. The Elders didn't realize what was happening until after they drank up and re-plugged their pouches.

And when they saw the four humans all hooked together, they still didn't know what to do. Should they run or should they drink? They looked to each other for an answer. A quick drink will help them decide.

Before the Elders drank, Duffy stumbled and the Ex-Lieutenant lost his grip. The Doc put his arms around them, held them tight. But it was too much for them. They took one more step and tumbled forward. It was all they could manage. A few feet and they had worn themselves out. As they fell, they turned to Uncle Brucker, and he realized they did it all for him.

They had planned his escape! First they had scattered the rats, now they were showing him the way out!

"Crawl, Sergeant. . . ," Downie started the sentence, and the Doc finished it, ". . . Brucker. Crawl!"

"Which way?"

"This way," the Doc said, and Downie pointed. "Center hole, left side!" said Midnight.

# 60

Uncle Brucker took a long, deep breath and gathered up a heap of fortitude, and he crawled through the center hole, left side.

He dug into the dirt with his fingers and pushed forward with his toes. He crawled past sleeping rats and hoarding holes stuffed with shiny things. He saw piles of jewelry and old stopped watches and shined-up silver dollars stored in the richest of rat holes.

He crawled past dead soldiers holed-up and forgotten since the first Uprising, and he heard the moaning of the dead. The earthly moans have echoed through the rat holes for many dark years. And they waited to be heard by someone, anyone, from their own dimension. That someone turned out to be my Uncle Brucker. Now they can finally rest.

He crawled passed boxes of fresh rat cakes, addressed to: NY City, Atlanta, Washington DC, ready to be shipped out. He used up a lot of fortitude fast, and it's not easy to get back. By the time he got to the entrance hole he was pretty much out of fortitude, and his mind drifted away. He didn't realize it, but he was starting to feel the effect of all those rat cakes.

As it turned out, Midnight sent him through an old alley hole that angled upward to the heart of Rat City. He wiped the dirt from his eyes and poked his head out of the hole.

But something was wrong. No, everything was wrong! The back alleys, store fronts, light poles, everything was crooked! He wiped his eyes again but it didn't straighten things out because in Rat Land nothing stands up straight. Everything is crooked.

The rats sang and danced and humped in dark alleys. A six-rat band playing patched-up instruments jammed in the corner. A drunken wharf rat plucked a sour note on an electric guitar. The musicians saw Uncle Brucker crawl out of the hole, and they came over.

A mean-looking dandy rat stood in front of him. It was dead-rat quiet.

Uncle Brucker knew he better think up something fast, or it will be over for him. But he had trouble thinking. Then when he tried to talk, it was hard to get the words out, his throat was so dry.

So he said the only thing he could say, "*Ka-ta-che.*" Good morning, dandy rat.

"*Ka-ta ch'ta-to.*" Good morning to you, Impostor, the dandy rat replied.

Because that's what they thought my Uncle was, a damn good impostor. The rats had never encountered a real human in their dimension, but they sure were used to impostors. What human could talk rat, anyway? He was a tall impostor.

The band played on. The rats humped and danced and danced and humped, but it lasted only for a little while. One hour until dawn, the night is nearly done, and the rats were plenty tired.

The dandy rat waltzed around his sleep hole. He didn't look so mean when he danced. He kicked some dirt out of his hole, then he went inside for the day.

Uncle Brucker felt he should get out of the hole and dance with them, but his back ached from sleeping in the dirt and his legs ached from crawling. One or the other, he would have joined in.

Instead, he wandered off into Rat Land.

# 61

Gone. Missing. Stolen. Disappeared.

Call it what you want, but words won't help me find it. Uncle Brucker's War Medal is gone, and I better find it and bring it back.

Someone who was at the party Saturday knows the answer. The Medal didn't crawl off on its own. Somebody gave it a lift and nobody's talking about it. I phoned everybody I invited to the party and others who just showed up, and I scheduled a meeting at the Old House. Wednesday evening. Eight o'clock.

I will never give up. I won't stop until I find it.

As a symbolic gesture, I decided to give up lunch until I get the Medal back.

Charlee, JJ, Ida Lena, Lee May, Bethany, Manny, Bones, Leroy, Arnie, Bunky and Phil attended the meeting. I made everybody sign in.

Only one person other than Vernie Verna didn't show up, and he was my main suspect: Kip.

We assembled in the kitchen where I had prepared a demonstration.

The demonstration involved a hammer and an apple. I put a carving board on the table and placed the apple on the board. I held the hammer in my right hand.

"I find who took it, this is what I'll do to his head."

Then I smashed the apple with the hammer and the apple splattered all over the kitchen and everyone at the meeting.

"See that?" I asked.

Everybody saw it.

"Bunky, you see that?"

"Sure, I saw it."

"Any questions?"

"Just one. Do aliens get pimples?" he asked.

Ida Lena and Bones stuck around after Charlee and everybody else left. Ida Lena and Bones had something to talk over.

Ida Lena said, "We just want to say we're sorry what happened to the Medal and we had nuthin' to do with it anyway. We know what it means to you and your Uncle. And we hope it never happens again."

"Thank you, thank you. That's a real big help," I said.

"What you should do," Ida Lena told me, "is hire a cleanin' service. They find lots of stuff. You can bet they'll find that Medal if it's still here, and if they don't you know it ain't."

"A cleaning service?" I said.

"That's my advice," Ida Lena said.

Advice. I get advice. Like advice will get off its fat ass and find that Medal for me.

"There's more," said Ida Lena on the way out. "Renata told me to tell you she's sorry too. She's real sorry and she wants to see you at Tuskies after the meeting."

# 62

It didn't take long to drive down to Tuskies. I combed my hair, brushed my teeth, put on my best Nikes and started up the

Eagle. I took the shortcut at Holmes, made a right on Center, and I was downtown in eleven minutes.

I couldn't wait to see Renata again, her long dark hair, those slinky eyes. I had a lot to think about but my mind always came back to her.

I parked across the street from Tuskies, Identifiers on. I figured I'd do some identifying before it got dark. The glasses slipped down on my nose, so I bent the plastic around my ears and they were fine.

There she is, all in black. She stood in front of Tuskies with her girlfriends. When she saw me in the Eagle she said goodbye to them, and they all looked my way as she walked across the street.

Then it happened again. My Identifiers fogged up!

I wiped them off but it didn't work because the fog was under the glass. I wore them in the afternoon and all evening. Maybe I wore them out. I threw them in the glove compartment before she got any closer.

"You took off your cool glasses," she said when she got in the car. "How come?"

"Oh, I don't know. Don't wanna be too cool, I guess."

"My father don't like me hangin' out with you," she said. "He says say goodbye and get over it."

"My Uncle says you ain't my type at all."

"What do you think?"

"What do they know?" I said.

"Kiss me," she said.

# 63

We cruised around for a while, taking the back streets to avoid the cop cars. But it was a night of empty streets and the cops were not around. I turned right onto Main and drove down Center and back to Meridian again.

All this time I said about three words to Renata. She did all the talking. She told me about her favorite pop star, Lyca, and got me interested. Lyca was an Idol. Renata had all her records except the first two but she'll get them. I never heard of Lyca and I never heard her sing but she was Renata's favorite and that was good enough for me.

I thought about the missing War Medal and I had a wrestling match with myself. In one corner I had this superhot girl I couldn't get my mind off. In the other corner was my Uncle's War Medal and I was all tied-up inside about that.

Renata is smart, very smart. She spoke like every word cost a million dollars. She knew a lot and she had lots of opinions. I just like the way she talks.

"Everybody's got their own opinion," she said. "But if you ask me it's all in the planets. Planets line up in a row, you got it made. Study the planets, you can figure out anythin'. When I get to college I'm thinkin' I'll major maybe in Jupiter."

We drove up to the Heights and she showed me her house on Crown, a brown house on a corner with big bushes out front and a circular driveway.

We had wasted enough time and I wanted to get back to the house. She said she would stay for a while. On the by-pass back to town I took the Eagle up to 75.

"So what's the problem?" Renata asked.

"What problem?"

"Somethin's goin' on. You're like an itch waitin' for a scratch," she said.

I told her about my Uncle's missing Medal, and she said she didn't hear anything about it, she'll keep an ear out.

"We goin' back now?" I asked.

"I don't know. I think maybe not," she said.

"You said you want to go back to the house."

"I do."

"So what are we waitin' for?"

Someone in the rear seat said, "We gotta be home by ten."

"Who are you?"

"Dwight meet Walt, Walt meet Dwight. He's my brother," Renata said.

"Half-brother," said Dwight.

"When did he get in?"

"I don't know, he gets in."

Dwight sat behind me in the dark. He was the brother she got when her mother re-married. He was a year and a half younger. I tilted the rearview down but I couldn't see much back there. He wore a baseball cap and he had a high voice and he was bigger than you think.

"What kinda car is this?" he asked me.

"This is an Eagle," I said.

"Never heard of an Eagle before."

"They don't make 'em no more," I said.

"Those blinkin' lights come with it?"

"No, I screwed them in the dash myself."

"Looks like they come with the car," he said.

I wanted to take Renata back to the house but Dwight insisted they had to be home by ten, so I dropped them off.

When Dwight got out he said, "Hire a cleaning service."

# 64

I saw Kip driving alone on Center Street and I followed him to Mid-City Lanes. He parked his little Mazda 3 in the lot. I parked the Eagle on the street where he couldn't see me. I watched him get out and when he walked across the lot I came up behind him.

He heard me and turned around. I socked him in the jaw first thing and tried to get him in a headlock, but that didn't work and he tripped me and knocked me down on the concrete but I flipped him and now I had him face down with my knee on his back.

"Time out! Time out!" Kip said. "Let me up, will ya? I ain't fightin' you no more."

"You don't have a choice," I said.

"No more fightin' till I know why we're fightin'," he said. "It's dumb fightin' somebody you don't know what for."

"My Uncle's War Medal, that's why. You were lookin' at it at the party and I want it back."

"Lookin' ain't no crime."

"You were lookin' to steal," I said. "Hand it over."

"Listen, dude. If I took that Medal I'd get up and punch your creepy face in. But I don't see no point in fightin' over somethin' I didn't do. You wanna fight, find out who took it. Or come at me for what I did do."

I let Kip go and we got up on our feet. He was breathing hard, making wheezing noises as he tried to catch his breath.

He sat on the fender of a silver Accord and wheezed and looked me over.

"You put up a good fight for a little guy," he said with a smile.

"I ain't little, I just look little. Man, I'm hungry."

"You ain't hungry like me."

"I could eat a medium pie with extra cheese," I said.

"Dogs are good too," he said.

Around the corner, we ate Texas footlongs at Scotty's Dog House. I dumped on a heap of kraut and squeezed out lots of mustard. It's the way I like it. Kip squirted mustard on his dog and he put ketchup on it too. I never heard of ketchup on a dog before, but Kip got around. He was an OK guy and no longer a suspect. Last year he went to Paris with his parents for two weeks and he got to know the country. Ketchup and mustard, it's how they eat their dogs in France.

What happened to my Uncle's Medal? He didn't know, so quit asking. But he knew someone who'll help me out and ten bucks an hour ain't a lot to ask.

# 65

Ron-Dell's Cleaning Service used to charge ten dollars an hour, but that was years ago, the woman on the phone told me. Now it was up to twenty on weekdays. It was twenty-four dollars an hour on the weekends. But she said she'd give me Monday's rate on Saturday if I paid her in cash today.

It would have cost ninety-six bucks to vacuum and dust the whole house, upstairs and down, which was more than I could spend. So I told her fifty dollars was clean enough. The cleaning lady's name was Distilda. She was about forty. She wore two earrings in each ear and she had extra holes for more. She told me she used to live in the city where she cleaned the penthouses of playboys.

Distilda came over Saturday at ten, took a break at twelve and worked until two. Before she went home she gave me a shopping bag with some things she found. I was hoping for about a hundred in cash, a couple of gold rings, two wrist watches, a stuffed wallet and Uncle Brucker's Medal. But all she had was two-forty in change and an old cigarette case she said might be worth something. No gold rings, no Medal.

"Are you sure?" I asked her. "About this big, says SECOND UPRISING, BATTLE OF THE BYPASS."

"Didn't see nuthin' like that around here," she said, thinking back. "But come to think of it, I saw one that might fit that description in a house I cleaned last week. Up at the Heights."

"Brown house on the corner, circular driveway?"

"That's the one. He asked me if I did yard work. You know anybody does yard work?"

"Who asked you? Guy with a bad leg?"

"He walked a limp, if that's what you mean."

Corner house up at the Heights. Circular driveway. Guy walks with a limp. It all added up. It was Renata's house, and he was her father.

Uncle Brucker was right. I should have kept my big mouth shut.

# 66

After Uncle Brucker escaped from the Rat Factory, he wandered through the crooked alleys of Rat Land.

It was total amnesia every step of the way. He didn't know who he was. He didn't know where he was. He didn't know where he was going. He figured if he walked far enough he'd get to a place he knew. Then, once he knew where he was, he could figure out who he was. In that manner he would find his way back to himself.

It's one thing being lost in your own dimension—then at least you have a home base. Try getting lost in another dimension where you've never been before and then throw in amnesia as an extra.

He was lost, totally lost, inside and out.

Rats can't build a damn thing, but they are real good at renovating. That's why they live in abandoned dimensions. Only their way of renovating is moving in and destroying. Put one rat hole in the basement, it's no big deal. Put ten, twenty, your house begins to crumble. They already wrecked one dimension and now they're looking toward ours.

He learned things as he wandered. What he had mistaken for a rat festival was actually a daily celebration—it's how they live their carefree lives. No rent. No taxes. Slobbering down rat juice. Fat rats peddling stew and selling trinkets, humping in the corners and celebrating. Hemp rats toking up.

He wandered through the alleys and down the hill to Boone's Dockand the rotting pier. He walked past the dock house and out on the crooked pier where the rats lay around. Here he sat among the lazy wharf rats, and he felt that he belonged.

"Hello, impostor," the wharf rat said. He was licking stew from a filthy stew pot.

"Hello."

"Hungry?" asked the wharf rat.

"Don't I look it?"

"Next lick's for you, impostor."

From step to step he changed inside, switching from man to rat and back again. One step man, next step rat. He walked through dirty back alleys, between the ugly rat hole buildings, everything crooked, foul smell in the air. Next step the alley is clean and straight and the air is sweet because that's how it smells to the rat in him. Now he was beginning to feel the effect of the rat cakes he'd eaten. His follow-up thoughts, his rat thoughts, came on strong.

Look at things the rat way. Rats didn't wreck this dimension; it was in bad shape when they got here. They fixed things up and made them better. The holes they sleep in are not simply "dug" or "burrowed." They're intricate rat hotels with rooms on many levels. Rats are as good at fixing as men are at making, but you have to be a rat to notice.

He sat on the dirty/clean curb in the shadows of the crooked/straight buildings, inhaling the fresh/musty air of a place called Rat Land.

Sunlight poked through the rat holes in the buildings behind him, spotting up the alley. As the sun came up, the spots criss-crossed in front of him. Those spots were heading somewhere he wanted to go. He moved his hand in and out of one bright circle and his hand glowed yellow in the sun. He wished he could sail off with that warm yellow spot to the other side of here.

He had been wandering for nearly a week and he still didn't know who he was. You could say he was exhausted, but the rat in him was always eager to get up and go.

He sat on the curb with his knees together, resting as best as he could under the circumstances. And for a moment, just one moment, the pulling stopped. One knee got a little jittery, but if that's all, he's doing pretty good.

Relax, Uncle Brucker. Don't try to get up. You must rest between steps. Stay there for a count of one hundred, at least. That's a minute and a half, counting slow. Back again, it's three. And keep your knees together.

The sun came up behind the tall impostor, but he hardly knew it. He sat on the curb and his shadow slowly came out in front of him. He got up and walked up the hill as the sun rose and his shadow came up fast. Now his great impostor shadow stretched out far in front of him on the sidewalk, bent across the alley and climbed up the rat hole buildings.

Even the shadows are crooked in Rat Land.

# 67

Night time in Rat Land. Uncle Brucker sat on the edge of the wharf, eating and generally minding his own business.

Eating? You can call it eating. With his finger he scraped the bottom of a filthy stew bowl. Licking that little bit of food off his bony finger had all his attention. He looked down into that filthy bowl. There were still a few licks left.

The tide went out three days ago and finally came in that evening. Driftwood floated to the shore, crates and trash all beaten by the sea. Scrawny ship rats jumped onto the dock and scrambled up the mooring lines. The lazy fog rose up slowly and hung around the bulkhead. In the sky above the dark water, a half moon hung exactly where it had hung the night before. It looked like it was pasted to a thick black curtain by the rats.

A couple of wharf rats ran over to him. They weren't so stinky any more.

"Come on, impostor!" said a wharfie.

"Whatcha sittin' here for?" said another.

He couldn't think of a good reason, so he followed the wharf rats down the pier. The rotting pier creaked and bobbed with each step, and the sand crabs scattered underneath. Farther down, rats sold potent rat juice and shined up trinkets for sale. Fat rats sat at crate tables and played a card game called Flippo.

At the far end of the pier a crowd had gathered under the tall dock light.

A wrestling match!

The tall impostor watched from the edge of the crowd.

The rats had thrown down hay and squared off the ring with rotten dock planks and hemp rope. A huge rat strutted into the ring, GRUDGE printed in black across his torn-up shirt. Black tail and stubby ears, close to 100 pounds, Grudge was an Old Guinea King Rat who finished off his opponents with a running head kick.

"Who's havin' a go at me? Who'll be next?" Grudge challenged the crowd. "How about you?"

The crowd quickly made its choice—a little hemp rat hanging off the ropes. The little rat dropped down to the pier and tried to run off, but the crowd closed in and pushed him to the ring.

That poor little hemp rat didn't want to wrestle Grudge. He shut his eyes. When he opened them he was in the ring. Grudge looked down at him and grinned, and that was the last thing the little rat saw.

The tall impostor hated the big rat. Grudge was all brag. Uncle Brucker once said, "I'm the best in the world at one thing (rat killing) but I never brag about it." When you're the best you don't have to brag. Brag too much, you'll never be best.

After the match, Grudge flipped to his front feet. He strutted around the ring upside down, showing off his sharp white teeth, and his upside down eyes were scary. He frightened the younger rats, and they ran to their sleep holes and didn't come out for the rest of the night.

But in the back of the crowd someone snickered. It was my Uncle, the tall impostor!

"Who's havin' a go at me? How about you, impostor?"

The crowd cleared a path and the tall impostor quietly made his way to the ring. Grudge stood up on his rear legs, ready to make his move. At the ring ropes the tall impostor looked deep into the eyes of the big rat. He wasn't trying to stare Grudge down, he was looking for insight.

The tall impostor didn't speak right away. He took some time to think and more to calm down.

He cleared his throat and said, "First of all, let's be sure what we're talkin' about here, cause I'll admit right off I can't beat you at every game. For instance, if it's a reekin' match, you got me beat. I'll forfeit right now cause you're stinkin' up the whole wharf. Whew! And I'd lose to you in a boastin' match too, cause I see you're one of the best at that, and I just don't have the experience. But we're talkin' about wrestlin' here, and in any fair wrestlin' match I'll knock you down in the first round and I'll beat you in the second. . . . So let's have a go at it!"

# 68

The tall impostor hired a rat promoter for thirty-three percent and a sleep hole.

"Let's see that hole," said the tall impostor.

The promoter was an ancient gray rat with cloudy eyes and a skip limp that moved from leg to leg. He was so old he forgot his birth name but it didn't matter. Everyone called him Scratch, and that's who he was.

The tall impostor followed Scratch to the sleep hole. The old rat moved slowly and painfully. His left rear leg cramped up most of the time, but sometimes it skipped to the right, and he dragged his crippled leg around after him. He stopped every few yards to rest, and he looked at Uncle Brucker with sad eyes.

The old promoter had a pouch full of delicious rat cakes that the impostor favored. Each time they stopped he reached into his pouch and gave Uncle Brucker one more cake. Again and again Uncle Brucker straightened out the old rat's legs. Finally he lifted the old rat by his rear legs and held him like a wheel-barrow.

The tall impostor wheel-barrowed the crippled old promoter down the alley.

"Turn me left. Turn me left!"

The tall impostor turned left, and they stopped at a busy drink hole.

Rats walked into the hole, rats crawled out on their fat bellies. Inside, a dugout room with a dirt bar and dirt shelves.

They stepped up to the bar. On the dirt shelves, a collection of broken plates, glasses, bottles. Rats on their way to the uprising stopped here for one last drink at a dirt mound table where they played Flippo.

A couple of impostors sat around making jokes and trying to be the center of attention. They thought they were convincing until they saw who came in the door.

Scratch ordered two rat juice cocktails. He chose a lickoff plate. The tall impostor preferred a chipped beer bottle. The wet-nose barkeep poured the drink. A clump of wet dirt fell from the ceiling onto Scratch's lickoff plate. The barkeep spit on the plate and cleaned the dirt off, then he nosed it over to Scratch.

"To the Incredible Impostor," said Scratch.

"Who?" Uncle Brucker looked around.

"That's you. It's your wrestlin' name. I thunk it up right now." The barkeep pushed two drinks across the bar.

"To the Asteroid," Scratch said. "May it crash tonight!"

Scratch licked the last of his plate.

"Rat-o-rat that's good juice!" he said.

There was something about the old rat that the Incredible Impostor couldn't figure out. . . . White whiskers. Cloudy eyes. When his eyes got used to the dark he realized what it was: the old rat was blind.

"You can't see a damn thing, can you?" Uncle Brucker said.

Scratch took a wrestling contract out of a pouch strapped to his waist.

"Don't have to see it when I can hear it. Every wrestler's got his own thump, I've heard it all before. I can tell by the thump, and you got a winner's thump. I tell you which round, you thump 'em in that round. You think you can do that? Sign here and drink up on me."

The Incredible Impostor looked at the contract, which was a filthy page ripped from a notebook. The nose writing was too smudged to read. He signed it anyway.

A wanted poster hung on the dirt wall opposite the bar. On the poster was a sketch of a man. The man had great powerful arms with huge muscles. He held a pistol in one hand and a big league bat in the other. He was as tall as the sky, broader than a building, and he straddled a wide open rat hole.

The caption said, WANTED, THE BAD MAN.

The man looked familiar to the Incredible Impostor.

"Who's the man on the poster?" the Incredible Impostor asked Scratch.

"That man? I don't know what they call him where you're from. We call him the Bad Man around here. He's the bastard that started it. Kilt sixty-three rats just hangin' around. Poor little critters, shot them in the butt for no reason. And that's how The Uprisin' started."

The barkeep poured another drink for each of them and two more to go.

"To the sixty-three!" Scratch said.

"This one's on the hole," said the barkeep, and he nosed two drinks across the bar.

# 69

"I'm only blind lookin' frontways," Scratch said on their way to the tailor. "My sideways vision's OK. I can't see where I'm goin', but I know where I'm at."

Scratch was a cranky old rat who hissed and snapped at everyone, but that was just his way. He told the Incredible Impostor he was the oldest rat in Rat City. In fact he may be the oldest rat in Rat Land. He started counting the years when he became Scratch and stopped when he reached 120, but he didn't know how long ago that was. He thought that he would probably live forever, so why count?

On a busy alley corner Scratch opened up his rat pouch and they drank the juice to go. Scratch drank it down quickly, then crawled off to a humping hole on the corner. By the time the Incredible Impostor finished his drink, Scratch visited two more humping holes and came back with a smile.

"To the tailor hole," said Scratch. "You got a name, now you need a suit. There's nuthin' like seein' ya win in a good suit."

A sign in the dirt wall above the hole said, STAR TAILOR WRESTLING SUITS—TWO MINNET FIT.

The Incredible Impostor would soon find out that rats are excellent stitchers as well as cutters.

The chief tailor greeted them at the entrance. He wore a torn-off piece of measuring tape around his neck. Through narrowed eyes he examined the Incredible Impostor, and he sniffed him up, down and sideways. On a piece of cardboard, the tailor rat drew a wet nose sketch of a costume. Scratch hissed dissatisfaction at him, then out of his pack he took the sketch of his own. They borrowed from one sketch, added to the other. In that manner they created the costume for the Incredible Impostor.

THE IMPOSTOR, it said, big gold letters on the front and on the back.

Scratch took two steps back and studied it.

"That ain't right," said Scratch.

From a storage hole the chief tailor dragged out a can of gold paint and he opened the paint can and added another word to the costume. He took his time and he used a lot of paint. Finished, he stepped back and now it said THE INCREDIBLE IMPOSTOR.

The tailor stuck the design on the dirt wall.

He scratched the dirt floor and six gray rats came out of another hole, spools of black thread stuck around their sharp tails. They shuttled up and down, back and forth, crisscrossing the tall impostor. They sewed the costume right on him using their needle tails.

The sign outside the tailor's hole is correct. In two minutes they had a perfect fit.

"He's a big rat," said the rat tailor. "I charge extra for materials."

Outside, Uncle Brucker stood at the store front, admiring his new suit in the mirrors. Two silver mirrors stood side by side. The mirror on the right was broken. He saw the reflection of a man in the left mirror. In the cracked mirror on the right he saw the reflection of a rat. Man, rat, man, rat, and on and on.

Rat Land was a strange and beautiful place to Uncle Brucker. Beautiful to the rat in him and strange to the man in him.

# 70

I didn't know what to say to Renata. It's been four long days since I talked to her. She didn't call me and I didn't call her. Will somebody please tell me what I should do? It's bad enough when a stranger steals from you, but when the evidence points to your girlfriend's father it's got to be worse.

Around eight I drove up to her house on the heights. It was already dark. I figured I'd park down the block and sit for a while until the lights went on, then I'd sneak to the side window. Who knows, maybe I'd get a look at the War Medal sitting up on a shelf.

If the front door is unlocked I'll run in, grab it, and return the Medal to its proper place.

The lights went on in the living room, then in the kitchen around back. But I couldn't get out of the car. I couldn't move from the seat. I just didn't want to find out what I might find out. I was stuck there for thirty-eight minutes before I broke free and drove away.

On the way back I stopped at Tuskies.

I had made up my mind again—I'd go in, find Renata, go for a ride and we'd talk it over. By the end of the night I'll have that Medal back on the shelf where it belongs.

But when I tried to get out of the car I ran into the same problem. I couldn't move. My mind wanted to go but my body wouldn't let me. I couldn't do anything except drive away.

When I should have done something, anything, I drove home and did nothing at all.

# 71

With eyes closed I walk from the Eagle to the back door of the old house. I hoped to find the Ram back in its spot when I opened them.

Halfway down the driveway, I open my eyes.

No Ram. I guess it doesn't work out that way.

Then I thought maybe he's at the kitchen table, drinking his Boomers and eating a raisin cake. The Ram broke down and he got a ride from Keith or Reed Weir. That's why the Ram's not in the driveway.

"Yeah, yeah I know. I shouldn't be drivin'," I'll tell him. "But I fixed the headlights and I had to test them out," I'll tell him when I see him in the kitchen.

But he's not in the kitchen. He ain't in the pantry or out back in the hammock either. He's probably upstairs, dead asleep face down on the bed.

But I never got a single ticket and I never dented a fender or chipped the paint of the Eagle or any other car.

"Well, shit," I'll say. "Back already?"

But he doesn't hear me because he's not here. Can't talk to a guy who's not here.

I know it's just a game and leave me the fuck alone.

# 72

I was running out of money fast. I spent a lot on the party and I didn't keep track of the rest. Uncle Brucker left a note: money in the drawer, so I checked every drawer in the house. I found 26 dollars and change in the kitchen drawers. Upstairs in his dresser I found 37 more. The kitchen money I saved for pizza. The upstairs money I used for gas.

In the afternoon I searched through the cabinet that was hidden behind boxes of old newspapers and magazines he stored in the hall. I found his two thought-up books in one of the drawers. True Rat Tales From Around The World and The Specialized Rat Encyclopedia.

I call them books but they're not books yet. Handwritten pages mixed in with typed pages, numbered but in no particular order. The Specialized Rat Encyclopedia Vol. #1 had only 26 entries, one for each letter of the alphabet. Most of those pages were typed. True Rat Stories From Around The World was all jumbled up, some pages typed, some pages written.

In the bottom drawer of the dresser I found the coins. He said it was his coin collection. Now I realized what he meant. No snap-in coin books, just loose coins. What sort of collection was this? I counted it upstairs. $110.78 total. I was ready to spend it.

In bed that night I figured it out, and I got out of bed and went downstairs and emptied the drawer out on the kitchen table to test my theory. I sorted the coins by year, and that's when I realized why it was a collection.

The coins went back fifty-eight years. That was the year Uncle Brucker was born. He had saved a penny, nickel, dime, quarter, half dollar and silver dollar from every year of his life. $1.91 per year for fifty-eight years. Uncle Brucker was $110.78 old when he went off on his special assignment.

That was Uncle Brucker's coin collection, and I would never take a penny. I put it all back in the drawer where I found it, every cent. When Uncle Brucker finally comes back from his two week assignment it will all be there.

If I run real low I might take out twenty silver dollars and replace it with a bill.

The next evening around eight I filled my pockets with coins, and I drove to Tuskies, no freezing up. I had a lot to talk to Renata about and that kept me moving along.

I parked the Eagle out front, left my Identifiers in the glovebox, walked in, and sat at the counter and ate a slice with mushrooms. Then I sat in a booth and ate another slice, extra cheese. All the while I'm on the lookout for Renata. I saw a couple of her girlfriends but she's not here.

When I got back to the Eagle, Dwight was hiding in the back seat.

"You call that hidin'?"

"They're after me!"

"Who's after you?"

"It don't matter who. They find me, my face won't look the same. Just get in and drive me home, I'll fix that old TV your Uncle gave you. Deal?"

I took the back streets through town. I drove slow and made easy turns so I wouldn't turn any heads. Dwight sat low in back. I checked the rearview, but nobody followed us from what I could see.

"I seen you drivin' by the house," he said. "Coupla times."

"Your sister been lookin' for me?"

"Not her style. She don't have to look."

"We got an expert on girls in the back seat today."

"I just know about my sister. And I know if she ain't home or in school, she's hangin' down at Tuskies. You don't see her because she don't want you to."

# 73

After I dropped Dwight off at his house, I drove straight to Tuskies. Renata didn't expect me to come in twice in one night and she wasn't on the lookout. I saw her the second I opened the door and walked in. She was sitting at the last table with her back to me. Her long hair fell over the back of the chair. She didn't see me walk in, but her girlfriends did.

By the time I got to the table, they had all cleared out and it was just me and Renata.

"My father's a good man," she said. "He won't do nuthin' wrong he knows about. He's got a bad knee he can't ever get fixed. He's a good man with a bad knee and he don't have your Uncle's Medal."

"I ain't sayin' he took it," I told her. "I'm just lookin' for someone who might know where it is."

"He's the the best man I know. He says they hold it against him. People see you got a bad knee and you stumble around, they think you're lazy and stupid. But what they're thinkin' ain't true. You can bet they don't treat you like that on the planet Jupiter."

"Renata, they're ain't nobody been to Jupiter."

"What are they waitin' for?" she said. "It ain't gonna come over here."

The dark-eyed slinky girl settled in her chair, and there was a sadness in her face and that made me sad too. She sipped her soda but the bottle was empty. She sipped and there was nothing left. I got up and came back in a minute with another bottle from the cooler, and I twisted off the cap and gave the bottle to her.

Her eyes were brown, dark brown, and her hair was black with reddish brown streaks going through it. She had the kind of mouth where her front teeth always show a little. She didn't have one freckle.

I didn't expect her to cry.

She took a little silver case out of her purse and flipped it open with her black nail thumb. There was a mirror inside. Her eye makeup trickled down her cheeks. I gave her a napkin to wipe her eyes and cheeks. She took the napkin but she didn't wipe, she dabbed. She looked at herself in the little mirror and dabbed. I gave her another napkin and she looked in the mirror and dabbed with the new napkin.

"You really come down here lookin' for me ten times?" she asked.

"Eleven."

"You ain't eaten lunch yet?"

"I don't care how long it takes, I ain't eatin' lunch until I get that Medal back. Until then I eat early dinners."

# 74

Under the tall dock light, a wrestling match had just begun. The fog turned to rain all around the light. Salt water slapped against the bulkhead like big dogs licking. You can't see the boats in that foggy rain, but you can hear the fog horns as the boats came close to shore. *BLAAHHH! BLAAAHHH!* Like that. The rotten bulkhead sagged under the weight of the huge crowd. The tide couldn't decide whether to come in or go out. The cowardly sand crabs hid in the dark under the pier, and the squawky gulls circled high up over the bay. They never flew close to shore because of the flying rats.

First match: The Incredible Impostor vs the Squealer.

"Place your bets over here," Scratch announced from the betting booth outside the ring.

The Squealer jumped into the ring. He was a beat-up old rat and a long-time wrestler, and he rarely lost a match. The scabs of a thousand wounds stuck to his fur. His upper lip had split apart, and most of the nails were missing from his broken, twisted claws.

"Thump 'em in five," Scratch whispered to the Incredible Impostor.

The Incredible Impostor thumped the Squealer in round five.

"You owe me for the suit," Scratch said after a three straight wins.

"But you said it's your expense."

"To lay out. That don't mean I pay for it. And there's a small layin' out charge."

Scratch piled up the cash he had won that night, divided the pile in half, in half again, and now he had four smaller piles. The first three piles accounted for his percentage, the wrestling suit, and the laying out charge, and he gave the last pile to the Incredible Impostor.

The wrestling suit looked sharp and it felt sharp so he didn't mind paying for the layout and the additional layout charges. It was his suit and he got to keep it.

The first time Scratch saw the Incredible Impostor wrestle he knew he was different. He carried his extra weight with no effort and he moved with ease for a big rat. He wrestled like no other rat that had ever entered the ring. The Incredible Impostor was merely a puzzle right now, but a puzzle can easily turn into a predicament. Who was this big rat that never lost a match?

As long as Scratch fed him the Rat Cakes he bought on the black market, the Incredible Impostor wrestled without complaint.

Rat brains are tiny compared to big-brain humans, which leaves little room for thinking. But that doesn't give humans the edge. One thing rats learned over the years is think quickly. Old thoughts move on out and make room for what's next.

Quick-thinking rats give up and charge ahead while big brain humans stick around and figure it out. Humans have big brains, but they're small minded, so what good is that?

Scratch learned this a long time ago: when you ask a question you better be ready for the answer. Be sure you're ready or don't ask.

The Incredible Impostor got Scratch thinking, but not for long. Time to move along. Now you know how it is with rats. He had other things to think about right now, but he'll be back.

Mountain rats, bull rats, grizzlies, elephant rats, Fat Rat, Mean Rat, Slim Deluxe, Bonko, Jynx, and the Blender.

The Incredible Impostor thumped them all.

## 75

Scratch was a show promoter all his life and he never saw anything like it. The rats traveled from the far corners of Rat Land to see the Incredible Impostor. Scratch's pouches were not deep enough to hold all the cash.

Scratch didn't trust bank holes and he hated the sneaky rats who worked there. He hid his money in hidey-holes instead. By the middle of next week attendance had doubled. Scratch didn't give out numbers, but on Thursday he took in a hole and a half.

To make more money he had to spend money, and Scratch had money to spare. With leftover bricks and junkyard wood he built a new wrestling ring on the far end of the pier. Unemployed wharf rats worked for nothing and a promise. They climbed up the dock light pole and replaced the bulb in the dock light. A thin coat of leftover paint made the ringside benches look new from a distance, and that was good enough for Scratch.

Yes, life was fat, fat and smooth, very smooth for the wise old promoter. Life couldn't be shinier. As long as the Incredible Impostor ate his daily dose of rat cakes, he was content.

Wealthy patrons who wore fine rags and expensive trinkets paid big bucks to sit on the ringside benches and drink watered down rat juice. Scratch doubled his stand-up fee and he added two more shows. Now there are wrestling matches on the first, third and last Thursday of the week.

The Incredible Impostor took his share and moved into a fancy new sleep hole. Scratch helped him find a luxury hole where the rich rats lived up on Cove Cliff. In the mornings before the Incredible Impostor went inside and fell asleep, he sat on a warm rock on the edge of the Cliff and munched on a rat cake Scratch brought over.

And so it went, Thursday after Thursday after Thursday. It felt like a lifetime had passed, but if you check the clock it was only a week. The flying rats slept in the trees and the gulls were very quiet. It was too early to squawk. If he listened carefully, he could hear the waves roll home to the shore. And beyond the foggy mist? A spectacular view of the sea, from Cliff Cove to the Rip Rocks on Craggy Shore.

Foreign memories, memories of some other time and a different place, stopped by and scratched on his door during these quiet times, but the old memories were not welcome. They didn't fit in with what he is now, and so they moved on.

After Scratch returned from a match, he pulled up a sitting rock and drank potent rat juice with the neighbors, and they dealt him in for an ancient card game called "*ta-ch'ti*," or Flippo.

The Incredible Impostor never quite got the hang of Flippo. Most of the hearts and diamonds were missing, and they started out with 32 spades and only 14 clubs. At the end of each hand the rats added up the cards and argued over the total.

When they chose a winner, they all jumped up and yelled Flippo! Then they ate the spades.

One night a little sweetie wandered over to the sitting rocks and moved a nice way. Her soft reddish whiskers curled without a tangle and she sure was sweet. She looked on quietly. She was not a chattery rat. The friendly card players of Cove Cliff pulled up a rock and invited her to sit in.

Soft hair, long red whiskers, starry eyes.

Her starry eyes fell on the Incredible Impostor. She walked the Cliff in the morning early, and he saw her from time to time once or twice. He recognized her from the wrestling matches, too, a familiar face beyond the ring ropes. She reminded him of an almost-remembered person who lived on the other side of a door he could not open. She played Flippo like a starry-eyed pro.

The Incredible Impostor never learned how to play that damn card game and he never found out why the rats jumped and cried "Flippo." And he couldn't understand why they ate the spades and left the hearts and diamonds uneaten.

He lost a lot of money and wanted to quit, but his neighbors would not have it. Hang in there, Impostor, they chimed in, your luck will change. You'll come back with a winning streak. You'll see.

The sun came up over the Cliff and the friendly rats said good day to all, and they returned to their sleep holes for the day.

Except the sweet rat. She didn't have a name. Her parents died when she was little and they never gave her a name, and she didn't feel right about taking one.

She sat with the Incredible Impostor on the rocks of Cove Cliff. She didn't say much, at first, and she kept to herself, for a while, except when he had a question.

"Nuther juice?" he asked.

"Make it double," she answered.

"One more game?" he asked.

"Two's better," she answered.

The game went on and then without saying, she got up from her sitting rock and went off to gather sticks. She saw a big one over there, and she got it. She found another big stick but not as big, and she got it. She dragged the sticks to the edge of Cove Cliff where she kicked them over one by one and watched them tumble down. The sticks tumbled end over end and they rolled and tumbled off Cove Cliff.

She came back and told the Incredible Impostor what she thought of him.

"You sure know how to wrestle but you ain't too good at Flippo and you got nice sticks," she said.

# 76

Thursday morning at the wrestling ring. The sun came up quietly without a cloud, and the shadow of Cove Cliff spread over the Cove. The night's final match is over and done. The Incredible Impostor won three in a row. Scratch totaled it up and put the score on the Big Board: 56 wins, 0 losses.

The vendors shut down and packed up, and the rats crawled through the alleys and went home to their sleep holes, and the hemp rats roamed the pier in search of lost trinkets. Two dandies fought over a leather wallet at the edge of the pier, cursing like wharfies. A fat gray rat joined in. *Splash-splash. Splash!* They were gone.

Scratch noticed a skinny rat at the far corner of the ring. The rat looked familiar.

They called him the Inspector. He had worked for the government during the first Uprising, looking for the strange, questioning the unusual, and otherwise snooping around. When he quit his job years later he took his reputation with him. Now he worked for any rat who had a question and the cash to pay for an answer. His expertise: digging up important info. His specialty: hard cases.

The skinny rat leaned against a ring post under the night sky. He was a smoker with a wet butt dangling from his lip.

Scratch didn't trust the skinny Inspector. His sunken eyes just might be hiding from something. Cross out might. Scratch was sure of it!

Scratch didn't trust him and he didn't like him, but that won't get in the way if money can be made.

The Inspector wore on his chest a rusty badge that said Inspector. Rats call it a badge—an aluminum pop top with a pull open tab. He tapped it with a ringed claw like it meant something.

The Inspector came with a reason. He never traveled without one, and he always carried a spare. Today he came with a Special One-Time Offer.

"A moment of your time is all I ask," he said with a smile stuck to his face.

The Inspector did not wait for an invite. He pitched.

"Every rat's lookin' for answers to somethin' he just can't figure," said he. "Might be a little thing puzzlin' him over and over, or a big 'un just popped up. You go it alone, best of luck to you, my long tail friend. You'll get no satisfaction and no guarantee from me. Today I'm here on a special basis with a three part offer for one time only. I'll supply satisfaction and include a no-charge guarantee. Act now, and I'll throw in inconsistencies, also no charge. Time out to mention it's a beautiful mornin'."

The Inspector paused and sniffed the fresh morning air. Scratch sniffed too. Not bad.

"You've seen the badge. Now take a look at my card," said the Inspector.

He pulled a packet of business cards from his pocket pouch and picked one out.

"Which 'un?"

The Inspector showed Scratch a card.

"This 'un."

"Ain't too fancy, that 'un."

"No need to be fancy when you already got respect," the Inspector said for sure.

What the Inspector said was true. Scratch did not know how truthful the Inspector was all-around. He had no way to measure the truth of what the Inspector might say, but Scratch saw the truth of this.

Once you've earned your respect, you don't need no official name tag, you don't need a fancy card or flashy badge. When you have respect, don't proclaim it, or you'll lose that respect for obvious reasons.

Scratch never thought of it this way, and with the truth of it all he warmed to the Inspector. Scratch knew that one truth often follows another and carries a sense of what's fair. The Inspector made more sense than most rats, a lot more.

Scratch thought seriously about his offer and the things that were bugging him. One hard case came to mind, and that was the Incredible Impostor. Scratch had invested much on an unknown quantity. After a week of figuring he couldn't figure him out.A tall impostor who doesn't talk much and never loses a match. What is his secret? Where does this strange rat come from? How did he get those scars on his back?

"That Special One-Time Offer still available?" he asked the Inspector.

"If time ain't run out."

"Guaranteed?"

"Included."

"Inconsistencies?"

"Thrown in."

# 77

Scratch had a friend named Drag who was a wrestling fan and wanted to meet the Incredible Impostor. Drag made his money in real estate, and he was a very rich rat, far richer than

Scratch, but thanks to the Incredible Impostor, Scratch was catching up.

Drag came to the pier almost every night to view the matches and sniff around with his nose high, and he spent a lot of money on rat juice and in the betting booths.

He was born with a roving eye, a thick head, and a knack for figuring things out. His right eye saw the world straight-on while his left eye snooped around. When he looked your way, you knew he was sizing you up. And when his roving eye quit snooping and settled down, his thick head had figured you out.

The night the Incredible Impostor beat Slim Deluxe three times in three separate matches, Drag invited Scratch and the Incredible Impostor to share a delicious stew dinner in his house hole.

Drag lived in a king's hole up on Cove Cliff, high above Cliff Cove, in the richest part in Rat Land, and he was not happy.

Born to a dirt poor family of scavengers, he made up for what they lacked in every way. His great hole had two of everything when only one would do. Two servants in the bedroom. Two waiters at each dirt table. Two gold rings on each claw.

Still, with all of this, Drag was not happy.

At dinner the rich rat ate two tasty appetizers and drank two mugs of potent rat juice, and for his entree he gobbled down two bowls of delicious rat stew, and he introduced the Incredible Impostor to his lovely twin wives, Fassola and Latido.

Fassola and Latido were petite rats of great natural beauty. Their whiskers grew long and their eyelashes curled delicately. Their soft fur glowed like heaven at sunset. They were the most beautiful rats the Incredible Impostor had ever seen, perhaps the most beautiful in all Rat Land.

And Drag was a proud rat and Drag was a grateful rat, but he was not happy.

"So they call you the Incredible Impostor," said Fassola. She too was a wrestling fan.

"Incredible will do," he said.

Scratch noticed his wrestling champ was a little shaky. His fingers tapped on the table and his teeth chattered. Scratch touched the Incredible Impostor's shoulder and passed a rat cake under the table. The Incredible Impostor broke up the cake and sprinkled it on the ground. He didn't tell Scratch he was cutting down.

After dinner Scratch sat at the table and entertained Drag's beautiful wives with true stories of his life as a wrestling promoter, but it didn't come off as it should.

In the middle of one story, Fassola got up from the table and walked off with a hiss and a spit. A few minutes later Latido slapped him in the face and snapped at him and walked out.

Meanwhile Drag took the Incredible Impostor on a short tour of his storage holes. The tall impostor followed the fat rich rat from hole to spacious hole. No chipped dinner plates or bent silverware in this rat's hole. Drag filled the storage holes with bins, and he stuffed the bins with beauties.

With the pride of a fat rat he showed the Incredible Impostor his collection of beauties.

The Incredible Impostor couldn't keep track of everything, but here's what he remembered: one four by four foot bin filled with sea shell beauties collected off the shores of Cliff Cove, another bin filled with corkscrews of many shapes and sizes, a beauty box of stopped watches for the wrist and pocket, twenty-two glass door knobs purpled by the sun, and two sealed decks of Flippo cards never to be opened.

Drag admired his box of beautiful stopped watches. He had his favorite bins and this was his most favorite. It filled his heart in ways you can't imagine, so don't try. Some of his favorites: 4:29, 8:20, 7:19, 2:29, 8:08. He wondered what does it mean? How did these beauties stop, and why?

Then, two excited messengers appeared out of a small hole and poked the fat rat.

"Trouble in hole #79, Mr. Drag."

Drag left his friend without a goodbye and followed the messengers through the tunnel.

Not long after, a rat appeared out of the dark and brushed up against the Incredible Impostor. It was Fassola, Drag's beautiful wife.

"Come with me, Incredible," she said. "Quickly, come and see."

The Incredible Impostor and Fassola walked through the tunnel to a storage hole of her own.

Empty boxes lined the walls of the special hole. The boxes once housed beautiful plates and cups and saucers. Somehow, somewhere, the plates got smashed. The smashed-up chips made a great heap on the floor of her storage hole.

This was Fassola's personal hole, and, like herself, a thing of beauty. Everything here is special. Special boxes meant to hold one thing of many pieces, the wonderful ceramic chips, no two alike, asleep in the heap in the bottom of her hole.

"Drag says throw the junk out, it's all broke up. But that's him, not me. It's true you can't keep apart what's meant to get together. And it's also true that parts always come back to form a whole. Someday my jumbled-up pile of chips will wake up and go lookin' for their home boxes. In time the pile will disappear and the plates will be back at home just like before, and it will be like that again, and like that it will stay."

Drag's house hole was the size of a Rocky Mountain cave. Side holes led to bottom holes that fed into tunnels that angled up and over. It was all interconnected. It went on and on forever or close to it. There was much to show his new friend.

But right now, Drag had a few questions.

"Look at me, Impostor. What do you see?"

The Incredible Impostor looked into the pampered face of his rich new friend. Short cut whiskers, curly hair clipped neat. His eye roved around but couldn't find a damn thing to focus on. Then it settled back.

"I see a rat who has two of everythin'. A very content rat," said the Incredible Impostor.

"Did you say content?"

"I say what I see."

"Then you ain't lookin' at me. You're lookin' past me. Look closer and you'll see just how content I ain't. Now why would a rat who has everythin' be discontent? How can this be?"

"Must be somethin' buggin' the hell out of him."

"Look closer."

"Somethin' big time he can't get away from."

"Closer."

"Can't look no closer, my eyes are crossin'!"

"It seems like I've got it all, don't it? I have a king's hole for my home. I double up meal after meal. I'm twice the rat I used to be! It's been a long and prosperous road but I missed the turnoff for happiness. The truth is I'll never be happy; I'll always be miserable until I kill the human who spared my life."

# 78

It happened so long ago it should be forgotten, but in all that time it never left Drag's mind for a minute. And what he couldn't fit in his thoughts when he was awake, he made room for in his dreams at night. No, Drag will never forget, his memory grew stronger every day, and his dreams brought him new details at night.

He was a young rat, barely out of his hole when it happened. It had rained for so long the sun was a mystery and clouds were what he knew. Then one day the rain stopped, the clouds spread apart and the sun came through.

It was a time to feast, a time to dance and rejoice.

But there was thunder in the air, and all around him lay the dead. His mother, his father, his neighbors and friends. Sixty-three rats total. He tried to nuzzle them awake, for maybe they were sleeping, but their bodies were as cold as his heart was lonely. They were dead, all dead.

Sometimes it takes a rat a while to understand the obvious, but, give them enough time, they figure it out. The poor little rats had been killed without reason by a bad man with a thunder gun. They called him the Rat Killer.

And Drag will be his next victim.

Caught out in the open field, Drag ran from hole to hole. But he found no sanctuary, for the holes were stuffed with the dead. The Rat Killer fired his thunder gun once more and missed. He fired again and missed but not by much. Then a shadow came over Drag. He scratched the dirt in a blind rat panic, but he could not move.

With his foot on the little rat's tail, Uncle Brucker looked down the long barrel of his .22 and pulled the trigger. But the gun didn't fire. He pulled the trigger again. He was out of bullets.

"You lucky bastard," he said to the rat under his foot. "Put it on the calendar. Today is your day."

He removed his foot from the rat's tail and the little rat ran off into the field and through the bush.

And now, years later, he stood next to the Incredible Impostor in his grand hole, and tears came quickly to Drag's eyes and his nose twitched with the sting of sad memories.

"Yes, I should have been number sixty-four. I was left out, stepped over, excluded. I'm not the rat I should be, I don't even know who that rat is. The future ain't mine and the past belongs to some other rat. Now I'm livin' in a world where I ain't supposed to be, doin' things I ain't meant to do. The Rat Killer stole a fate from me that should have been mine and gave me one that ain't."

It was a sad story that Drag told, so very sad, filled with tears and sorrow and topped off with hatred.

After listening to Drag's sad story, the Incredible Impostor felt a pain in his heart, a great sad pain such as he had never felt before.

He hated the Rat Killer almost as much as Drag hated him. He was the sort of creature that makes the entire planet look bad just because he walks upon it.

"Recently," said Drag, "I came upon some information that leads me to believe the Rat Killer may have crossed over from his dimension and he's hidin' out around here. And if this is true, I'm gonna make sure he ain't goin' back. It's only a matter of time before I catch up to him and make things right. Then I'll know what happiness is. At last I will be happy."

The Incredible Impostor saw the toll it took on Drag, a lifetime of should-have-been's. There must be something he can do to help the poor rich unhappy rat.

"Is there anythin', any way at all I can help get you out of your misery?"

Drag was overcome by the Incredible Impostor's heartfelt offer. Most rats are stingy and rarely gave so much of themselves, but Drag knew from the start that the Incredible Impostor was no ordinary rat. In fact, he was no rat at all.

When someone looks down his gun barrel at you, ready to pull the trigger, it's a sight you will never forget. Drag recognized the Rat Killer the moment he saw him in the wrestling ring.

"How nice of you to ask." Drag faltered. "But I already got my plans laid out."

Drag didn't quite understand why, but he was having second thoughts. Now that he finally met the man he wanted to kill, he wasn't sure that he should go through with it.

There was a tear in Drag's eye and he didn't know how it got there. One lonely tear, stuck in his eye, and it wouldn't slide. But one tear cannot wash away a life of misery. Drag didn't come this far to let a tear talk him out of his lifelong quest.

In the end he decided to proceed with his original plan.

"On Thursday night after the match I will finally kill the man who saved my life. But that Thursday isn't here yet. Until then," he took out the deck of cards he carried in his pouch, "join me in a pleasant game of Flippo."

# 79

Scratch left the ring early Thursday morning and went back home to count his money. Game over, the Incredible Impostor shed his wrestling suit. He said goodbye to the promoter and walked to the ring ropes where he greeted his faithful stick-around fans. The sweet rat with no name stuck around.

A rat spoke from the dark of the ring.

"Yo, Impostor!"

The Inspector stepped forward into the glow of the dock light. A wet butt stuck to his lips.

"Hello," he said. "I said hello."

"I heard you the second time," said the Incredible Impostor.

"A quick response would spare your ears some listenin' time."

"Other than givin' out small advice about the unimportant, is the Inspector here for a particular reason?"

"Just doin' my Everyday Job, of course, and meantime I'm doin' my Meantime Job. My Everyday is all about lookin' for the Strange and questionin' the Unusual, and in the Meantime I do anythin' I want. Usually I separate the two, except today I'm doublin' up for an important reason."

"Why? More money this way?"

"No. Sore feet."

The Inspector rambled on. It was slick talk meant to confuse while he circled around and went straight to the point. He had a way of rambling the information out of you and you didn't know you gave it up.

The Incredible Impostor was a particularly hard case. It was like trying to get money from an empty hidey-hole. The Inspector had never encountered a rat like this before. He tried and tried but he just couldn't break through.

The Inspector took some time-out to sniff the air and relax, but when he started up again something seemed to crack inside his head, and through the crack, a Realization came into his mind.

It was a Realization powerful yet simple, something he knew but he didn't know he knew it. If the Incredible Impostor is the only rat the Inspector couldn't open up, the reason just might be because he isn't a rat at all.

The Incredible Impostor is no impostor. He is the real thing. And the Inspector realized why his technique could never work. He was using a rat's key to unlock a human's door.

The Inspector turned and walked along the pier. The Incredible Impostor walked off in the other direction. The Inspector was heading to a bar hole past the rail tracks and a meeting with Scratch. He had a lot to discuss with Scratch, and it was not all good. But the Inspector was skilled in making good out of a bad situation. Sometimes bad is good.

The Inspector walked slowly like a rat whose troubles had fallen off Cove Cliff and scattered into the ocean. It was a good feeling and he wanted to keep it forever.

As he walked he noticed his reflection in a mirror in a shop window, and he hated his hair. He found a fishbone comb in his pouch and combed a lick down but he couldn't get it right. He combed that lick again and he still he couldn't get it right, but now he didn't mind.

# 80

Scratch slurped up three lick-off plates of top shelf juice. The Inspector also had three, top shelf. Buy two more and I'll charge you for four, offered the wet nose barkeep. The Inspector had the cash and Scratch ordered two more drinks.

They were sitting at a dirt mound table in a tiny bar hole called Drinkets, just north of the rail tracks. Ship rats and wharfies hung out here, and the hemp rats crawled around. The hemp rats had droopy ears and low voices, and they danced with the wharfies, but they didn't dance with the ship rats. The ship rats danced with the barkeep behind the counter and in between drinks.

The two rats had agreed to meet at Drinkets and discuss the Inspector's special offer.

Scratch was concerned. The Incredible Impostor had lost steam in the last few days. He talked not much at all and he sunk inside himself. On Thursday he lost his first match ever to Grudge, and they had to change the banners because the Incredible Impostor was no longer undefeated. The victorious Grudge walked out of the ring with his chest sticking out like a rooster, and the rats cheered.

Scratch waited patiently for the Inspector's report on the strange impostor, but his patience wore off quickly. Scratch enjoyed a drink as much as the next rat, but he hated to wait around.

Scratch's lips pull back and his fangs pop out and he shows his teeth when he's impatient, like most rats.

Said the Inspector, "Sad news is a shot of whisky. Good news is whisky with a chaser. What do you call a double shot and a chaser?"

"I call it stallin'," said Scratch.

"Another drink, we'll both be ready."

"It ain't right keepin' me waitin', despite what I'm drinkin'. But then we ain't goin' by my version of what's right, are we?"

"Another round, barkeep!"

"Ready to give me my report?" asked Scratch.

The Inspector was ready for anything, but first he had good news for Scratch: there will be no charge for his service. It's absolutely free, and the reason is Stipulation #33. The Inspector charges for findin' out, but there's no charge for what he realizes, so the Inspector can't charge Scratch because it ain't fair: Stipulation #33.

"Very nice. Got my report?"

"That's where I'm gettin' to. There ain't no report. The report ain't cummin' up because of Stipulation #33A. Stipulation #33A is No Charge/No Report."

"I had concerns, very strong concerns and you ain't done nuthin' to relieve me. What are you doin' for my concerns, ratso?"

Scratch was riled. But that didn't bother the Inspector. He was used to it.

"Fold up your concerns and put them in your pouch. You may never take them out again," said the Inspector.

Free of charge, the Inspector told Scatch what was on his mind, and Scratch understood the implications. Scratch was a promoter of rat on rat competition, and he was subject to the strict rules of the Wrestling Board. If the Commission found out The Incredible Impostor was not an Impostor, Scratch would have a high price to pay. The Board would take away his license and fine him heavily. Wrestling fans all over Rat Land would turn against him. The rats will demand a refund of the full ticket price and a surcharge for being cheated. If that happens, the Inspector said he would help Scratch out.

Scratch was depressed. His business went with the Impostor, his life shattered.His ears sagged and he wanted to bite off his own tail, spit it out and bite it off again.

But Scratch knew very well that there's money to be made from every situation. He just forgot it for a little while until the Inspector reminded him.

"You better eat your spades before you lose the game, cause they're gonna find out about that Impostor." The Inspector continued. "I've done a lot of thinkin' on the way over here. You got to make one last bundle and change your game before it's too late, and I got it all figured out."

Scratch looked at his empty, licked-off plate, and he looked at the Inspector. The Inspector was a rat with ideas that pop into his head, and he was always looking for something new.

Scratch was the opposite type, he held onto what he had. Right now he wished he was more like the Inspector. A real good idea makes him smile. The Inspector's head popped a good one and Scratchs' tail stuck out straight as a board when he saw that great big smile.

The Inspector ordered two more drinks from the barkeep, an the barkeep poured and delivered the drinks. Scratch was touched that the Inspector was willing to share.

The Inspector said, "I'm willin' to share cause that's what partners do."

"You mean we're partners?" Scratch said.

"Sign the dotted line, we are."

They searched the bar hole but they couldn't find a dotted line, or a sheet of paper to draw a line on, or a pencil to draw with. The barkeep said they could sign the dirt mound table with their noses—for a small fee.

"Your new partner has big thoughts, and from big thoughts come big plans. He's thinkin' of a big match." The Inspector was talking about himself.

"How big a match?" Scratch asked.

"Biggest match I can think of," said the Inspector.

"Can it be grand?"

"Bigger than big and grander than grand."

"Would it be bigger than Slim Deluxe versus the Porker?" Scratch asked.

"Makes that look like a mouse match," said the Inspector.

"Will it have banners and lights?"

"Banners that stretch across the city. I'll find out about the lights."

"A marchin' band?"

"Included."

"Parade?"

"Essential."

"So tell me about this most fabulous match, Inspector. But don't spurt it out all at once like a fathead human. Take your time and spread it out like a rat," said Scratch.

# 81

Dwight carried the old rat TV up from the basement and put it on the floor in the dining room under the 100 watt bulb. He had no use for tables and benches. He did his best work on the floor.

Dwight got down on his knees and took the old TV apart.

I tried to fix it weeks ago when Uncle Brucker gave it to me. Now it's Dwight's turn. He owed me one repair because I gave him a ride home last week and for driving him around in general.

Dwight brought a tool set with him along with two shopping bags with leftover parts. The parts came from many different appliances. If he can't repair a TV with TV parts, maybe he can fix it with a mixer.

It's been three and a half weeks and no word from Uncle Brucker. He said he might be late but I don't think he meant this late. When I came to live with him, I never thought things would pile up like this, so high I can't climb out. I was tired of people coming around when I didn't invite them. I hated being in charge and making all the decisions. On top of it all Uncle Brucker's War Medal was still missing and I didn't eat lunch all last week.

And with everything else going on I had slacked off on my Identifying. The government could ask for my list anytime. It was written down in the government contract, and I better be ready to hand it in. Don't forget to sign it. No matter what, it had to be neat.

Dwight threw the leftover parts in the bags. We put the TV on a chair and plugged it in. Dwight went into the kitchen in search of food. I pressed a button under the picture tube and waited.

The TV hummed to itself as the ancient tubes and out-dated transistors warmed up. A pinhole of light appeared in the center of the screen, and the hole expanded and the screen came alive with a circus of static.

Long lines of horizontal static stretched across the back and short vertical lines of static moved in the foreground. And there was shortline static of different sizes and shapes twisting around all over the screen, and zigzagging static with shortline static mixed in.

I moved up close to the screen and I found a dial on the side and tried to tune it in but what I got was clear static, and I figured out why.

The rats see the world through a different kind of eyes than we do, and that means a different kind of vision. I'll never get rid of the static because it's what their vision is based on. Rats have static vision.

There's a whole other dimension filled with rats on the other side of the screen. Rats went about their daily lives in their world just like we did in ours. I'd like to climb into the picture tube and clean it up.

Then I got an idea, and while Dwight looked for food in the kitchen, I put on my Identifiers.

As soon as I put them on, the static disappeared, the picture cleared up, and I got my first look at a very strange and dismal place.

The camera showed a dark alley with dark crooked buildings where the rats crawled freely. Across the alley stretched a long banner. I don't know much about nose writing but I could read this: GRUDGE MATCH THURSDAY AT EIGHT. It was a wresting channel, and so was the next channel. In Rat Land, every channel is dedicated to wrestling. I watched for a while, and a man walked in front of the banner.

He wore a real cool wrestling suit that read THE INCREDIBLE IMPOSTOR, and in that suit was my Uncle.

He was miles beyond tired. He was beat-up tired, old age tired. One ear was swollen from a left foot drop kick and he had a black eye from a knuckle punch that knocked him to the mat. His bent nose had taken a beating and now it was bent in the other direction. He lost some weight. His eyes were wide open crazy, wild, wounded jungle animal eyes.

But I must say he looked pretty damn good in that suit.

"Who was that guy in the static?" asked Dwight.

I did't notice him come in from the kitchen. He was standing by the door.

"Oh, him. That's my Uncle," I said.
"Awesome," Dwight said.

# 82

Uncle Brucker helped me out by taking me in. What's mine is yours, he said. He gave me everything he had and he taught me everything he knew. It's a lot to give and now it's my turn to give it back. I had to go into the rat dimension and get him.

Usually I fall asleep quickly. Tonight I turned over in bed. I did a lot of thinking and rethinking, and it buzzed around inside my brain. I couldn't sleep, so I got up and found Uncle Brucker's Specialized Rat Encyclopedia in the dresser and I got out my reverse map, and I brought them to the kitchen and sat at the table, and I went through the Encyclopedia and studied the map and I wrote a page of map notes to help me out, and I formulated a Plan of Rescue for Uncle Brucker.

First I covered sneaking through the no man's land surrounding the Portal, which I labeled Portal Approach. Then I moved onto climbing up the Nowhere Road to the top of the Portal, which I labeled Portal Ascent, then up there on the Portal my plan stalled.

I could study the book and my notes and look over the map until I burned a hole in my forehead, but it won't mean anything because it's all based on hearsay. The Portal, the Nowhere Road, the Platform were just rumors people only heard about because the Army classified it top secret.

I made small progress but I made some good labels and I learned two things:

(1) Don't waste time on labels.

(2) A good plan has a life of its own because you can't plan for the unknown. A plan changes as it moves along. Plan all you want, but that doesn't mean you're prepared.

True, I lacked a good solid plan. But I knew what not to do and I realized that I wasn't prepared.

Tomorrow's the go date. Don't knock on my door because I won't be here. As far as I'm concerned, I have something better than any think-ahead certified 100 point plan.

I have a reverse map and an open mind.

# 83

Thursday at 7PM I parked the Eagle on the rise at the edge of town and waited for Dwight to show up.

From up there I had a view of the valley. Route 94 curved around the Galleria and the water tower, then headed west into the night. All the lights were off in the county office building, except for one or two and the first floor.

The Nowhere Road from Base Camp, the portal that led to the next dimension, the bridge that connected to the tunnel—nobody knew it was down there because it was camouflaged and classified as Top Secret, but was all discovered by Uncle Brucker and me.

We followed the homing rat. We made the reverse map and discovered the rift between dimensions. We notified the General through the LL.

General Hardesty's Army Engineers dug the rift out and widened it, covered it with camouflage, self-reflecting mirrors, and other high tech military trickery. With the aid of Dwight and my reverse map, I will sneak into the rat dimension and make my way through the camouflage and mirrors and the trickery, and find my Uncle and take him back home.

It's 7:25. Where's Dwight? I sat in the car and studied the reverse map and waited for Dwight. I practiced my Rat Talk. *Chi-'za-ba*. Out of the way, Ratso! *Tze'-che-te*. Get packing!

Dwight had tuned in the TV, and by adjusting the contrast and light he chased away some of the static, and we got a better look at my Uncle. I didn't ask Dwight, he volunteered to go with me. If he doesn't get here in the next few minutes, it will be too dark to make our way through the woods and I'll have to abort until tomorrow.

I put the Eagle in first and I was ready to drive off when I heard footsteps on the sidewalk. Dwight came out of the bushes, and Renata was with him.

"What are you doin' here?" I asked.

"She's goin', I'm not."

Dwight turned and showed me the left side of his face. Whoever was looking for him, found him, and I didn't want to know why. His left eye was black and blue and swollen shut, and it made him look tough and dumb. Tough enough to take a punch, but too dumb to avoid it.

"I'll fix the timer and start it up for you," Dwight said. "Don't wanna go into no extra dimension lookin' like this."

"That's why I'm goin'," said Renata.

"You don't want to go, and I don't want you with me," I told Renata.

She showed me the name tag she made just for me, and it was fancy and beautiful and it looked like it belonged to somebody important. The name WALT stuck out the top in neat letters like the Eleventh Commandment. Blue ribbons with sparkles and green ribbons with stars hung halfway down my chest.

The rats don't care much for awards and diplomas, but they do have a lot of respect for a fancy name tag or an important-looking badge or an impressive business card.

"I won't let you go without me," she said.

# 84

"**L**et's go," I said.

I took the lead with my reverse map in my hand. It's not an exact map, but it pointed me in the right direction. And if I keep an open mind, it will get me where I want to go.

Dwight grabbed his tools and one parts bag and Renata grabbed a bag with dials and meters, and we made our way through the woods to the Portal.

We passed weary soldiers limping back to base camp. More soldiers rode past us in military vehicles. Their bandaged legs hung off the tailgate. Rat-shocked MPs walked past us unaware, and headed to the med tent. Farther on, we entered the no man's land patrolled by the rats.

But no rats patrolled. The restless rats had wandered off hours ago, and they left the patrolling to impatient rats, who left soon after and retreated to the storage room. After a while we came to the bridge support. Dwight found the service door and we went into the dark room.

In the storage room the pathetic rats slobbered down Rat Juice, smoked hemp and sang tuneless songs of victory.

The pitiful drunken rats did not know their limits. Most had passed out on the cold concrete floor, beer cans and Flippo cards scattered around them. On a table in the center of the room sat a metal box. A heavy black electric cord connected the metal box to the wall outlet. The metal box contained the timer.

"Gotta take it down," said Dwight. "Put it on the floor. Can't fix it on no table."

Dwight and I tried to lift it, then Renata helped us and we managed to move it off the table.

Wasting no time, Dwight opened his parts bag and set to work. He unscrewed the cover, looked inside, and like an a-list mechanic, he removed the main switch and the timing mechanism.

The rats had taken the timer apart and put it back together, but they couldn't make it work. The lights on the Portal had not been on for many weeks.

"That baseball cap he's wearin'," Renata whispered. "He takes it off and switches it around means he fixed it. If he don't switch, nobody can fix it."

Dwight threw out the parts he didn't need, borrowed a few parts from the toaster bag, fit the other parts back in.

"Pin!" said Dwight.

Renata dug into her purse and handed Dwight a safety pin.

"No. Bobby!" he said, and she found a bobby pin. Dwight reassembled the timing mechanism and installed the main switch and put the bobby pin where he needed it. He screwed the cover back on and turned his cap around.

Fixed!

Dwight set the timer.

Ten minutes!

"Let's go, Walt. Let's climb up the Portal!" said Renata.

A stairway on the right went all the way up to the top platform.

Renata grabbed my hand and pulled me along with her. She held it all the way to the top. She didn't let go.

As we climbed the stairs I gave her some advice. Don't make any sudden movements. Don't smile, cause rats never smile. I knew some rat talk so let me do the talking.

I hadn't planned on taking her with me, and I didn't want her to go. But everything got switched around, and now she was taking me with her.

Up we climbed like indoor mountain goats, two steps at a time.

"I love climbin'," she said as we neared the top. "I see stairs I gotta go up 'em. I just love gettin' to the top a things. When you're up there, you're higher than what you climbed. Nobody can say nuthin' to ya. You look down at everythin'!"

At the top of the stairs, before we opened the door to the platform, we pinned on our name tags and waited in the stairwell for the lights on the Portal to go on.

A moment passed, then two. The timer clicked, the lights went on, and a great rat cheer filled the air. Rat feet tore up the dirt as the rats gathered outside the Portal to view the spectacular light show.

"Let's go!"

I pushed open the iron door.

A huge mean-looking grizzly stood before us. Muscles bulged all over his hard body, a yellow stripe ran down his nose. He must have weighed eighty pounds or more. The stripe means he's a member of the Elite Guard. It also means he doesn't back down.

But his attitude changed when he saw our impressive name tags. His mean look softened. He smiled like a chipmunk and held the door as we went through. You have to be special if you wear a name tag like this.

The wind blew our hair and tugged our name tags as we held onto the rail. Renata closed her eyes as tight as she could. The whistling wind howled. Her hair flew back like a movie star in the best film of the year.

Next stop: Rat Land.

"Remember, I gotta be home by ten," Renata said.

# 85

Uncle Brucker awoke to a different Thursday.

It was a difference so familiar he couldn't see it at first, as strange as a memory that was new to him. It took him all evening to piece it together and he came to the conclusion that the difference was inside him. Everything around him was exactly the same, therefore he must be different.

He didn't tell Scratch, but three days ago he had eaten his last rat cake. He had made up his mind he would never eat another one. Scratch gave him a bag full of cakes every morning and Uncle Brucker fed them to the crabs and seagulls. Each day he went without, another foggy layer peeled off his mind and it became clear there was somebody else underneath.

He didn't know how he got into this mess, but he had to find a way out of it. But before he could get out he had to figure out who he was.

When all the layers were peeled off and he could finally see himself, who would he see?

He wheel-barrowed Scratch down the crowded alley. Grudge Match at 8:00.

"I'm done with sleepin' in rat holes and crawlin' around in the dirt," Uncle Brucker told Scratch. "And as far as my contract goes, we gotta renegotiate."

"Renegotiate? There ain't no such thing. What's done is done and it can't be redone. Turn me right."

The night was cool and quiet. The breeze took the evening off and mulled around offshore. The fog gathered in the distance and waited for a cue, while the mist scouted through the alleys. The street lights came on at sundown and the rats left their holes in the twilight. Polished by the misty air, everything was shiny. A good night for snooping around. A special night.

The flying rats circled overhead, too excited to land. The squawky gulls saw their chance and swooped down at the sand crabs. The curious moon came in for a closer look and pulled the tide over the pier and all the way up to the dock house. And the filthy ship rats stepped off the driftwood and tiptoed onto the shore. They were heading to the Grudge Match.

The rotten pier groaned under the weight of the huge crowd. Beyond the old storm drains, decorated with streamers and lights, a special wrestling ring had been built on solid ground. A magnificent banner stretched from building to building high above the alley: GRUDGE VS THE INCREDIBLE IMPOSTOR.

"That banner is my partner's idea," said Scratch. "Gotta admit, it draws a big crowd." Scratch turned to the skinny rat who stood next to him. "Right, partner?"

Uncle Brucker didn't recognize the skinny rat until he turned around.

"That's right, partner," said the Inspector. "Thump him in three."

# 86

"I want to go home," Renata said.

The rats crawled out of their holes and headed down to the docks and the wrestling ring. They hissed and snapped and fought to get ahead, and they scrambled through the crooked buildings and down into the crooked alleys and spread out onto the crooked streets of Rat Land.

Dirt-nose tunnel rats left their holes for the first time in years, joined by poor dump rats who had saved for months to buy just one ticket. Slick dandies walked with their spouses, who wore fancy trinkets and displayed their shiniest pins for the occasion.

The elder rats crawled out of their sleep holes on scrawny legs, and they all went down to the docks and the wrestling ring where the Grudge Match will soon begin.

Renata and I backed into an abandoned storefront next to a pile of crate wood. The rats were not interested in Renata and me. We were just a couple of impostors and our fancy name tags were beautiful.

I had my arms around her and she held onto me just as tight as she could.

Rat Land isn't all that bad if you have a girl like Renata with you.

Renata trembled.

"I want to go home," she said. "I don't want to be here."

"We'll go back after we do what we came to do," I said.

"I liked climbin' up and gettin' here. But now we're here we ain't goin' up no more. There's too many rats around here."

"Listen!"

A rat orchestra started up somewhere down the alley. The rat trumpeters attempted a tune while the rat cellists searched for a note. A marching band appeared from around the corner, and Renata's mood quickly changed.

"Look, Walt! It's a parade, Walt! A parade!"

Rats love a parade almost as much as a wrestling match. When you combine the two it adds up to one hell of an event. The rats waited to buy premium bench-seat tickets. A heap of money will be made at the betting booths and the card tables. The Promoter was going to make a killing tonight.

From the top of a dirt mound we watched the parade go by.

An orchestra of 100 instruments came down the alley. Bongo beaters marched out of sync with the horn blowers. Twenty-one hum drummers drummed and harmonized to the backbeat. An Old Guinea King rat plucked a three–string junkyard banjo. The drunken cellists tripped on their instruments and fought with the bony flutists, and the hemp rats grabbed the penny whistles and blew a note.

Next, after the orchestra, 101 high-stepping dandies marched down the alley, spinning ragged top hats on bushstick canes. And then came twenty-two tunnel rats with jingling silver bells tied to their pointed tails, followed by fifty-five tap-dancing sewer rats with crowns of red roses.

No rat in Rat Land had seen a parade like this before. Little rats and their mothers and their grandmothers came out too, and they watched with eyes wide and mouths open.

And their eyes grew bigger and their mouths opened wider when they saw what came next.

Pulled by teams of thick-necked wharf rats with ropes tied on their backs, Grudge and the Incredible Impostor arrived, each on their own rolling platform. Grudge was first, flexing his muscles and posing like he's the the big winner.

Next, the Incredible Impostor, fan favorite. He stood on the platform with his shoulders sagging and his head down. The front wheels of the platform hit a bump. The platform shifted. He lost his balance and almost fell over. The crowd gasped, then cheered. The banner flapped in the wind.

It was an even match before the game, but the odds changed when everyone saw the sad-looking impostor. Now the bookmakers favored Grudge five to one.

But where was Renata?

"Look at these bracelets!" she said.

Renata forgot all about the rat parade when she found what she really came for. She was going through a box of colorful bracelets a little dockside vendor had opened up for her.

"Come on, Renata. We gotta tell my Uncle I'm here."

"What's the rat sayin'?"

"He's says take the whole box, he'll give you a deal. Let's go!"

"How much?"

"Two and a half cents each for a beautiful impostor like you, he says."

"Ask him if he'll go down to two."

The platform carrying Uncle Brucker passed before us. I shouted out in Rat Talk but he couldn't hear me above the crowd. The drummers pounded on their patched-up drums. The junkyard banjo player found the string and plucked it, and the parade continued down the alley under the street banner to the wrestling ring.

Uncle Brucker was getting away.

"I came here to get my Uncle, and that's what I'm gonna do," I told Renata. And I left her at the trinket vendor and made my way to the wrestling ring by myself.

# 87

R ound One:

"Who's havin' a go at me?" Grudge asked the crowd.

And the crowd replied, "The Incredible Impostor!"

Grudge had changed his image. Now he wore a new black wrestling suit with GRUDGE printed in gold on the front and back. He had been working out lately, drinking less. He had filed his teeth down and they were razor-sharp. His neck was as thick as a truck tire, legs like a tiny rhino. He looked like he was made of a harder material.

He circled around Uncle Brucker, hunched down low and ready to spring. Uncle Brucker just stood there with his arms folded at his chest. For a second Grudge hesitated—this could be a trick—then he turned around and knocked Uncle Brucker down with a double back kick.

Uncle Brucker got up and brushed himself off. There was something important he had to remember, of the highest priority. It was coming back to him now, words written on a box.

"Give me m-more!" he said.

And Grudge gave him more. He came at him with a right leg head kick, and then another back kick, and with each kick another piece of Uncle Brucker's memory came loose.

Round Two:

A few more flips. Another kick. Two more. The wrestling ring sailed over his head and my Uncle landed on his back. His memory loosened up—but only for a few seconds—then it jammed again.

One more kick, Uncle Brucker thought, looking up at banner and the spinning night sky. One more kick should do it. Then I'll get my memory back. Then I'll fight back and win.

Round Three:

"Hit me harder!" he told Grudge.

Uncle Brucker was losing the match, but he was winning his memory back.

"That ain't hard enough!" he told Grudge.

Grudge leaned back against the ropes and studied his opponent. The crowd knew what was coming next.

Running head kick!

As Uncle Brucker sailed backwards through the air, thoughts spun around inside his head, all broken up, daring him to put them together.

The Factory. The rat cakes. The Professor. An address. A package. 1600 Pennsylvania Ave. Now the White House spun by. The President stood at the front door! What's that in his hand? A Rat Cake!

Uncle Brucker hit the ground, bounced once, twice. Grudge walked over to him as he lay face-up on the mat. And as Grudge walked toward him he looked up and read the banner for the first time, and he knew who he was and he made the connection.

He was the Rat Killer and the Professor had shipped Rat Cakes to the White House!

And now it all came back to my Uncle. He knew exactly who he was and he knew where he had to go and he knew what he must do.

He was Uncle Brucker the Rat Killer, and he was tired and he was losing and the rats were eyeing me and becoming suspicious and I realized my name tag was missing.

There was only one thing I could think of that might save my Uncle, only one thing left to say. I had held it in reserve. Now it was time to bring it out.

"Look out!" I yelled to the crowd. I yelled like never before. "Look out! Up there, in the sky! The Asteroid is cummin'!"

# 88

For a moment, time froze. The mist stopped short in the alleys and the waves lined up offshore. The squawky gulls quit

squawking and the rats held their breath. Then, in a single movement, the rats looked to the night sky.

"The Asteroid? Where?" Grudge asked.

"Over there!" The Incredible Impostor crawled out from
under the big rat. "Don't you see it?"

"I'm lookin'," said Grudge.

"It's stuck in the clouds!" said a rat.

"It's hidin' behind the moon!" said another.

"It won't be long now!"

"*Te'-ta* Asteroid! It's the One Big Night!"

The bar holes filled up in minutes. Fat-gut barkeeps mixed
their drinks and nosed them across the bar. Chipped glasses
clinked against lick-off plates as ten thousand rats toasted the
Asteroid. The barkeeps poured one more for themselves, and
the Flippo cards were dealt. The hum drummers drummed and
hummed. Folk rats strummed their patched-up guitars and played
the bongos to a happy beat. Dandy rats waltzed around the rims
of their sleep holes and they invited the tunnel rats to join in. Even
the little hemp rats got up on their feet and danced a jig, but they
couldn't keep up with the dandies.

Alley vendors who had waited all their lives for the One Big
Night set up shop and sold Asteroid trinkets for big bucks, and
they didn't have to shine them up.

Every rat lost interest in the wrestling match, including
Grudge.

"This is it, the night we been waitin' for," Grudge said. "Easy
now, fella. Hope I didn't do any permanent damage. Come on,
I'm buyin'."

With a warm smile and steady claw he helped the Incredible
Impostor to his feet, and they headed to the nearest bar hole.

"What did I tell ya?" Scratch said, slapping five with his partner, the Inspector. The Inspector exhaled like it had been a long
day, week, month, year. Scratch smiled so wide his fangs popped
out. It was a record-breaking crowd. They had surely made a bundle. "Some night, eh? So, what are your plans, Inspector?"

The Inspector leaned back against the ring ropes, scratched his ear, gazed up at the stars.

"You know," he said. "I've thought and thought about it over the years. We all knew this night was cummin', but now that it's here, I still don't have a clue. . . . What will you do now that everythin's changed?"

Scratch yawned and sniffed the air for an answer.

"Tell you the truth, I figure it's about time I got out of the wrestlin' business. There's a quiet country hole north of the tracks. I used to crawl around there when I was a pup. I'll dig it out a bit more, find me a sweetie, make a little palace out of that hole. It's a fine place to take it easy and wait out the cloud. I hear it gets pretty chilly durin' the One Big Night, and the moon don't light up a thing. . . . Or maybe I'll stick around Rat City and work out a new line. Got one idea just now. The Asteroid is cummin'! Pick a time! Pick a place! Place your bets over here!"

Scratch looked down at his legs like they were up to something, and they were.

"Well if that don't beat all. . . . My skip limp is gone!"

All the excitement had re-charged his muscles and brought his legs back to life, and now they moved on their own, picking up speed, taking giant steps, swinging his body around and around.

"I'm dancin'! I'm dancin' like a dandy!"

And on his two back feet Scratch danced through the crowd.

"Win big in the Asteroid Lottery!" he cried. "Two chances to win. Pick a time, pick a place. Win big in the Asteroid Lottery. Place your bets over here!"

# 89

"Don't get me wrong," Grudge told Uncle Brucker as they left the busy bar hole. "I love wrestlin', and I'm damn good at it, but my real expertise is dentistry. Filed these down myself."

He grinned and exposed his needle-sharp teeth.

"Goes with the image," said Uncle Brucker, tired but impressed.

Grudge grinned handsomely and eyed the crowd. Uncle Brucker got to know him over a few drinks, and Grudge wasn't at all what he expected. His real name wasn't Grudge. Everybody called him Snookie. He used Grudge for wrestling because Snookie didn't fit. And he was a lover, not a fighter. He left his mean streak in the ring.

The rats carried their Asteroid trinkets down the alleys and headed to the wharves. Some mighty fine-looking rats, Grudge noticed. He loved the cute little ones with the soft whiskers. He loved them all.

"That Asteroid's on its way," he said. "Think I'll stick around here and see what I can dig up. Remember what I told you? Just follow the map on your back," Grudge reminded him, then he noticed a wild-eyed cutie walking his way. "Hey, sweetie pie! I been waitin' for you!" He whistled through his fine sharp teeth.

"There's a map on your back," Grudge had told him back in the drink hole. "Draw a line from cut to bruise, you'll know how to get back to the Portal. That's a curb stone made that long cut on your shoulder. That bruise underneath is from a sewer gratin'. And here's where you crossed the rails, that welt right there on your spine. Bent spike did that. Sorry, didn't mean to poke ya. Find that spike, you know you're on the right track. So, you see, even though you got no memory of it, you always knew how to get where you came from. You got a built-in map on your back."

Everywhere the rats had dragged him, it was all written on his back. After the rats caught him in the tunnel, they tied him up and dragged him down a dark alley and over the rails. They stopped at a drink hole, and they came out and dragged him over the chipped curb stones. All he had to do was find the sewer and work his way back to the rails. And when he got to the rails, the Portal couldn't be far!

# 90

The fog spent the evening offshore, getting thick and lazy. Sometime around nine it finally wandered into town. It spread out from the wharves and squeezed through the alleys and traveled farther than ever before. A sea breeze rose up and pushed it even farther, and now it was stuck in the narrow alleys around the Portal and couldn't find its way back to the sea.

Uncle Brucker pushed through the crowd of rats and spread the news.

"The Asteroid is cummin'! Out of your holes! The Asteroid is cummin'!"

He located the broken sewer grating and the chipped curb stones a few alleys back. Only the bent spike remained. The fog was so thick he could hardly see. As he made his way down the slippery alleys, he felt a pain in his back. He went a little farther and it faded. He backwalked and the pain got worse.

Follow the pain!

He turned left and it was like they were dragging him on his back again. A few more steps and it hurt so much he fell to his knees, and through the fog he saw it. The old railroad track! He brushed the fog out of the way and made his way forward. A few more yards and he came to the bent spike.

He touched the cold spike and the pain went out of him. It left his body and went back into the rusty spike where it came from.

Up ahead, the entrance to the Portal. The rats had planted bushes and trees for camouflage, but they didn't water them so the camouflage died off. The entrance ramp went down into the tunnel, and the tunnel went deep underground and ended in a wall of nothing. But Uncle Brucker knew it really didn't end, it matched up with the bridge back home in the other dimension.

A few scraggly rats hung around the entrance and drank and toasted the Return. Across the alley a young rat sang slow, tear-filled songs while the other rats dreamed on. As the Incredible Impostor walked past they watched him with misty eyes.

"*Te'-ta*-Asteroid!" said Uncle Brucker.

"*Te'-ta*."

He entered the dark tunnel. The fog followed, hoping to find a way out. The tunnel angled down and the fog rolled back and took the warmth from the air. Water dripped from the ceiling to the slick floor, and the tunnel grew darker.

He was hungry, cold and tired, and the tunnel was filled with what if's. What if Grudge lied? What if the tunnel doesn't match up with the bridge? What if it leads deep into the hollowed-out earth instead? What will happen if he is trapped in Rat Land forever?

Maybe he should turn back.

Turn back! Turn back!

Then he felt it . . . a breeze. No, more than a breeze—a wind.

And he heard it too. That was no ordinary wind. It's the Whistling Wind! The Portal had to be up ahead where the crosswinds meet and the wind whistles. He rushed forward and the tune changed. Now it was a sour rat tune, and the drumbeat of footsteps joined in.

Someone had followed him into the tunnel.

Uncle Brucker backed against the wet wall. The footsteps came closer, and a fat rat stepped out of the dark.

"Hello there, Drag," said Uncle Brucker.

Drag stopped short.

"Well, hello there!" Drag said.

"Surprise, surprise. It gets me thinkin' you might be followin' me."

"No, sir. I got my own way a goin' wherever I go. I don't follow nobody, and when I get where I'm goin', I go back my own way."

"Sure looks like you're followin'. I mean anyone would think."

"I ain't denyin' what it looks like. I got no time for definitions, and I can't help what you think. After all, we are walkin' in the same general area, goin' in a similar direction. But that ain't the same as followin'."

"It's damn close."

"But even if I was followin' I'd be done with it now, wouldn't I? Here I am, and now that I'm here it's time to do what I come to do."

The fat rich rat looked Uncle Brucker in the eye. My Uncle caught that look and threw it back. He didn't scare my Uncle.

"Let me guess," said Uncle Brucker, scratching his bearded chin.

"You came here to kill the man who spared your life. And only then will you be happy. Think that'll work out for you, ratso?"

"I got nuthin' else worth tryin'," said the rat.

The rich rat rose up on his rear legs. And as he rose he let out a powerful roar that spread through all the tunnels in Rat Land.

Drag pounced on Uncle Brucker. With his two front claws he grabbed him by the neck. He threw him against the tunnel wall. He pinned him to the ground. He picked him up and threw him against the wall again. Uncle Brucker was taking a beating, but he wouldn't lift a hand to fight back. Uncle Brucker just wouldn't give in. He fought back by not fighting back.

A few yards away, in the dark of the tunnel, someone watched the rat and the man fight. It was a person with determination and fortitude, someone who had come a long way for a good reason. It was someone from another dimension who couldn't let Drag hurt the Uncle he loved.

Out of the dark, I said, "Get your claws off my Uncle, you dirty stinkin' rat!"

And I grabbed Drag by his tail and I spun him around and around until my Uncle said, "Let the rat go, Walt!"

"But I got him good! I'll break his legs for ya, Unc!"

Uncle Brucker sat on the tunnel floor. He was beaten and bruised and he had a dizzying headache, but his Incredible Impostor suit still looked sharp.

"I said let him go."

"I'll pull off his tail! We can hang it up in the hall!"

"You don't want to kill him. You don't even want to hurt him. I got somethin' worse in mind."

"I know what's cummin'," said Drag. "You don't have to say it."

"I'm gonna say it anyway," said my Uncle. "Get up on your feet. Go home and be miserable. I just saved your life again."

Drag got up on his legs and stumbled along down the tunnel, a miserable broken rat. I thought he might try something sneaky. I was ready, but he didn't.

He looked back over his shoulder, and his beady rat eyes had tears in them when he said, "Ain't there a limit to the misery one rat can take? I spent my whole life plannin' my revenge. Only I didn't realize I was plannin' my revenge on me."

# 91

Drag slowly went down the tunnel to the entrance hole. I sat down next to my Uncle. Our legs hung over the edge and dangled in the air.

"There ain't really no Asteroid, you know," I told him.

"I suspected."

"It was me who called it in."

"I figured."

"We fooled 'em, Unc. We fooled 'em good."

"It ain't hard to fool a rat, Walt, so don't pat yourself on the back too hard. We only fooled 'em for a minute or two, and a minute ain't long for foolin'."

"I guess we better get outta here. And we better get outta here fast," I said.

Uncle Brucker picked a nasty twig out of his beard and caught up with another he'd been looking for. I was ready to take him home to the old house with me. I had nursed him back before, and I'll do it again. It won't be long before we were home and he was the old Uncle Brucker again.

"Listen to me, Walt," he said. "There's somethin' I gotta tell ya. If you told me you was cummin', I woulda said stay away. You see, I got my own special assignment, Walt. I took it upon myself cause it's the utmost importance because it goes all the way to the top. I got me a brand new obligation to uphold, and if I don't follow through I ain't me. Now I gotta go. I'm sorry, but I can't go back home with you tonight, son. See ya when the job is done."

Uncle Brucker stood on the platform at the end of the tunnel, one foot on the ground, one foot hanging off into nowhere.

I sat around but not for too long. I had come a long way to do two things. (1) Help him out and (2) Bring him back. (1) I didn't do and (2) I never accomplished.

He stood there for so long he could be a statue.

The wind whistled and the tunnel shuddered. He took a deep breath and stepped into nowhere, and I went back to get Renata.

# 92

I don't know how long it took to walk back from the Portal, but it took a lot longer than going there. We took the tunnel to the stairs and went out the service door. The Portal was empty except for us and a few drunken dandies lying around on the stairs, reeking of liquor and smoking hemp. All the other rats were down at the wharves, drinking rat juice and celebrating the return of the Asteroid.

Renata and I just shuffled along through the woods. I was about sixty percent tired and forty percent beat, but I didn't let her know that.

When she asked me how I was doing I said, "Fine."

"I'm fine too," she said.

Renata thanked me for a great time, and she put her arm around me and kissed me on the cheek as we walked. Traveling back and forth between dimensions wasn't as bad as she thought it would be. But the rats belong in their dimension. We agreed we would never tell anybody we went there, not even for a special report on TV, and we'd never go back again.

She had filled two shoe boxes with trinkets and bracelets the rats left behind. Now she was going to make some money. We each carried a shoe box under our arm. With the other arm we held onto each other.

Going into another dimension takes a lot out of you in ways you don't expect. I don't have the energy to go into it right now.

Unless you're set on repeating my experience, just take it from me and stay home.

Time passes differently in the other dimension. It doesn't line up exactly like it does here. It sort of slows down and jumps along. When Renata and I got back to the Eagle it was only 8:15, even though we'd been away for hours.

I had something to say to Renata. I had thought about it for a while. It was important to get it out right, and I was thinking of the best way to say it.

Renata knew something was coming her way. It's hard to say what she said or did that tipped me off, but I could tell we were thinking in the same direction.

As we drove home in the Eagle I was still trying to figure it out.

She turned to me and said, "You got somethin' to say, say it. I can't stand it no more."

I had thought up a million ways to put it and I went over them in my head as we walked from the Portal, but driving home now in the Eagle I could think of only one.

What I said was, "It's about time you brought back my Uncle's War Medal, Renata. Just give it to me and I'll forget it ever happened. Fair enough?"

She froze up when she heard that, stiff as a north pole icicle and she stared straight ahead. Last week I saw her stash a pair of earrings in her purse in Half Price Stores when she didn't think I was looking. She also had a habit of taking money from the tips left on the tables at Tuskies. Yesterday I was sure her father stole the War Medal from the shelf in the living room. I'm not counting him out, but now I was leaning more toward Renata. Either way, I felt sure she had to know about it.

It was just a hunch when I said it, but I knew by the way she reacted that I was right. "All I want is my Uncle's Medal back," I said.

She kept her eyes away from me but I could see they were wet. She was almost crying. Almost, but she didn't quite get there.

"Want to go back to my house now?"

"Take me home, please," she said.

"You don't want to go back to my house?"

"Take me home please. Now."

"Guess I'll take you home," I said.

I dropped her off at the house on the heights. I figured she would go inside and get the Medal and bring it back to the car. She'd say she was sorry, and I'll see her tomorrow at Tuskie's pizza.

But it didn't happen that way.

She got out of the car quickly and carried her shoe boxes to the front door. I waited a while and when she didn't come back to the car I took off and headed back to the old house.

Every time I drove over a bump the passenger door rattled because Renata didn't close it all the way. I was too tired to stop and fix it. The door rattled until I got to West Second street. About half way down I hit a bump just waiting for somebody like me to drive over it. The Eagle lurched forward and the suspension bottomed out. The door got stuck and I couldn't pry it open, but I never heard that rattle again.

# 93

It was late afternoon when Uncle Brucker arrived in Washington, DC. He spent his last five on gas somewhere out on the highway and he drove into the city with the gauge on empty. On Pennsylvania Avenue outside the White House, people waited on line for the day's last tour.

No time to find a parking space. The guards were closing the gate!

Uncle Brucker left the keys in the ignition and ran across the street and stood on the end of the tourist line.

The White House has one bowling alley, two swimming pools, a barber shop and thirteen bathrooms named after the thirteen colonies. Uncle Brucker made a quick stop at the Pennsylvania bathroom, and he joined the group and learned a few interesting facts, but he wasn't here for sightseeing.

He had more important things on his mind.

"I got information for the President," he said, and he elbowed his way through the crowd.

Down the hall from Uncle Brucker, the President walked with the VP. They had just been to a briefing and the President looked a little frustrated. Once again, he had asked his advisors: What are the rats working on now? Still, no answers. The President stopped at a vending machine outside the Oval Office.

At times like this he needed a snack.

"Who ordered these cup cakes?" the President asked, puzzled by the new selection.

"Why, you did, Mr. President. Don't you remember?" said the VP. He found four shiny new quarters in his pocket. "I got it covered." He put the quarters in the slot and pushed the button.

The cake slid down to the little door at the bottom of the machine.

Uncle Brucker broke through the crowd and ran down the hall. With a force he did not know, he pushed a Marine guard out of the way. Another guard leaped out of nowhere, two more up ahead, but they could not bring him down.

The President unwrapped what appeared to be a premium cup cake. It smelled so sweet and fresh. He brought the cake to his mouth, but before he could take a bite, Uncle Brucker cried, "Hold on, Mr. President! That's a rat cake you're eatin'!"

# 94

The President had a firm jaw that was pure leadership, and he had a trim moustache you don't notice on TV. With a neatly folded handkerchief he brushed a few crumbs from his mouth.

"So that's what they're working on," he said. "The rat cake!"

The President shook my Uncle's hand. Out of the corner of his eye he took in the whole picture, and he noticed the worn-out pair of shoes my Uncle wore.

"Come with me." He spoke to the man who had saved his life. "I'll introduce you to the Boss."

And together they rode the elevator down below the White House.

Like all elevators in the White House, it doesn't go straight up and down, it zigzags from floor to floor for security reasons. Uncle Brucker watched a spectacular display of lights and arrows on the control panel, and he thought of what he wanted to tell the President.

The President answered three calls on his cell phone. Each time he apologized to my Uncle with a we'll-talk-later wave of his hand. They zigzagged past a swimming pool and the bowling alley, and they stopped at a floor with no number that few people know about.

The Boss is an unsmiling white-haired woman of few words who took charge of the floors beneath the white house. In a military uniform of no particular rank or service, she greeted them at the elevator. Other than the 9mm automatic and the Master Key, she carried two flashlights on her belt, one marked Boss and the other marked Emergency President. She had worked in the White House for ages and everyone called her the Boss.

At the end of the hall, the Boss unlocked the door to a special room. Inside, shelves and shelves of shoes left behind by the Presidents throughout the years.

"Find a pair that fits," said the President. "The Boss will sign them over. It's my way of saying thanks."

Uncle Bucker looked through the room of shoes while the Boss and the President waited outside. A few minutes later Uncle Brucker stepped into the elevator wearing a pair of brown wing-tips with fancy stitching and old-fashioned leather heels.

"Who do you think wore them?" he asked the President. "Could it be Roosevelt? Maybe Lincoln himself?"

"Hell, I wouldn't know," said the President. "You have to match-up the sizes."

As it turned out, the President was a great guy who carried the burden of responsibility with total control, and he invited Uncle Brucker to stick around the White House for a few days as a Special Guest of The Administration or Special Advisor, he hadn't decided which.

Uncle Brucker was scheduled to attend the Awards Dinner on Thursday. No sense going home only to rush back. Meanwhile he'll take it easy, walk in the garden, get to know the place. Who knows, if he feels confident, maybe he'll get himself an official blue suit and a name badge and volunteer to give a few tours.

And so he did.

No house compares with the White House. In hospitality, heritage and accommodations, it has to be on top of the list. In a short time he built up confidence to spare, and he learned a lot of inside info that made for a great tour. And the tourists recognized his easy confidence as something special. Combine this with his insider insight, and you'll see why his tours were popular from the start.

Uncle Brucker bought a new blue tour suit. The White House barber trimmed my Uncle's beard. Ten-dollar tie. Official Presidential shoes. The line of tourists stretched out the door and all the way across the lawn and through the gate and halfway down the street where the Ram had stalled.

"The elevators zigzag for security reasons," he told the crowd as they entered the lobby. His words bounced off the marble columns and came back as solid reminders. "And the Oval Office we know about isn't the real Oval Office. The real Oval Office is on the other side of a hidden door, and that's where the President does his thinkin'."

# 95

The President rushed from briefing to briefing. Uncle Brucker led the tours. They passed each other in the halls of the White House. The President had no time for hello's, only for advice. But Uncle Brucker said hello every time they passed, and he always had time to advise the President.

"Hi, Mr. President!"

"What do you think of my domestic agenda?"

"Stick to it and don't waver."

"Foreign?"

"That's their concern. But I got proposals to discuss with ya—when you got the time."

"How about now? I don't have to rush to every briefing," said the President.

"In that case I've got some spare time too," the VP said.

"I was talkin' to the President," Uncle Brucker told him.

# 96

In the real Oval Office, the President and Uncle Brucker sat in soft leather chairs and discussed a few prime proposals. The President smiled and said it wasn't his department, he would see what he could do. He answered one cell call, one slight wave of his hand. After that he let the phone ring and they discussed everything from rat tracking to politics.

The President thought he'd be a bad rat tracker. He just didn't understand the nuances. Uncle Brucker smiled and said you'll be surprised what you're good at. Keep your eyes on the big things, don't worry about the nuances. Beneath it all, Uncle Brucker and the President were very much alike.

He noticed that the President and the VP were so different. The President could communicate so much through a simple gesture. The VP will talk for hours and not be understood. The President had the light bouncy walk of a tennis pro. He didn't play tennis, it came naturally to him, and the President had an agenda. The VP stumbled from briefing to briefing. He never seemed to go anywhere in particular, and he was sneaky.

Uncle Brucker moved his chair close to the President, and he told the President what he thought of the VP.

"I got my suspicions, Mr. President."

"Shhhh! He's standing outside the door."

Uncle Brucker whispered, "I'm not sayin' I know everythin', but what I don't know is pretty easy to figure out."

"No, you can't know everything," said the President. "But there's lots of stuff you can skip."

"I'm not callin' him a rat, but he does have certain ambitions I don't have to mention. Everybody wants to be President, Mr. President."

Elbows resting on soft leather, fingers curled under his chin, the President was deep in thought, also a little tired. To Uncle Brucker he looked like a sleepy addition to Mount Rushmore.

"The VP ordered the rat cakes," the President recalled. "He ordered the cakes, not me."

"You'd a remembered, right?"

"And he had a pocketful of change, as I recall."

"So's I noticed. . . . And that gun under his jacket."

"Pistol?"

"Automatic."

"No!"

"I seen it bulgin'!"

"He knows I won't tolerate that! I put signs up accordingly!"

"Signs?" Uncle Brucker stood up and took the signs from his pants pockets. Front pocket, PRESIDENT ONLY. Left rear, NO GUNS ALLOWED. Right rear, NO VENDING. The sneaky VP had stashed the signs behind a radiator in the Vermont bathroom. "Signs! You're trustin' him with signs?"

The President sprung from the chair like a man on fire. You could see his mustache clearly when he got mad, and his eyebrows looked a little like a mustache too.

"That settles it," he said. "The bastard's been hanging on my coattails for four long years. Come November I'm showing him the door! That means there'll be an opening for the Number Two spot pretty damn soon. But before I make my move I'd like to know I got my replacement. A Washington outsider, somebody who's easy and confident. . . . Yes, Brucker, I've seen your tours, and I've noticed how the people respond. Just give me the word. I'm proud to have you on the team."

It was a lot to spring on my Uncle, but at this point in his life he was prepared for just about anything. He didn't have to think about it for long. He made his decisions quickly and he stuck by them.

"I appreciate the offer, Mr. President, but I'm tellin' ya I can't accept. Another place, another time maybe, but offhand I can't tell you where or if ever. I got a serious affliction that's draggin' me down, my two-week assignment's takin' about a month longer than expected, and I got a boy at home could be starvin' on my account. But I can recommend someone just as good, and he's got the experience."

# 97

The next VP presided at the Awards Dinner in the main dining room of he White House on Thursday.

Arriving early, Uncle Brucker found his table in the back of the room. He thought he knew everything about the White House, but he did not know the dining room expanded as the guests arrived. Curtains spread apart, walls retracted, Starburst chandeliers hung from the ceiling. An eight-piece ensemble performed on a slide-out stage. Two hundred tables. Eight hundred guests.

After the intro, the next VP sat at the table with Uncle Brucker. The VP was General Hardesty.

"I couldn't ask for a better recommendation," he said.

"There ain't nobody better to recommend," Uncle Brucker replied.

Soup. Salad. Entree. Dinner was nearly done. When would they present him with his award?

He had prepared an important speech. He would accept not for himself but for his men. For Ex-Lieutenant Willett, the Doc, Duffy, Midnight and Downie, for how they suffered and what they gave. It was all thought-out in his speech. The Boss let him practice that afternoon downstairs in the Guest Speaker's Room.

But after a while Uncle Brucker realized he wouldn't get a chance to give his speech. The meal was over and they didn't seem to be handing out any awards. Three Martinis, one more beer. Cigars were lit around the table: the VP, a scientist, and a diplomat.

Uncle Brucker stood up. "Hey, where's my award? I mean, for my squad. For my squad! I got a speech prepared for the occasion." He was loud.

The violin stalled on a low note and the music faded out. Somewhere in the kitchen a busboy dropped a plate. Everybody looked toward my Uncle. General Hardesty realized my Uncle was upset. He put his arm around his old friend and drew him close.

As the music started up again he said, "The President doesn't give out awards anymore, or even citations. Sometimes it's just the meal. Your choice of dessert."

Uncle Brucker only told me part of his speech and I have nothing to go by for filling in the rest.

But I know where to go if you want to check it out.

The entire speech is available on disc in the Guest Speaker's Room on an unmarked floor somewhere beneath the White House. Public access, private booths. You can go there and listen Monday through Friday. First I'd check the hours.

Just take the zigzagging elevator down to the floor nobody knows about. At the end of the hallway there's a door without a sign. The Boss is the old woman with the keys on her belt and no name tag. She'll look you over without a smile, but don't let it bother you. If the door is locked she'll let you in.

# 98

Uncle Brucker finally made it home early Friday morning before I went to school. His two-week assignment had lasted thirty-six days.

I got out of bed and went to the window when I heard the President's Limousine pull into the driveway. The Ram pulled in behind it.

The door swung open and the President got out the back with a coffee mug in his hand. Uncle Brucker followed. One secret service man came out the passenger side and another climbed out of the Ram. They stood by the limo in the shade of the willow and drank their coffee and talked.

The President drank from a mug marked President. The license plate on the limo also said President. My Uncle drank from a paper cup with a cardboard sleeve. The Secret Service men used plain, sleeveless, unmarked cups.

I didn't know how he met the President or why he came home with him until later, but I figured correctly it was all about his Special Assignment. Somewhere along the way my Uncle took a bath and cleaned himself up. He looked a lot better than last time I saw him in the tunnel, that's for sure.

Before the President returned to the limo, he shook my Uncle's hand warmly, and he thanked him for saving his life and helping out around the White House, if only for a little while.

"Now that you're gone," said the President, "the White House just isn't the same. I think I'll relocate."

"But you're the President and the President lives in the White House."

"The President lives where he wants. It's in the contract. Keep a bed ready for me, Brucker," he said.

"Always."

"Feather pillows?"

"You bet."

And then the President and the Secret Service men got back in the limo and backed out of the driveway, and I saw it all from the bedroom window in the old house.

# 99

Uncle Brucker went directly to the refrigerator, grabbed a can of Boomers and popped it open with his thumb before the refrigerator door closed. Next he took the beer into the bathroom and stayed there for two flushes. He came out with a cigarette in his mouth and sat at the kitchen table and went through the mail and drank and smoked.

With eyes half shut he checked out the kitchen, and everything was the way he left it. The pile of mail on the kitchen floor by the closet. The ceiling tiles hanging down over the refrigerator, the water stains on the floor from when the pipes burst, the Heritage Mugs on top of the fridge.

A photograph of Grandma and Grandpa Thompson hung between the windows on the kitchen wall. It was taken thirty-six years ago and Grandma and Grandpa were old even back then. They stood hand in hand in front of the barn like they were welcoming him back home.

"Welcome back from the Rat Wars," Grandpa Thompson said. And Grandma Thompson, "Brucker, you look more like your dad every day!"

And it's true, now that he is as old as Grandpa in the picture. Shave off his beard, and I bet you can't tell them apart.

At this point I might have dozed off for few minutes, but when Uncle Brucker opened my bedroom door I was back in bed with the sheet over my head.

I pulled off the sheet and sat up.

"Hiya, Unc!"

He fell back and bumped into the dresser, terrified, and he put his arms up to shield his face.

"Don't spring at me!" he said.

"Sorry, Unc."

"I come home, first thing he does, he springs at me!"

I should have realized right off that something was wrong by the frightened look on his face. It was a good joke, we should be laughing, but he was just plain scared. I should have known it, but I was so happy to see him I didn't give it much thought, and I let it slip away.

Breakfast: bacon and eggs and toast. Coffee? Ready in minutes, steaming in his World's Greatest Uncle Cup. Milk, sugar, spoon, plenty of napkins.

192 | Leslie Peter Wulff

"More sugar, Unc?"

"That'll do."

"Any time," I said. And then I had to ask him. "Was that who I think it is in the driveway?"

Uncle Brucker didn't answer. He put a finger to his lips instead, which meant it's not my place to ask.

He drank and I watched. He was slow sipping the coffee, slow eating the raisin cake. His eyelids were wrinkled old blankets that covered his sleepy eyes. I thought of what he went through the last few weeks and I forgot for a minute that I was with him.

Then he noticed the empty shelf in the living room, the high shelf where the War Medal should be.

"How's my War Medal?"

"Fine," I said.

"Dust it?"

"I don't go near it"

"Bring it here, let's see."

This morning before sunrise I heard footsteps on the porch. Through the window I saw somebody running under the willows. When I went outside I found a paper bag by the door. The War Medal was inside. I took it in but I didn't put it on the shelf yet. I left it in the bag on the counter.

"I ain't been dustin' it," I said. "I moved it to dust around it."

I grabbed the bag and backed into the living room and quickly put it back on the high shelf where it belonged.

I poured another cup. He drank about half and in the middle of it his half-shut eyes closed all the way, and he tilted forward.

His two-week assignment was over. During that time he traveled to another dimension, fought the rats, wrestled a few, and he drove to Washington DC and met the President. Why shouldn't he be tired? Sleep caught up with him, and he couldn't stay awake any longer.

I caught his cup before it spilled and eased his head down on the table. I didn't wake him up or try to move him. Instead I went to the living room and got a pillow from the couch and put it under his head.

And he slept in the kitchen with his head on the pillow all morning. All morning long he slept, and he was still asleep on the table when I got home from school at 3:15.

# 100

The Ram was steady on the highway, as solid as a tank, but the Eagle had its peculiarities. It stalled out if you wake it up too early. Just let it sleep until ten o'clock before you turn the key, and don't pump it.

The distress calls had piled up while he was gone. We had a lot of stops to make. The rats were causing trouble, and my Uncle insisted we get out early Saturday and waste no time.

"The Eagle ain't an early car," I told him. "It ain't goin' nowhere 'till ten."

It was only 9:35.

He stuck the key in the ignition and turned it a few times but the engine didn't catch. The battery wore down in no time and the engine flooded out. That's when I noticed the fat cop driving down the road. A minute later, he pulled into the driveway.

"If we took the Ram we'd be out of here," I said. "You had to take the Eagle and you flooded it. Meet Mr. Trooper."

"What did you do that sent him here?"

"Didn't do nuthin'."

"Then sit up straight and look him in the eye."

The fat cop got out of the Police GT and closed the door. Uncle Brucker walked over and they shook hands. The cop said a few words to Uncle Brucker. Uncle Brucker said a few words to the cop. The cop leaned back against his car. Uncle Brucker leaned back too. The name on his sheriff's shield was Trooper L. Ditton.

I don't know if they were old friends, but you'd think so, the way they smiled and leaned and talked like they shared a lot of memories and hadn't seen each other for a while.

Uncle Brucker had a way with cops. If they weren't old friends already, they would be pretty soon.

As they talked Trooper Ditton glanced in my direction. His slicked-back hair looked like he just painted it on. He held his hat in his left hand and with his right he patted his hair to check if the paint was dry.

Then he put his hat back on and he walked over to the Eagle.

"This ain't the first time I been here," he said to me. "Out of the car, please."

"Yes, sir."

I'm in for it this time. He has something on me I didn't know about, and it's bad news. He going to arrest me for sure. The handcuffs hung from the Trooper Ditton's belt. I got out of the car and put my hands out. Guilty.

But instead of cuffing me, he looked down at me with a toothy smile and said, "May I shake your hand, son?"

He held out his big, meaty hand, and I shook it.

"You must be proud of yourself," said Trooper Ditton.

"Me? A little, I guess."

"A little, he says a little."

"I mean a lot."

"Well, you should be." He looked at me like I was a hero who just saved the town from giant killer insects. "And you're . . . how old? Only sixteen?"

"Sixteen's pretty old. I mean it's old for me."

"Smart for your age too, are ya? Readin' on anuther level. I guess your education can wait a while, bein' you're advanced. But not for long or you got a weasel nippin' at your ass. You know what I'm sayin'? Well, listen to me good, or you'll find out first hand what you only want to hear about."

Trooper Ditton's front teeth stuck out on top and he had a goofy look on his face when he talked. He was a real friendly cop, the friendliest. He probably had a bunch of little troopers at home, and they loved him and he gave them bb guns and bikes for Christmas.

"You gotta stay educated no matter what," I said. "Make up the time in night school. Or Saturday's good."

"Take all the equivalent courses you can," said Trooper Ditton, "It'll add up in your favor. Where there's a will, there's a way, and I know you got the will. I can tell by your bright eyes. OK, I call you Bright Eyes? In the meantime keep up the good work. You hear me, Bright Eyes?"

"I hear you."

"I know you hear me. What I'm askin' is, you gonna keep up the good work?"

"You know I will."

Trooper Ditton shook my hand again and said goodbye to his new old friend Uncle Brucker, and he took off his hat and tossed it on the front seat of the Police GT. The car sat kinda low with him in it. Better get new shocks. Try Koni adjustable. Or go on a diet.

Trooper Ditton started up his Town Car, and I went over and checked it out.

"What's under the hood? A two-sixty-five, six?" I asked.

"Not any more. They put a three-twenty-four in last year."

"Sure wish I could drive," I said as he backed out of the driveway. "But I guess I gotta wait till I'm seventeen. Next year, I hope."

Back in the Eagle. "What did you tell him, Unc?" I asked.

"Didn't tell him nuthin'."

"Did he say anythin' to you? Why's he lookin' for me?"

"He didn't bring up the subject and I didn't ask him."

"But you musta said somethin'."

"There ain't nuthin' you can tell a cop. You can only imply. I don't know what he got out of it, that's up to him. All I can do is point him in the right direction. It's a trick I'll teach you sometime."

"How about now?"

Then Uncle Brucker shut down again, just like before. Like somebody switched him off, he just shut down. Eyes shut, he opened his mouth and a word almost came out, but his head fell back against the headrest and a snore came out instead.

I'll never know why that cop was looking for me, and there's no way to find out. Unless somebody writes in.

I went inside the house and let him sleep. In a while I came out and then I went back in and let him sleep some more. Uncle Brucker the Rat Killer snored like a polar bear.

# 101

We sat around the house after dinner. I dozed off at the kitchen table and he moved to the living room couch. I came in when the TV woke me up and I sat in the recliner. He pointed a finger at my face and I brushed the table crumbs off my cheek. Then he got up and took a beer from the refrigerator. When he came back I had the couch and he went back to the recliner.

For a while we didn't talk. We didn't need to. It wasn't like I knew what he was thinking, more like he knew what I was about to say. So we just thought about what we'd say and took it from there. We didn't have to talk all the time, and we didn't really care what TV show we watched.

All this time the rat was growing inside him. But it wasn't straight-line, day after day growing. It grew and shrunk down and grew again. It grew in ways he didn't know about and can't explain, and it left him confused and tired-out. If he couldn't find some way to live with it, that rat would soon push the old Uncle Brucker out.

"Uncle Brucker," I had to ask him. "Can you be friends with a rat?"

"Friends? How can you be friends with a rat?"

"I mean if he gets inside you."

"Not when he's inside you pullin' the other way," he said.

"But even best friends argue."

"You figure a man and a rat ain't ever meant to get along."

"Put 'em in the same room they'll argue," I said. "Put 'em in the same body—"

"They'd fight!"

"Always?"

"Always."

"Is that a rat scratch?" I asked him.

"Where?"

"Right there. That cheek scratch."

He touched his cheek. "No, I'da knowed it."

"Well, can you?"

"What?"

"Be friends with a rat."

Uncle Brucker thought about it for a while. I always say that but who knows what he's thinking about really. Maybe he went on to something else and came back. Or maybe he just sat there.

He finished his beer, put the can on the floor next to the recliner. He lit a cigarette, leaned back and smoked, staring up at the ceiling and through the ceiling beyond the clouds past the moon.

His beard looked like it grew half an inch since yesterday. I know it must have grown somewhat, but I'm saying a lot.

Finally, cigarette halfway down, he said, "Best you can be is neighbors."

# 102

"OK, Unc. Let's cruise!"

Sunday morning and we're finally out on the road.

Sunny day + the Ram + a lot of people on the streets = a prime day for Identifying.

This is the day I've been waiting for. We had a lot of work to do and I was ready to go. We'll have a great time together, driving and counting and laughing at the miserable rats like we used to. Maybe we'll drive all the way to Conklin and eat a burger and twister fries, come back with a new high total.

They were sinking in all over. They hung out in front of Tuskies and Mid-City Lanes and on the corner of North and South Main. A dude in western boots and a too-big cowboy hat leaned against a utility pole. He pulled his hat down low. I'm sure he saw me noticing him, then he walked to the street corner and disappeared. Put him on the list.

I thought we were heading to Half Price Stores but instead Uncle Brucker turned right on Meridian and stopped at Food Saver.

"Good idea," I said as we walked to the store. "Stockin' up on food in case we get too busy countin' and we lose track a time. Just don't buy no perishables."

Uncle Brucker hated the supermarket. Usually he grabbed an armload of canned stuff from Aisle Two and raisin cakes from Aisle Nine and we were out in minutes.

Today was different. Today he found a cart outside the entrance and he took his time as he pushed it down the aisles. He checked out every item on the shelf like supermarkets were just invented and wow what a great place.

"Meet you in the car," I said.

He came out and we sat in the car. He didn't turn the ignition and we didn't drive anywhere. We sat in the car like I said.

After a while I spoke up.

"This car's got wheels, don't it? Got an engine too. You got the keys. Put the key in the ignition, turn on the engine, it spins the wheels and we'll get the hell outta here."

"We ain't goin' nowhere till I remember what I'm forgettin' to get," he said. "There's no sense drivin' around to get back here again."

I hadn't spoken to Renata for days. Last time we talked on the phone I told her I wasn't mad at her. Why is she avoiding me? It's over, I explained. My Uncle is home, I got the Medal back. Somebody dropped it off and I'll never know who and I don't want to know. I never forget, but I'm a forgiving guy and that's worth more than forgetting. So why doesn't she return my phone calls?

We cruised down Center, Uncle Brucker sat up straight and leaned over the wheel. He reminded me of a ship captain on a foggy night off the Outer Banks with his nose cold in the wind. I've never seen a ship captain lean over a wheel and I don't know where they point their noses, and I've never been to the Outer Banks, but that's how it seemed to me.

Vicks and Bones came out of Mid-City carrying their bowling bags and Bones saw the Ram right away. They watched us make the turn. Bones was a funny guy who held his nose when he farted. Vicks real name is Duane but everyone called him Vicks because his head was shaped like the cough drop. He smiled and pointed to Renata.

There she was, Renata, walking across the street.

But this time she wasn't standing around with her girlfriends. She was walking hand and hand with her new boyfriend, Kip. I slid down in the seat so she couldn't see me.

As usual, Uncle Brucker knows what's going on even though he doesn't show it.

"Some folks might say you lost your grip on the situation, but if you ask me it just ain't workin' out," he said.

"You don't have to say nuthin'. I didn't ask you nuthin'."

"Are you gonna listen to me next time?"

"Not a chance," I said.

Hunkered down in the seat where no one could see me, I realized my Identifiers weren't working. Something was wrong. Usually they jumped like crazy when I drive around town.

As soon as I took them off I saw what went wrong. No wonder they didn't work. I put on Uncle Brucker's old Identifiers by mistake!

What happened to mine?

I checked the glove box, the floor, under the seat. I found them stuck behind Uncle Brucker in the cushion of the front seat. When I pulled them out the case rattled. I opened it up and saw the pieces.

"Look what you did, Unc! You busted my Identifiers!"

Of all the things to bust, the one thing that can't be replaced. I'll never find another pair of Identifiers because there's only one rightful pair, and now they're busted. Busted!

"Sorry," he said.

"Yeah. Right. Sorry."

"I said I'm sorry."

"That does a lot a good."

I didn't say another word all the way back home. I was busy checking out my glasses. The right arm had snapped off the frame and both lenses were cracked. When I got home I tried to glue them back together. All night long I tried and I only said three words to my Uncle, including dinner.

"Pass the salt," I said, because he was a salt-hogger.

# 103

That night while Uncle Bucker slept, I took out my Rat Chart. I had started it a few days ago after Uncle Brucker returned and it was coming along pretty damn good.

It was all written down here on the chart. Symptoms, percentages. I made notes and added to it all week. Now I took a close look at it and made some minor adjustments. I switched a few symptoms around, evened out the percentages based on what I had recently observed. It's not perfect because nothing is, but it made a lot of sense to me.

This is what I came up with:

## RAT CHART

Percentage Rat/Symptoms

20%: occasional cravings (eating right from the refrigerator, "starvin"), rat dreams

30%: rat cravings everyday at ten (supermarket) and two, forgetfulness (Schnells), licking his lips, scratching and itching

40%: trouble with math, Rat naps at eleven and three, (dozing in the Eagle), ("I'm tired." "Gotta nap.")

50%: hoarding food in the supermarket (same as gluttony?), rat breath (foul breath)

60%: impulsive behavior, (slamming on brakes, stopping at Schnells), nibbling

70%: forgetfulness ("I wonder what I'm getting.")

80%: shoplifting?

90%: nose-writing?

A nd this:

He slept on and off during the day, never for very long. He ate at odd hours but nothing added up to a meal. The faraway look on his face meant something was going wrong on the inside.

Whatever he went through in Rat Land, it was nothing compared to the horror of what was happening to him now.

According to the chart, Transposition has taken over and Genomorphism is almost compete.

Uncle Brucker is turning into a rat.

# 104

H e said he's going down to Minks to see Dotty. He heard she was back in town. It was about 9:30 now. He'll be back in a while.

I waited fifteen minutes until nine forty-five, and I followed him to town in the Eagle. He never looks in his rearview when he drives, so I was right behind him all the way. He went past the diner, turned right on Lower Main, and came back.

There was a dumpster out back in the parking lot. He pulled in and parked next to it. I parked on the street. Uncle Brucker waited in the Ram until the cars moved on, and he got out and walked to the dumpster. In the Eagle behind a Cherokee Sport, I saw all I cared to see. He came in at 2:30 after a night of sniffing garbage, hanging out in dumpsters, drinking beer and peeing in the bushes all around town.

He was as quiet as he could be, which isn't very quiet. He bumped into the kitchen table. The ashtray fell off and rolled down the hall and crashed into my door, and I got out of bed.

"Is Dotty back yet?" I asked him in the kitchen.

"If she is, I ain't seen her."

"I guess you'd a seen her."

He opened the refrigerator and held onto the door, looking for something to eat. The refrigerator couldn't hold his weight. On top, the Heritage Mugs rattled.

"Stop leanin'. You're tippin' the fridge," I said.

"No I ain't."

"What do you call it when things fall over?"

"A lot a things tip and fall. It don't start out with me."

He held onto the refrigerator door and he mentioned other things that tip——like the leaning Tower of Pisa, for example. You can't blame that on him because he was never in the vicinity.

A quart of milk fell over on the bottom shelf. Tip the fridge a little more, those mugs will slide off the top and they won't bounce.

I knew what was bound to happen and I went to my room.

A few seconds later I heard the crash, but I didn't come out right away. I waited until he called.

"Walt?"

"What is it, Unc?"

"Accident, Walt."

# 105

At the kitchen table I worked on my New Rat Chart. The Old Rat Chart was just OK. It jumped out at you but it didn't grab your attention. I added to it and changed things around. I used a red Sharpie to highlight the numbers. I wrote the symptoms in black and underlined them in red so it would get his attention, and the New Rat Chart was both a jumper and a grabber.

I stepped back and looked at it and decided it needed one final touch, so I wrote DELUXE in red across the top.

By consulting my DELUXE Rat Chart, I could see how the inner rat moved in on Uncle Brucker. He could swing up to eighty percent rat in one day, and back again. Like a pendulum swinging out of control, each day he swings further.

You got to grab hold, Uncle Brucker. Take a good look at yourself. You can stop the swinging if you really try. Steady yourself, Unc. Balance will come naturally. If you don't stop the swingin one day you'll never come out.

I left the DELUXE Rat Chart on the kitchen table. Sooner or later he'll come for a beer.

"The hell's that?" he said.

"Oh, that. That's nuthin'," I said.

"Gotta be somethin' or I'm seein' things."

"Oh, you mean this chart? This here's my Rat Chart."

"No kiddin'? A Rat Chart, you say. Let me see."

He put the can of Boomers down on the table and pushed his glasses up on his nose. I had his attention and I was holding on.

"Take a good look at it, Unc. Basically it charts the swingin', which should be startin' up about ten."

He checked the wall clock: Nine fifty-five.

"You're right. Almost rat cravin' time, accordin' to this chart here. I could use a nibble myself."

"Nibble! You said nibble."

"So? So what," he said.

"Rats nibble. Humans eat. Hoardin' food at the supermarket. And forgetfulness. That's part of the swingin' too. It's all down here on my new chart. Take a look at yourself, Unc. Check out the X's."

"You went a little crazy with the X's."

"You won't go out Identifyin' cause rats can't count."

"What did you say?" he said.

"I said you don't wanna go countin' cause rats can't count."

"I thought you said that. Like a rat I am, a big ole rat. You make this chart by yourself?"

"Based on facts. I don't make up the facts, and I know what I see."

"The rat's movin' in on you, Unc. You ain't what you used to be. You gotta shake him out before he shakes you out. Let me help you try."

"I've been tryin', I really have, but I'll try again just for you," he said. He sounded like he meant it.

"I mean try, really try. Try hard."

"I'll do it for you, Walt."

"Show me hard."

"I'll show ya, Walt. I'll show ya hard!"

He grabbed the seat of the chair, spreads his legs out and steadied himself. He clamped his teeth down and his eyes went up under his lids and he groaned. He groaned like he was lifting a boulder out of hell's basement. Veins popped out on his hands and his forehead like wormy skin snakes.

But what good did it do?

When you get down to it, not a bit.

And what did he show me? He showed me how to make a face. That's no way to shake the rat out. Make a face. Grunt. And he didn't do it just for me. He did it for the rat inside him because that's who he does everything for nowadays.

He went to the living room and sat on the couch and opened the newspaper, ignoring me. He didn't want to listen to me any more.

"Bring me a beer, will ya, Walt?"

"Non I won't," I said. "Ask your rat to get it for you. You and him are pals."

And I left the Rat Chart on the kitchen table and went to my room for the night.

# 106

*S*cratch-Scratch Knock! Scratch Knock-Knock!*
He came out about four-thirty, snooping around the barn and scratching-up for a fight. I watched him from the kitchen window. He ran up to the house, teased me with a scratch, but I chased him away before he knocked.

Now it was twenty after seven and he was banging on the back door.

Uncle Brucker had melted into the recliner with the newspaper on his lap, and everything was the same as usual except the little things were different. For one thing, I didn't feel like picking up his empty beer cans. And Cole's Law had just ended and he didn't hum the theme song. A great show, you can't help humming. Right, Uncle Brucker? Those little things add up.

*Scratch-Scratch Knock! Scratch Knock-Knock!*

"Ain't you gonna say it?" I asked him. "Ain't you gonna say 'Don't tell me I gotta wrestle that damn rat now?' You always say it. Ain't you gonna wrestle that damn rat?"

Uncle Brucker just sat there.

"Part of me wants to go," he said, "but part of me just don't give a shit. And that ain't enough to get me on my feet, and barely enough to consider it."

*Scratch-Scratch Knock! Scratch Knock-Knock!* This time he couldn't do it. This time he had too much beer in him to do anything, four or five cans on the floor. He looked at me over the top of his reading glasses. His eyes were doing the talking and his mouth was just standing by.

"Well I guess it's my turn, innit?" I said. "You always said someday it might come down to me to carry on the tradition. I guess that day is today."

"It's up to you, Walt, but tradition don't work unless it's passed on."

It was a heavy decision because it carried the weight of everything that followed. But I knew my Uncle couldn't wrestle that damn rat forever. Now it was up to me. I had to go.

"I don't want to screw up tradition," I said.

*Scratch-Scratch Knock! Scratch Knock-Knock!*

"I'm cummin' to get ya, Wrestlin' Rat!"

"Remember," Uncle Brucker said. "Knee jab to the stomach. Left to the jaw. Go right to a Cherokee Chokehold. Don't follow him in no bushes. Fight him out in the open. He moves fast for a big rat."

"Don't worry, I won't lose. He's just a dirty old rat."

"One thing before you go, Walt. Upstairs in my dresser, take a look in the top drawer."

I ran up the stairs and opened the drawer. Don't ask me how, but I had an idea what it was on the way up. When I saw the gold lettering I knew I was right. I held it up in front of me in the mirror.

"Wow! An Incredible Impostor suit!"

In the mirror Uncle Brucker looked over my shoulder.

"Had this one made exactly like mine."

It was almost like Uncle Brucker's wrestling suit but not exactly. It was only the shirt and it didn't say Impostor. It just said Incredible, and it was too tight. I had to take off my undershirt to get it on. I guess it looked OK with my jeans.

"It's only half a suit. Where's the pants that go with it?"

"Gotta talk to 'em about the pants," he said.

# 107

*S*cratch-Scratch Knock! Scratch Knock-Knock!*

    I chased him off the porch. He ran behind the barn. I hid in the pig shed until he came out, then I went after him. He dashed across the back yard and I was right behind him.

He was a good runner, a good escaper. He had a lot of experience. But I was good too. I've always been fast and that cool suit helped me run faster. I chased him all the way to the pond. Twice I almost caught up with him but each time he got up on his rear legs and sprinted ahead. Once I fell in the dirt and that's when I hurt my elbow.

By the time I got to the pond I was out of breath and it was getting dark. I stopped at the rotten rowboat where the camper rats hung out. That's where I'd hide, under that upside-down boat. I flipped over the rotten boat with my foot. Nothing, just the old rusty grill and burnt-up charcoal.

Where is that damn rat?

*Scratch-Scratch Knock! Scratch Knock-Knock!*

And there he was! Hiding in the bushes next to the old rotten boat, ready to jump me. But I wasn't going in there after him, not with one bad arm and a warning.

"Come out, Wrestlin' Rat! I know you're in there."

"He-he!" he laughed.

I only wrote down he-he, but he laughed for a long time, a squealy high-pitched laugh that started off with he-he's and changed to ha-ha's halfway through. I just don't feel like writing down all those he-he's and ha-ha's.

"What are you laughin' at, Wrestlin' Rat?"

"That suit don't fit."

"Sure it does. How'd I get it on me?"

"Maybe you put it on when it did fit. Maybe it shrunk in the rain and you can't get out of it. Reasons don't always jump out at you. I gotta think about it. . . . Anyway, I'm tired of runnin'. Are you tired of chasin'?"

"I'm real tired of chasin'. I wish I'm the one who's gettin' away."

"Listen to the night," he said.

And for a while we sat and listened to the night. We listened but we couldn't hear anything. Not one cricket or a hound dog barking or a far-off radio, not even the cars on 94. I don't know how quiet the night can get, but it can't get more quiet than this. It's what the night sounds like when you take everything else away.

Then the crickets started up again, one at a time, filling in all around.

I rubbed my aching elbow. It's swelling up now.

"Look at that elbow!" he said. "This ain't no match for me. Now I gotta win by default, which means I lose. Oh, what am I gonna do? What am I gonna do? All these years we've been stretchin' it out. Your Uncle wins a match, I win the next. We planned it that way. I guess it had to happen sooner or later. I'm finished now. They're gonna make me retire. It's everythin' I ever been and now it's nuthin' I can be. You call that winnin'? Well this rat calls it losin'. There'll be a new Wrestlin' Rat and then who am I? I've been workin' out too."

"You been knockin' harder."

"I know."

I sat on a log next to him, but the log was too small. He kicked over another log. I put two logs together and made a pretty good seat.

We talked about our situation. I told him my real name is Walt, not Incredible like it says on my suit. He told me his real name is Wrestling Rat and the next rat's name is Wrestling Rat. It goes like that. He's the best wrestler of his generation because he's not all look and show, but he thought Uncle Brucker was only so-so.

"He's got the weight advantage but basically he wrestles like a man," he said.

And he laughed again, that squealy laugh, the kind of laugh you have to watch out or you'll laugh that way too. The whole bush shook.

Who would win a match between us? It's hard to say. On one hand, he had the experience. But on the other hand, I was determined to win. Experience vs determination. He thought he would win. I knew I would win—if I had two good arms, that is. With only one good arm it would be a tough match.

He could easily get out of a German Headlock, so he said, but he could be tricking me so I wouldn't use it on him. He had scratched-knocked on back doors all over the county, looking for a fight, but only Uncle Brucker took him up on his offer.

"And you, Incredible."

"Not Incredible. Walt."

"Don't believe everythin' men say about miserable rats cause I don't believe everythin' rats say about lazy men."

"The barn is a good place to hide out when you're scratchin' up for a fight," I told him.

"Especially the loft," he said.

# 108

We sat and listened to the night again. But now it was a different night filled with crickets and sirens and barking dogs and far-off radios and thunder from a hidden storm. He shook his head and his ears sagged, disappointed. I knew how he felt. We heard everything else but we couldn't hear the night.

"So, you wanna learn?" he asked.

"OK."

And he taught me how to scratch-knock.

"Basically it's an open-fist knock. Knock with the palm of your hand, then scratch down with your fingers. Remember that, you got it down."

"Like this?"

*Scratch-Scratch Knock! Scratch Knock-Knock!*

"There you go. You catch on real quick for a man," he told me. "Every rat's got his way of doin' things, and you can't always figure it out."

I said, "That goes for men too."

And I told him what happened to Uncle Brucker, holed-up in the Rat Factory for days. No food. No water. He had to eat those rat cakes. He had to eat them or he'd starve.

The Wrestling Rat gave me some very good advice.

"The rat inside your Uncle is actin up cause he's on a reverse schedule," he said. "He's up all day, sleepin' all night, when it should be the other way around. And his eatin' schedule's reversed too. It ain't so easy gettin' used to somethin' that's always been another way, and it's throwin' him off balance. The rat inside could be dyin' for lack of consideration, and if that happens, your Uncle goes with him. So you see, he's gotta go back through the Portal. If he don't go by himself, they'll send an Inspector to take him back. Get that schedule out of reverse and back in order, and everything will balance out. Every man's got a bit of a rat in him, you just gotta learn to live with it."

"Everybody?"

"Everybody. Just like every rat's got a bit of a man in him. We're stuck that way, bit parts of each other. But thirty rat cakes, I don't know. . . . That's gotta tip the balance."

"Wrestlin' Rat, are you thinkin' what I'm thinkin'?"

"Depends what you're thinkin'."

"I'm thinkin' nobody's keepin' score. And I don't see no refs around."

"There ain't nobody, just us. Even match?"

"That's what I'm thinkin'."

Now I heard someone coming from the far side of the pond. Footsteps coming closer, voices getting louder. Kids from Colony Park?

"Goodbye, Wrestlin' Rat," I said. "We better go."

"Yeah we better. Goodbye, Incredible."

"Not Incredible. Walt."

"You don't know who you are. I go by the suit."

The bush shook and he ran off, scratch-knocking on all the back doors down the road.

# 109

The rain came with no warning and the wind shook the rain off the trees as I walked back to the old house. I took my time all the way, even when it poured. The Wrestling Rat gave me a whole lot to think about.

Rain is good for thinking and so is walking. Walking moves your thoughts along while the rain washes your mind clear, and that makes for a new kind of thinking.

When you have a lot to consider, and it's wearing you down, do what I do: take a walk in the rain. You'll be surprised how good you'll feel when the rain washes everything clean.

I got home and I felt like a fresh new person who saw things in a new way.

And everything was quickly different. The back door suddenly needed a paint job. The hinges had a different squeak. The door latch hung on by one screw. How could I have missed that all these years?

"Hey, Unc!"

*Scratch-Scratch Knock! Scratch Knock-Knock!*

"Hear that, Unc?"

*Scratch-Scratch Knock! Scratch Knock-knock!*

"Fooled ya, didn't I? That's me scratch-knockin'. It ain't no rat. I been taking lessons from the master."

From the kitchen through the living room and into the hall I left a wet foot trail. But I didn't find my Uncle anywhere on the first floor. The old Rat Killer was probably upstairs.

I called up to him and told him the score, "I won one and he won one, just like always—if you know what I mean. So everythin's OK." And I climbed the stairs. "We got things to talk about, Unc. The Wrestlin' Rat told me, everybody's got a bit of a rat in him. Everybody. You and Renata and me. Them government lists don't mean nuthin' when you keep that in mind. You can rip them up and throw them in the wind. Whatever's inside you, you gotta learn to live with it."

At the top of the stairs I sat down and rubbed my sore elbow. I don't know why people do that because it doesn't do much good. It don't make it worse, so I rubbed it anyway.

'You can get a little confused when everything comes together,' Uncle Brucker said. 'Not everybody's right all the time because that would make you perfect, and nobody's perfect. And you can't figure everything out on your own, either.'

"Hey, Unc. Where are ya?"

Finally I checked the driveway and the Ram was gone.

# 110

Uncle Brucker didn't come home Thursday night.

It's not like him to stay out all night, and when he's late he'll leave a note.

I couldn't sleep. All night I lay on top of my bed with my clothes on and I listened for the Ram. I heard a couple F150s, and an ancient El Camino with a broken tailgate went up and down the hill, but no Ram.

The sun came through the kitchen window and I filled the thermos with coffee. Today I'm tracking down my Uncle. Cross school off my list—but not all the way off. Charlee and I are scheduled to give our report on World War II today. I'll show up when I find my uncle and I'll be there when I get there.

First stop: Minks. Maybe he passed out in the corner booth, and Dotty didn't notice him on her way out last night. I'll bust through the door and drag him to the Ram and pour him a hot cup.

Don't give up, I told myself when I saw Mink's empty lot. I'll find him somewhere. Or when I come back he'll be sitting on the porch with a smile and a beer.

After Minks, I checked the strip mall parking lot. Maybe he ran into his old-time drinking buddies, had a good time and passed out in the Ram. Or somebody took him in for the night. It's happened before. With the rat behind the wheel, he could be anywhere.

It was all too much for the poor old Eagle. It tried but it couldn't keep up. It wasn't just age that worked against it. Age held it down while rust punched it out and mileage worked it over. The next hill was a tough one. The Eagle lurched forward and stalled again.

The Eagle could have put in just a little more effort and helped me out, and I wouldn't be so mad. I drive hard, but you can't say I'm neglectful.

And I don't care what anybody says, four quarts of oil is plenty for any car. You want just enough or it's a waste of money. Pay no attention to the manual, use your brain instead. You can't overfill anymore than you can under fill.

The real trouble began after I stopped for gas in Otis. I turned the key and it wouldn't start up. Damn it, Eagle, I'm countin' on you! I jiggled the key and waited, which works for every other car, but not the Eagle. I pressed the pedal to the floor and pumped the gas and held the shifter in second. It caught on and we rolled along for a while. Then black smoke came up behind me. Engine light went on. Fuck you, Eagle! I know what's up next.

On 94 West the engine cut out and I pulled the Eagle over for the last time.

About the engine oil: I took two quarts out of the Monte Carlo and put one in the Eagle and one in the Camaro about a month ago. Maybe I should have put both quarts in the Eagle. But that's not the problem. The engine was dying and it would cut out no matter how many quarts I failed to put in.

I put on the parking brake and left the old clunker R.I.P. on the side of the road.

Here's what I didn't do: I didn't pat the faithful Eagle on the fender like in an old movie, and say "Good bye, pardner. See you later," with a tear in my eye.

"Fuck you, Eagle!" I said. "You let me down, you shit!"

On the corner, I stuck out my thumb.

One Altima, Accords, a Bronco, next a Subaru, then my father came down the street in the Malibu.

He stopped for the light and put on the right blinker not more than twenty feet from me. A woman with long dark hair sat in the passenger seat. It was Daphne, Raylene's other sister. She looked out her window and when she saw me she smiled.

My father waited for the light, pissed off as usual about I don't know what. He shook an angry finger in the air like a conductor who hated the orchestra. Daphne ignored him and winked at me. It was a very nice wink. She's three years older than Raylene and knows how to wink better.

The light changed. My father made a right on South Main and didn't see me, and they drove down Middle Road and I stood on the corner with my thumb out.

The Eagle is a shit car.

The shifter pops out at 3,000 rpms if I don't hold it in. Step on the brakes, the car veers to the right and you can't stop it. The trunk jams or it won't close at all. You need a crowbar to pry it open. The muffler has its own volume control. The starter motor works on occasion, so that's not so bad.

# 111

Charlee was sitting on the back steps when I got home. She had a bottle of spring water she always carries with her because she won't drink piped-in water. She set the bottle down on a step and stood up when she saw me in the driveway.

"What's going on?" she asked.

"My Uncle didn't come home last night," I told her. "I've been looking for him all day. He didn't leave a note. He didn't call. Maybe he got drunk and he's sleeping it off at a friend's place, I don't know, and now the Ram is gone and the Eagle's dead on the side of the road and my father drove by with his new girlfriend and nobody gave me a ride so I had to walk back home."

Charlee wore a new pair of jeans and a pull-over sweater. She never wore sloppy clothes and she put on extra makeup today because she had to stand in front of the class and give a report on WWII.

"How did World War II go today?" I asked her.

"Postponed until Tuesday."

"I'll let the Generals know," I said.

She drank from the bottle, then wiped it with a tissue and passed it to me.

"Spring water from Vermont," she said. She took it back and wiped it again before she drank it.

I had one lead. It wasn't much of a lead. Just a ripped off piece of paper that I found in my Uncle's dresser. On the paper my Uncle wrote this address: 357 Holster Street, Buckston. It was a long shot, and I could wait around here and hope he comes back, or I could drive out to Buckston right now and check it out.

"You cummin' with me?" I asked Charlee.

"You gonna drive all the way to Buckston? Without a license?" she said.

"I don't see nobody handin' 'em out, and I can't wait until next year."

"I'll go with you, but there's just one problem."

"Big one or a small one?"

"Big enough. Look around you, Walt. You don't have any cars left."

# 112

"What do you mean we got no cars left?" I said.

I turned the key and the Camaro started up with a pop and a growl. Charlee sat next to me with her mouth open. I stepped on the gas and revved it and Charlee smiled along with me. I can fix up any car that's worth fixing. Just give me the tools and throw in the owner's manual.

I knew the Camaro would start when I replaced the plugs and cleaned out the distributor cap last week. I was just waiting for the right moment to turn the key.

"Tie your seat belt in a knot!" I said.

"I can't believe it, Walt," she said. "You finally got it goin'."

"It took a long time but I got fast results."

"It ain't as fast as Cooter's Cougar."

"What car is?"

When you drive a great car you feel great, especially when you work hard and tune it yourself. It makes you proud, and I felt great and proud riding with Charlee in the Camaro.

Tight steering, quick brakes. Real quality control door-to-door and bumper-to-bumper.

Who knows? I get in the mood, maybe I'll drive out to Big Burger on Mustang Monday and show them what a real car looks like.

Charlee had a debit card that we used for gas. I put air in the tires, mostly the left front. The right front only needed a few pounds. She put her foot on the gas to prevent stalling when I filled it up.

"You got to take care of yourself," Charlee said on the road to Buckston.

My shirt got dirty driving around today. The bandage fell off my arm and I didn't know it. In Charlee's eyes I'd been through the Battle Of The Bulge.

"You ever go back home and see your father?" she asked.

"Why the hell you bring him up?"

"Just wonderin'. After all, he is your father."

"I don't consider him my father, so don't call him my father. Right now I'm lookin' for my Uncle."

It's a long way to Buckston. I'd never been there and I didn't have a map. But I know which roads to take and which roads to avoid in general. Uncle Brucker says that's not savvy, it's a gift.

The exterior of the Camaro looked great. That's my specialty. The interior is clean and the body looks great. At every stop sign and traffic light people looked over and admired the detail. Yes, I fixed it up myself. Yes, the original 327. Shined it up last week. You can smell the sweet wax two lanes over, down the block and across the street.

The Camaro ran beautifully with the silver balls hanging from the rearview and Renata's blue bracelet around the ignition. Charlee saw it hanging. She tickled it.

"Engaged?" she said.

"You can put it in the glovebox if you want."

I leaned over and opened the glovebox but it was stuck and I couldn't open it.

"I don't care where you put Renata's cheap bracelet," she said.

"How do you know it's hers?"

"How do I know anything I know? Your elbow looks like Jaws got it."

"I fell, that's all."

We stopped at RightWay Drugs, and Charlee went in and bought a bottle of spring water from South Dakota and box of Bandaids while I watched for cops and worried about my Uncle. No cops. Where the hell is my Uncle? Charlee got a variety box of

Bandaids because they didn't have large. She took the bandaids out and peeled off the paper and stuck them in a row on the console.

She had make-up around her eyes that I didn't notice. Not dark and slinky like Renata but nice, and she wore lipstick too.

I had kissed her in the Monte Carlo and we made out in the Eagle, and now I kissed her in the Camaro but we didn't have the time to make out. I held my arm up and she took the Bandaids from the console and stuck them on my elbow and smoothed them out, and she made a real nice pinwheel bandage on my elbow.

Charlee knew how to get around Buckston because she had relatives there, and she gave me directions to 357 Holster Street. Along the way she showed me a bakery that made great cupcakes. She also showed me Indian Rock. We made a lot of turns on the way.

"Next house on the left," she said.

357 Holster Street used to be a place where people lived until last year or the year before. Now it's not even a location. Who knows why it burned down, but the fire had a great time when it burned off the roof and most of the second floor.

The front doorway still has the number 357 at the top.

# 113

On the way back home we drove past the bakery Charlee said has great cupcakes, and again we saw Indian Rock. Charlee got the radio working and tuned in Classic Rock for me because I was bummed out. She tried to cheer me up with her positive attitude. Don't jump to any conclusions, she said, and she was still trying when we drove down Meridian and stopped for the light at Holmes.

A car pulled up next to us in the left lane.

The muffler played a serious tune. The driver revved the engine and revved it again. The first rev was a greeting. The second was a challenge.

I kept my cool and stared straight ahead and accepted the challenge with a rev of my own.

The light turned yellow on the cross street.

Charlee and I looked to the left lane.

It was Cooter's Cougar!

Cooter's metallic burgundy Mercury Cougar with the white racing stripe and 20 inch alloys is a super-fast turbocharged dream machine. Those alloy wheels cost a fortune. The front spoiler locked the front end to the ground. Sway bars front and rear and adjustable shocks, of course. But you'll find it in another guy's dream, not mine.

"It don't look so fast to me," I said.

The light turned green. I stepped on the gas. My tires spun and squealed. The Cougar with those 20's pulled ahead. I caught up with it a block later at Constant Value, and just past Billy's Bargain the Cougar slowed down, pulled over, and stopped at GasMart.

"Cooter's takin' a rest," I said.

We parked at the curb, and when we looked back the Cougar's emergency flashers went on.

Charlee and I got out and she took my hand and we walked back to Cooter's Cougar. I walked slowly and kept my cool because the Cougar was nothing special to me, just another car that's not a Camaro. Up close I caught a glimpse into the dim interior. The red lights on the radar detector blinked on top of the dash. A dancing skunk air refresher dangled from the rearview, and that's all I saw through the blackout windows.

Charlee squeezed my hand and whispered, "Nobody knows who Cooter is. Nobody's seen him. From now on they'll have to consult us. We are the experts."

Charlee learned how to build suspense in school last month when she gave her report on Vesuvius and Pompeii.

The window went all the way down and a gray-haired lady looked out from behind the wheel. She wore a white nurse's uniform with white gloves but she also wore a white scarf around her neck. She look like everybody's favorite aunt.

"Flo Rizotti, nurse practitioner," she said. She had a soft, clear voice. "Call me Dr. Flo."

Charlee said, "Hello, Dr. Flo," and I said, "Good afternoon," at the same time.

"Generally, I'm a happy person," Dr. Flo went on softly. "By that I mean ninety-nine percent of the time. Unfortunately, you caught me on a one percent day. If you have a few minutes to spare, I'd like to discuss the source of my unhappiness, which is this damn car, and what I can do about it. Do you mind?"

Charlee and I looked at each other. We had a few minutes. Of course we didn't mind.

The Cougar wasn't her car, it's her son's car. He took off a while ago with her Civic and it's the only car she has. She's already a day late for an operation in Saint Paul because of the Cougar, and the patient can't hold on much longer. She hates the damn car. The accelerator sticks and the clutch jumps out at her. The car zooms along like a strip racer, and she can't control it. She'd appreciate it if we'd inform everyone that the Cougar's not her car and she's no strip racer. In the meantime can we help her at the pump? She suffers from a rare affliction called petrolphobia which means fear of gas pumps.

"The tank's runnin' on empty and it's a long way to Saint Paul," she said.

"Sure, we can help you out," said Charlee.

Dr. Flo drove the Cougar to the gas pump.

She asked Charlee for another favor. If Charlee would use her charge card at the pump, she'd give her the cash—or else she'd have to walk all the way to the GasMart and pay at the register.

It didn't sound right to me, but it was Charlee's money. She took out her card and swiped it. I punched 93 octane and Charlee handed the nozzle to me and I put the it in the tank. Dr. Flo rolled up the window. Before it went up I saw an expensive Swiss racing watch on her left wrist, the kind with the extra dials and a timer.

I tapped on the window. Dr. Flo rolled it down. She had removed the watch from her wrist.

"Cooter your son's name?" I asked Dr. Flo.

"No. He's Earl," Dr. Flo said.

"Cooter his middle name?"

"He doesn't have a middle name."

"Wonder why they call it Cooter's Cougar."

"Didn't know they did."

"Your son buy it from a guy named Cooter?" I asked.

"Are you sure you're old enough to drive?" she said.

I didn't say anything. I turned around and cut her off at the pump. I put in 10.7 gallons but it would have been more. The gas cap closed automatically, and I returned the nozzle to the pump.

Dr. Flo hit a button and the window shot up. At the same time she turned the ignition key. She put the shifter in first, revved it up to 6,000, let out the clutch, and with the stink of burning rubber and her white scarf hanging out the window, Dr. Flo took off down the road.

"You don't have to say it. I know I've been cheated," said Charlee.

"Then why'd you do it?"

"She reminded me of my aunt," she said.

"She ain't like no aunt a mine."

# 114

Charlee went into the mart and bought a bottle of spring water. The police GT came down the road while she waited at the register. The cop made a U-turn and parked past the pumps next to where I stood. The door opened and Trooper Ditton got out.

"Bright Eyes!" he said. "How you been, my boy?"

"About the same as I've always been," I said.

Trooper Ditton had a hard day. Beads of sweat ran down his forehead and sweat stained his hat on a cool afternoon. He patted his slick black hair and put his hat on and walked past me to the curb, and he came back with Dr. Flo's white scarf in his hand.

"You see a Cougar go by, Bright Eyes?"

"I saw a Cougar with a nurse behind the wheel."

"That's a nurse, I've got a dozen more in the trunk."

He opened the trunk of the police car and threw the scarf in with the other scarfs, wigs, and hats she left behind.

"She's a librarian on Mondays and a security guard on Tuesdays. This is Friday, she's wearing her nurse's uniform. She's been runnin' up and down the strip for years now. She thinks she's tricked me but she don't know I caught on. She dropped the scarf going north and that means she's headin' south."

"I saw her headin' north, sir."

"She'll slip up and I'll catch her some day. But I can't do nuthin' if I can't get behind her disguise. So I guess I'm headin' south."

"She was headin' north, sir,"

He opened the driver's door and started to take off his hat, but something caught his eye.

"Sweet," he said. "That's what I call sweet."

"What's so sweet?"

"I'll show you what's sweet. A 327, dual carbs, fogs, vinyl top wrapped in a package called Camaro. That's sweet."

He walked over and checked out the Camaro with the word Admiration painted all over his face. He'd checked out hundreds of Camaros during his years on the force, but I'm sure he never saw a Camaro like this one.

What other Camaro has silver mud flaps, a vinyl top, light-up side view mirrors, fog lights, and a piston shift knob?

Charlee came out of the mart with her bottle of spring water. I signaled to her, stay away from the Camaro. She got the idea and turned around.

"You can tell a lot about people from their cars," I said. "A Camaro clean as this, he's gotta be a good man."

Trooper Ditton got back in his GT.

"You'll be here for a while, Bright Eyes? The owner comes back, tell him to come on down to the station and bring the Camaro. Will you do that for me, Bright Eyes?"

"That shouldn't be too difficult."

"Meanwhile, I'm goin' south."

"I saw her headin' north, sir."

"Maybe, but she's goin' south on my map."

And he drove off in his GT, made a U-turn and headed south. I got back in the Camaro and Charlee came over and got in.

"Spring water from Virginia," Charlee said, and she wiped off the bottle and passed it to me.

# 115

He sat stretched-out in the double rocker, relaxing like he was on an overdue vacation. His long legs hung over the railing, his hands folded behind his head. He wore wraparound sunglasses with a backstrap.

"Who are you?" I asked him.

He looked at me like I'd broken an important rule.

"I don't give out names, and nobody's authorized to give out my name," he said.

"How come?"

"Cause anybody can scratch in a name or get a fake name tag. But I got an official card says where I'm from."

He took the card out of his shirt pocket and showed it to me: US Gov't. Proposal Division. US Gov't in big black letters on top. Proposal Division hand written underneath.

"Ain't scratched in, see? It's written by officials at Division Headquarters," he said.

He put the card back in his shirt pocket and through his dark glasses he surveyed the yard. Mailbox, garbage cans, driveway, barn. When he got to the junked cars under the willows, he smiled like he finally understood something that had puzzled him for years.

The morning sun broke through the willow branches, shining up the Camaro and the Monte Carlo until they hid again in the shade. Last winter a willow branch fell through the back window of the Impala. When spring came it had taken root in the back seat. Leroy and I shoveled in dirt and manure we got out back, and the branch grew and now it was a willow tree as tall as the barn.

"Is Brucker Thompson at home?" he asked.

"Why you askin?"

"Might wanna talk to him if he's home. . . . Somethin' happen to your arm?"

"Well it ain't bandaged for nuthin'," I said.

"Could be for nuthin'. If you got extra bandages to use up, or if your arm is cold."

"Could be, but that ain't for nuthin'," I said.

He leaned back and rocked and said, "When your proposal gets accepted, it's a really big thing."

"My Uncle's proposal was accepted? His government money's cummin' in?"

"Now I didn't say nuthin' about money. I said I'm from Division is all, and I said really big thing. I can say there's movement, without pointin' in any direction, there's movement. Consider that my final word on the subject."

"My Uncle ain't home," I told him. "I don't know when or if he's cummin' back."

"Whatever. He ain't home is why I'm sittin' here. When you work for the government, you gotta do things the government way, even if it's confusin' and don't seem right. My instructions is sit right here."

"Government can't put instructions on every little thing," I said.

"No, it can't. You're right about that."

"Government says sit down. That don't mean you won't get up again, does it?"

"Maybe it does, maybe it don't. Here is where I'm sittin'."

"Suit yourself," I said. "Can I see that card again?" I asked him.

He took the card out of his shirt pocket and he was going to hand it to me, then, on second thought, he put it back in his pocket.

"It ain't changed none," he said.

# 116

The State Troopers out of Parville pulled Uncle Brucker from the Ram early Saturday morning. He lost control and went off the road sometime Friday night. North on 94, just south of Parville, the Ram swerved off the road and rolled over in a ditch. The Troopers said he must have blacked out. Uncle Brucker spent the night upside down in the Ram.

No registration. No drivers license. No insurance. No charge cards. No identification at all. The police had no idea who the hell he was and they couldn't understand a word he said. It was probably Rat Talk. They found in his wallet a torn off piece of paper with Keith's name and phone number. An ambulance took my Uncle to Mercy Hospital in Dexter, and a wrecker took the Ram to Sturdevants in Crawley.

The police called Keith and Keith called me.

"He got through it with a headache and a couple of bruises, but the cause of it all was a stroke," Keith said over the phone.

I hung up and a minute later I was backing out of the driveway in the Camaro. Halfway down I stopped by the porch.

The man with the official Government card sat in the rocker with his arms curled around his knees. His instructions were sit, and he sat. All night he sat. The strap around his neck kept his glasses from falling off. A burnt-out cigarette hung from his lip.

I rolled down the window.

"You want to snatch my Uncle and bring him back with you? Now's your chance. Get in the car, please, Inspector."

# 117

"**Y**ou can only fool another rat with that fake scribbled-in card," I told him on the way to the hospital. "Get yourself a Government hat, you'll be more convincin'. But them shades you're wearin' are rat cool."

The words flew past the Inspector. Getting used to another dimension isn't easy, and the strangeness of this new world overwhelmed him. All the buidings here are straight and upright. It puts you off-balance. They lack the crookedness that makes everything firm.

I asked him what's it like being an Impostor. Like everything in life, he said, it has its advantages and disadvantages, but for him it's only temporary. He was a shy kind of rat, sort of vaguely formed and rough around the edges and not how you might think an impostor would be.

"Do you know the Wrestling Rat, by any chance?" I asked him.

"Is heard about the same as knowin'?" he asked.

"Not really," I said.

"Then I guess not," he said.

We were already out on the highway past Conklin. I stuck to the left lane all the way, passing an Accord and a new Explorer that sped up to seventy-five, passing everybody.

Pressed against the door, the Inspector held onto the armrest.

"I guess I wasn't cut out for impostorin'." He yawned a big one.

"I don't like bein' what I'm not." He played with his broken seatbelt, clicking it on and off again like it was a toy. "Stick to what you're good at, is what I say to all."

"I'm a real good driver," I said.

"I got good ears," he said. "I can hear the Whistlin' Wind from two miles off. I been an Inspector most of my life, and I got my own code I never broke or strayed from. I'm good at lots of things, maybe one or two things I ain't. And I know what's fair and what's close to it."

"I got an idea," I said.

And I told him how I had rescued Uncle Brucker from this same hospital once before, and this time the doctors will be watching and waiting for me to make my move.

What the Wrestling Rat said made a lot of sense. I had to get Uncle Brucker back to the other dimension and make room for the rat within him or the rat would strangle him from the inside and they will both die. The Inspector had taken the job of escort, but he had no plan for busting my Uncle out. I had a plan but I couldn't do it all myself. I needed the Inspector's help, and he needed my help. He said he wasn't opposed to helping a human if he wasn't opposed to helping a rat. We had to do this together. For the good of my Uncle and for the rat inside him, the Inspector came to take my Uncle back.

By the time we pulled into the parking lot next to the hospital in downtown Dexter, we had agreed on a plan.

"If that ain't fair it's close to it," he said. "Where can I get me one of them Government hats?"

# 118

"**O**h, it's the White Palace for sure. . . ."

Mercy Hospital, Intensive Care, room A-27.

We stood outside in the hall and listened to my Uncle moan.

Except it wasn't really a moan because it didn't come from his throat. It came from someplace deep down and took a long time to get out, which made it worse and scary when it spread out into the hall. Moan is the best I can come up with.

It took a while to get up the nerve, then I went in to see my Uncle.

"Oh, there's no mistakin' it. The front door is wide open and the Palace lights are on. . . ."

I spread open the curtain and there he was, eyes shut tight, covers up to his chin. He looked bad, real bad. Hanging upside down all night made his face go all crooked and blotchy. One eyebrow went up, the other went down, and they didn't meet up in the center. He looked like he belonged in a late night spook show.

He opened one eye, saw me standing beside the bed and smiled a sneaky smile.

"Shut the door will ya, Walt? I don't really see no White Palace, and that ain't real genuine moanin'. It's a technique I'm perfectin' for scarin' doctors away."

His swollen tongue got in the way and he had trouble speaking, but I understood what he said.

I sat on the edge of the bed and told him what Keith told me. The Ram. The accident. The stroke.

"It's that rat actin' up is what it is," he said. "No matter what I do, he's got another way a doin' it, and that includes drivin'. No wonder I ended up in a ditch! I'll tell you somethin', Walt. It wasn't a stroke caused the accident. It was bringin' me to the hospital give me the stroke! My heart knew it was headin' back here and couldn't take the bad news. It ain't fair, Walt, creepin' up inside me, snipin' at my soul. Infiltratin'! Takin' over! I wish I never killed a rat, if that's what brung this upon me. And now I'm back in the hospital, trapped inside and out. I'm totaled, Walt. Like you said, I'm totaled."

"Not you. The Ram."

"Say again?"

"I said the Ram got totaled, not you. Only the Ram."

"I ain't totaled?"

"Not nearly. Matter of fact, you're lookin pretty good . . ."

"No kiddin'?"

"I got a hunch about somethin'," I said. I took the clipboard from the side of the bed and looked it over. "A-ha! I was right. Look, Unc!" I held up the chart and there it was, RS in big red letters across the top. "You know what RS means, Unc? It's doctor's code for Revitalizin' Stroke!"

He pushed his glasses up on his nose and squinted the chart into focus.

"Well I'll be damned. That ain't so bad, is it? In fact it's pretty good. Unplug me, Walt."

He peeled off a wire taped to his chest and he threw it to the floor. I peeled off a tube taped to his left arm. More tubes and more wires, thrown to the floor, I kicked them all under the bed where the doctors can't see it.

"Here, drink up. It'll do ya a world a good." I passed him a glass of water from the table. "Slow, Unc, drink it slow. Now sip from the other side. You gotta sip all around to get the full potential."

"You're right, Walt, I need all the potential."

He sipped and turned the glass, and his tongue loosened up. His eyebrows pulled together in a tight line of important thoughts, and his eyes cleared up and found something to look at.

"Gimme more," he said.

I held the glass and he drank. Half a glass later he was sitting up straight. I helped him get up from the bed. He was a little shaky at first, steadier as he stepped forward.

By the time he got to the closet he was on his own.

# 119

"**O**K, Unc, switch clothes!"
I opened up my bag and took out Uncle Brucker's blue suit and name tag. He took off his robe and put on the pants. I had no time to take the wrinkled suit to the cleaners. In the mirror he straightened the collar of his blue tour-guide suit.

I pinned on his name tag. Thompson, Brucker.

"Better get goin'. There's doctors comin'," I said, and I quickly got into the bed and he opened the door and walked out.

Face to face with the Inspector.

At this point the Inspector was supposed to say, "Is this the official tour?" And then he would join the tour and follow along behind Uncle Brucker. We went over it in the car.

But he just stood there looking scared and confused and hopeless. Uncle Brucker knew how the Inspector felt. He knew it because he lived it. It's tough being stuck in another dimension where everything's different and you have no home base.

"Yes, this is the official tour," Uncle Brucker said, and he started off down the hall, hoping the Inspector will take the hint and follow. An elderly couple got on line and followed, but the Inspector stayed behind motionless. "Follow me, please. This tour goes in one direction only."

The next time he looked back, the Inspector had caught up and joined the tour.

"There's operatin' rooms on the left. That's where they do the fixin'," said Uncle Brucker. "Intensive Care is on the right, and that's where they do the curin'. Someday they'll combine the two and speed up the process. That's the front desk up ahead. Call it main desk or front desk, they'll know what you mean. The tour starts and ends right here. Thank you and stay well."

By the time they reached the front desk, the group had grown to eight people.

The door opened and two doctors came into my room. Their name tags said Dr. Yula Von Delpa and Dr. Gail Gustarino. They had pens in their pockets and they carried tablets with lots of information. Dr. Von Delpa wore a tiny ice cream cone earring on her left ear. Her right ear had a stick pop. Dr. Gustarino wore no earrings at all. They took my pulse and checked the monitors and the chart.

Then left their pens in their pockets and they tapped on their computer tablets and consulted each other.

"Not my choice for the picture of health gallery," said Dr. Von Delpa with the earrings.

"And he's been talkin' about the White Palace," said Dr. Gustarino who was earring free.

"Lights on, doors open?"

"That's what he says."

"There's not much we can do when the lights are on and all the doors to the Palace are open."

"Suggestions?"

"Coffee?"

"I concur."

The doctors put their tablets in their pockets and hung the clipboard on the bed, and they didn't use their pens at all.

After they left I counted to one hundred, got out of bed and went into the hall. The two doctors were all the way down by the cafeteria. At the front desk people inquired about the twelve o'clock tour.

I took the stairs down to the parking lot. There was a window on every floor. Through the third floor window I saw my Uncle and the Inspector walking slowly across the tree lawn. Second floor, they headed toward the road. Next floor down I couldn't see them through the bushes. Down the hall and out to the parking lot. I got in the Camaro, tied my seatbelt in a knot, and took off.

# 120

Uncle Brucker and the Inspector walked across the tree lawn in the cool shade of the maples and birch. Out in the sun they followed the sidewalk downtown. The Inspector knew exactly where he had to go. He wasn't sure how to get there, but he had a good sense of direction and he had no trouble finding his way around.

By the time they got to Main Street, Uncle Brucker had worn himself out. His leg muscles ached and his heart beat like a sump pump, and he needed to catch his breath.

They came to a yellow bench at the corner bus stop. An elderly lady moved over and they sat next to her. They talked about the weather. Everyone agreed it's a most beautiful day, and that's as far as the conversation went. The sparrows spread out on the telephone wires, all pointed in the same direction. A mother pushed her twin daughters in a sidewalk double stroller. The siren went off at noon.

On their feet again, the Inspector and Uncle Brucker talked about the difference between dimensions and what makes a good stew.

"It's in the stirrin'," said the Inspector. "Cook it even all around."

"Ingredients," said Uncle Brucker. "Or it don't matter that you're stirrin'."

The Inspector complemented Uncle Brucker on his Rat Talk. "Close my eyes, I'd swear I'm talkin' to a rat."

Uncle Brucker thought the Inspector had a real good sense of direction. Outstanding, considering he was from a different dimension. The Inspector got around better than a lot of people from this dimension that my Uncle could mention.

"But to be honest, Inspector, as an impostor you won't make my ten best list."

"Have you seen my card?" The Inspector smiled like a bandit and took his US Gov't Proposal Division card from his pocket and passed it to my Uncle. "What do you think of that?"

They laughed at the smudged-up nosewriting. Fake!

"But that don't mean nuthin' against my proposal."

"They could be workin' on it right now."

"It's about time," Uncle Brucker said, and he bent over in pain.

"Oh, no, he's actin' up again!" He stumbled, but the Inspector didn't let him fall. "G-G-Goddamit, Inspector. I thought you was findin' us a Portal!"

Years ago there used to be a fish mart on the corner of Main and Third, but the store burned down and the owners never rebuilt. Uncle Brucker and the Inspector walked cross the old parking lot where the weeds grew high through the crumpled cement. The Inspector stopped and listened. A few steps further, one more, a little to the right. He stopped again.

"Hear anythin'?" asked the Inspector.

"Just you whistlin'."

"It ain't me whistlin'. It ain't nobody at all."

In the tall weeds of the grown-over parking lot behind the old Main Street Fish Mart not far from Mercy hospital in downtown Dexter, there has always been a Portal to the next dimension. Look for it if you want, but you'll never find it unless you have the Inspector to help you out.

"You sure know your way around," said Uncle Brucker.

"After you," the Inspector said.

# 121

On 94, past Conklin, I slipped the Camaro into fourth and got into the left lane. Farther down on 94 I went 70mph in a 55 zone. A cop car pulled up behind me and I slowed down. He followed me for a mile, then he put his directional on. He got off at the exit and I stepped on the gas. At 70mph my thoughts turned to Renata.

At the edge of town I stopped at the Shell station. I went into the shop, couldn't find anything I wanted to eat, bought a Coke and walked out. Then I headed through town to Tuskies.

It was a busy afternoon. For every guy that hung out, three girls walked the street. A cherry red Impala cruised down Center and turned right at South Main, and a red T-bird made a lonely picture with its hood open in front of Half Price Stores. The Impala is a cool car, but not as cool as the Camaro.

An accident tied up the entrance to the strip mall. The cops blocked the road and they set up detour signs. I made a right and followed the signs back to Center.

I don't know how Dwight got in the back seat, but I wasn't surprised when I saw his face in the rearview mirror.

"Hidin' out, Dwight?"

"I wouldn't call it hidin'," he said.

"It's my car, I do the callin'."

"I suppose you're lookin' for my sister."

"Maybe I am, maybe I ain't. Your sister got anythin' to say to me?"

"I don't know what goes on in her mind, but I know she's sorry. She's sorry she took your Uncle's War Medal. She's sorry about lyin'. She took it for our father cause he never got nuthin' 'cept a bad leg. And I'm tellin' you she split up with Kip and I don't know how long before she's back with him. You ain't been callin' or cummin' around."

"I got reasons."

"She gave back the Medal. It ain't stealin' when you give it back."

"It's stealin' until you give it back. And what do you mean, she? You brought it back for her, probably took it for her too. I saw you or your twin brother runnin' from the house that mornin'."

That stumped him but only for a second.

"She's my sister and I'll do anythin' for her," he said. "She wants you to come down to Tuskies. She's been down there every day, waitin' and you ain't showed up. She ain't gonna wait forever and she ain't the type to go lookin' for company."

I parked across from Mid-City Lanes, turned the engine off and there we sat with the radio off. We sat for so long I grew about an inch and a half. Dwight said nothing to me, and I didn't speak to Dwight because I get quiet when my mind is busy.

A real cool black Charger with a white racing stripe and a hood scoop went by. A not-so-cool red El Camino played a doo-wop tune at the stop light. I hate that doo-wop crap when they don't know what to sing.

They can't figure out the words so they doo-wop it up.

Dwight got out the passenger side and I almost got out with him. I had my seatbelt tied but that's not what held me back.

"She's waitin'," Dwight said. His black eye had cleared up a little, not much. A shiner like that takes time to clear up. "You cummin'?" he asked.

My fingers played with the ignition key.

"She's waitin'," he said.

"I heard you."

"This car ain't no Mustang."

"It's a Camaro."

"Mustang's faster."

"Not without a turbo and a filter-charger it ain't."

"I'd rather have a Mustang."

"So write it on your forehead and shut up about it."

Dwight took his cap off and adjusted it and put it back on his head.

"It looks better the other way," I said.

"Like this?"

"Yeah. Tilt it like that."

"Anythin' you got to say?" he asked.

"Nope."

"Nuthin' at all?"

"On second thought there is one thing." I turned the ignition key.

The battery got the message. The starter motor passed it on. The spark plugs sparked and the Camaro started up like a dream-mobile on the highway to heaven. "Tell her I'll see her on the next shuttle to Jupiter."

I pulled out onto Center. The accident by the strip mall had cleared up and the police cars drove off. I cruised through town and outside town I pressed the pedal to the floor. Dual carbs, four on the floor, two new plugs and wires. If the Camaro had wings, I'd be flying.

# 122

I woke up Saturday morning with the sun on my face. I had no memory of coming home or when I got into bed, but I had a clear picture of what led up to it: driving to the hospital in the Camaro with the Inspector, tricking the doctors and hiding under the bed sheets, sneaking Uncle Brucker out of the hospital in his official blue suit.

Three months ago I left my father and my home and moved into the old house with my Uncle. So much has happened since then, it seems much longer. All my plans were my Uncle's plans. And now that he's gone, what's next?

Who am I now that he's gone?

I have no mother. She's been gone so long, she'll never come back. I hate my father and he hates me, and there's no getting around it. My Uncle has gone off to another dimension for the good of the rat in him or they'd both be dead. I have no money. I spent every cent Uncle Brucker left me, including his coin collection. I have no food. I'm out of gas. No wax for the Camaro. The old house is no bargain now that I'm on my own. Living here means oil bills and water bills. And electricity costs too, doesn't it? If I want to stay here I'll have to find a way to make money, or check me in at the Park Bench Hotel.

Uncle Brucker had been a rat killer all his life, and what does he have to show for it?

A pile of appliances on one side of the basement labeled Fixable.

A second pile near the furnace labeled Forget it. And a third pile of garden tools and patio furniture and hedge trimmers in the barn. Thirty-four blenders, sixteen microwaves, twenty-three toasters.

I wandered into the kitchen and searched through the cabinets and checked the refrigerator, but I didn't find much. Leroy drank all the milk. Manny fried all the eggs and Bones ate the bread and peanut butter. There's a half-box of Cheerios I hid under the sink, and cans of soup that Charlee brought over. The half-gallon of milk went sour while I was in the next dimension looking for Uncle Brucker. I guess I'll throw it out.

I sat at the kitchen table and poured the Cheerios into a bowl. It's not half a box, only a cup. I poured in some invisible milk from a brand new quart. I had a few spoonfuls and it wasn't bad. It would taste better with invisible sugar. Make room for me on the bench.

I finished breakfast at seven forty-five. The phone started ringing at eight.

Harriet Grooner phoned first. She lived in a rat-infested area on East Raynor Street. An ugly rat with a chewed-off ear moved into her mailbox where it was waiting to attack her when she opened it up. She has been unable to get the mail for two weeks. Could the Rat Killer please come over and destroy this ugly one-ear rat?

She had offered the Rat Killer one toaster oven and one Mix-Master the last time he helped her out, but it wasn't enough. "You want 'em dead, give me the Blender," he said. Times are tough and she needs all her appliances. Could the Rat Killer please let her pay with cash?

"I'll pay fifty dollars," she says.

"The Rat Killer ain't here," I said.

"Please?"

Ward Balk called next. He lived in an apartment on Lower Main. The apartment building next door had burned down and forty-one rats moved into his basement. He trapped thirteen, killed seventeen, but eleven got away. Could the Rat Killer come over and teach those rats a lesson? How does ten bucks a rat sound? OK, he'll go fifteen, but he'll be damned if he'll trade another tool set.

The Rat Killer had neglected his business for more than a month. The emergencies piled up. Customers were nervous, and from nervous they became frantic.

Frantic customers sat with open bottles of aspirin on their tables and fingers tapping Redial. A lady with a raspy voice saw a roof rat that resembled her dead husband. Could the Rat Killer come over and catch him? She had a thing or two she wanted to tell that lazy rat. Another man saw three gas station rats drive off in his Mini. Two rats worked the pedals and the third steered the car. Somebody saw the Mini in Dengrove. How does two hundred sound to drive out there and help him get it back?

These people had relied on Uncle Brucker for many years but he couldn't help them this time. The rats are acting up again. Somebody better stop them or they'll get out of hand. Trouble has a long tail and crawls around on four feet. Somebody better step up and do what must be done.

The phone rang. It was Mrs. Grooner again. Now two rats are hiding out in her mailbox. The ugly one-ear rat and an uglier nipped-nose rat. And they were doing things she'd rather not talk about.

"One hundred dollars! Each!" she says.

The sun came in through the morning window. Dust floated in the kitchen air. A rectangle of yellow sunlight climbed up the wall and stopped at the photograph of Grandpa and Grandma Thompson. The half-empty can of Boomers stood on the edge of the counter, exactly where Uncle Brucker left it. A breeze blew the squeaky kitchen door halfway open. It stopped mid-squeak. The ceiling light sputtered and the refrigerator went on. Uncle Brucker's rat rifle leaned up against the wall next to the closet door.

His leather work gloves hung on a nail in the wall behind the door.

The rifle needs a cleaning, but I don't have time for that now. I better load it up and take an extra box of cartridges with me, don't forget the leather gloves, and head on out to Raynor Street and exterminate those two ugly rats. Mrs. Grooner has a big house and plenty of money and I won't let her down.

I'll work long hours on the weekends, and I'll make emergency calls after school until I catch up. And I'll change to a cash-only policy, effective immediately. I'll rise early and set my traps before I go to school. Charlee will take care of the schedule and go to the supermarket and keep things in order. We'll move the boxes filled with old magazines off the stairs and put them in the basement and find a broom and clean up the old house. But first we'll move Uncle Brucker's big bed into my room and put clean sheets on the mattress and we'll test it out and test it out some more.

Our birthdays come up in two weeks.

I thought about some of the things my Uncle had taught me: Always wear gloves when handling a rat. Keep your eyes on the rat's eyes. They look from side to side before they make a move. The German Headlock. The Cherokee Chokehold.

The phone rang. Mrs. Grooner again.

"This is the Rat Killer speakin'," I said. "You got a rat problem, dumplin'? Talk to me."

# Epilogue

### "The Old Impostor and the Skinny Rat"
True Rat Stories From Around The World
by Brucker Thompson

At one time rats came from all over Rat Land to visit the Old Impostor. No arrows pointed in his direction and not one road sign marked the way, but every rat knew how to get there.

Take the first alley past the ripped-up railroad tracks, turn right by Boone's Dock where the wharfies once lived, turn left where the dock house used to be. If you remember what used to be you can figure out what was. The crooked pier where the wrestling ring used to be drifted out to sea a long time ago, and Renovation is the big new word.

Try and find a sleep hole there now, if you can afford it.

But back then, where the old dock light used to be. . . .

He sat all day in a unfolding chair outside a sleep hole where he never slept.

Now listen to this. Every rat knew the Old Impostor was really the Rat Killer. He never said he was and he never said he wasn't, but they all know the truth. Rats aren't as dumb as humans say. They've got humans fooled most of the time, and humans fool themselves with what's left.

No one expected him to admit he was the Rat Killer, but every rat wanted to be there when he did. There were no signs that said Rat Killer either. Of course you wouldn't expect that.

A trim rat who had traveled for a long time from very far away came up to him. The trim rat looked him over and said, "They say you're the Rat Killer."

"No, I'm just a really good Impostor."

"They say the Rat Killer never says he's the Rat Killer. They say he sits in a chair and catches up on his beauty sleep."

"What chair?"

"This chair."

"Who says?"

"Everybody."

"They're wrong, then. Every one of 'em."

The trim rat who had traveled a very long way ducked down low. The squawky gulls swooped at him, and the look on his face said go away you dumb birds, or something like that. He wished he could jump up high and scatter the gulls away. You couldn't tell that from his face, you just knew it.

"I don't see how everybody can be wrong," he said.

"No, I guess you don't."

The old Impostor lived on beer and butts, at least that's what they say. He bought them with the fortune he made as a wrestler. Beer and cigarettes filled up his sleep hole. That's why he sat outside in the unfolding chair. Empty cans and butts scattered on the ground all around the hole. Take one as a souvenir.

If you could come over here and look into that hole, see for yourself. Then you'll know for sure, won't you? Come closer. Over here. . . . See? It's empty.

Not one can, not one pack. Not a wrapper nor a butt.

Maybe a long time ago it was true what they say. Maybe a long long time ago he had ten thousand cases of beer and one million cartons of cigarettes, like they say, smuggled in from another dimension and stuffed in that rat hole. Maybe he was a Five-Alarm

Fire Chief, too, or a World-Class Stew Chef. There's no end to maybes.

The skinny rat came by again. Above all, he enjoyed a smoke after a hearty meal. He wanted a smoke but he needed a light. He refused to eat a hearty meal only to be served disappointment for dessert. The Skinny Rat quit eating a while ago. He sure was hungry, but hunger just didn't stack up against disappointment. Anybody got a light?

The Skinny Rat had something on his mind he never mentioned. The Old Impostor saw something other than what he was looking at. The Skinny Rat thought he knew what the Old Impostor was searching for. The Old Impostor thought he knew what was on the Skinny Rat's mind. They didn't know anything for sure.

"No, I don't got a light," the Old Impostor told the Skinny Rat.

"I ain't asked yet," the Skinny Rat replied.

"But you were gonna . . . I saved you the trouble."

"I might ask anyway, cause it's really no trouble."

"You wouldn't be so skinny if you didn't smoke."

"No, it's why I'm skinny cause I can't smoke."

The Old Impostor ran out of beer a long time ago. Scavenger rats took the empty cans. He smoked his last cigarette. The smoker rats carried the butts away. There go the souvenirs.

Maybe at one time he really did store cigarettes in his sleep hole, and beer, too. But ten thousand cases? One million cartons?

Impossible! That would be one hell of a hole. You need an army of rats to dig a hole so deep, and it would stretch around the world again and again. It would take more than a lifetime to complete a project so big. But when it's finished it will be another Great Wonder of the World, no maybes about it. Great Wonder #8, if you put it at the end. Could be any number if you stick it in between.

That Skinny Rat was awfully skinny. The Old Impostor felt bad. Not all the time, on occasion, about his skinniness.

Finally, one day the Old Imposter said, "Light up!"

The Old Impostor struck a match and lit the butt for the Skinny Rat. The Skinny Rat smoked the butt and his smiled faded, and smilelessly he looked to the stars and the moon and wished he had eaten a hearty meal.

"Knock-knock. Who's there?"

A Sweet Rat asked that question.

"No, no. You got it wrong." The Old Impostor sat in his chair and shook his head. "First you say 'Knock-knock,' then I say 'Who's there?' Got it? Let's try it again. . . . OK, go!"

"Knock-knock. Who's there?"

"Forget it."

"Forget what?"

The Sweet Rat found a stick. She found another stick. She was a happy rat, and she made a pile of sticks at the water's edge, and she jumped and ran in circles when the waves came in and took the sticks away.

"Think you got enough sticks there, sweetie?" asked the Old Impostor.

A handsome rat dragged a magnificent stick along the edge of Cove Cliff and over the edge and down into the Cove. The rats gathered around. It was a long, beautiful, hard-to-find, one-of-a-kind stick for all to see.

The Sweet Rat walked toward him.

"I'd introduce myself, but I got no name for reference. Nice stick," she said, and she followed him.

The Old Impostor grew older. He sat in his unfolding chair for so long it was the only place in the world. He could not imagine anywhere else and he didn't care to be anywhere else. He felt like he'd been here forever, yet he knew it couldn't be forever because forever has a long ways to go, and it went back a long ways too. He spent the rest of his life where he didn't want to spend it, but he forgot where that was about the same time he forgot who he was.

The Sweet Rat returned with the beautiful stick or another stick just like it. She threw it on the pile. The street cleaner rats came by and went to work with their curb rakes and gutter shovels, and with street brooms they swept the pile of sticks away.

"Where's your stick?" asked the Old Impostor of the Sweet Rat.

"You are my stick," she said.

The Old Impostor never thought life would be like this.

The flying rats flew off in a squall and never came back. The squawky gulls swooped down low and filled their bellies and they had nothing to squawk about. The crooked old pier grew tired of floating around without a reason and sank to the ocean floor. In time the sand crabs repaired the old pier and it floated to the surface. The wharf rats strung the ring ropes, and old Scratch started up the wrestling matches once again.

Eight p.m. Every Thursday.

# About the Author

Leslie Peter Wulff lives with his lovely wife Sandy in a small college town in upstate New York. Other than reading great literature and watching great films, he enjoys building stone walls—and taking breaks from building stone walls. All his life he wanted to be a writer. Some years ago he quit his job because of Parkinson's disease. Now he's a writer.